Idle Deceptions

Oliver E. Cadam

Copyright © 2016 Oliver E. Cadam

All rights reserved, including the right to reproduce this book, or portions thereof in any form. No part of this text may be reproduced, transmitted, downloaded, decompiled, reverse engineered, or stored, in any form or introduced into any information storage and retrieval system, in any form or by any means, whether electronic or mechanical without the express written permission of the author.

This is a work of fiction. Names and characters are the product of the author's imagination and any resemblance to actual persons, living or dead, is entirely coincidental.

ISBN: 978-1-326-63914-3

PublishNation
www.publishnation.co.uk

Acknowledgements

My warmest thanks to all those readers who took the time and trouble to give me detailed feedback, either verbally or via email and social media, on my first novel, 'Once Too Many Times'. It seems to have been well received, and I hope I have included much of your advice in this Murder Mystery, **'Idle Deceptions'**.

There are simply too many such readers to mention you all by name, but special thanks must go to Chris C, Chris S, Sally, Quentin, Austen, Oliver, Barbara, Bea, Heidi, Kerry, Peter, Ken & Michaela, Dorothy, Frances, Bruce & Michele, Jim, Carol, Dave & Lou my brow-beaten guinea pigs, Margaret, Julie, Penny, Scott and Jason.

For Alison

Also by Oliver E. Cadam :-

'Once Too Many Times', a Mystery Thriller.

Synopsis for 'Once Too Many Times'

Ray just couldn't work it out. When had their lives together started to unravel? Where had it all gone so wrong, and why so soon? He had lived his tedious uneventful life right alongside her for almost twenty years, watching her, craving and yearning for her, and never really believing that she could ever be his. And then, out of nowhere, and only through tragic personal circumstances were his emotional shackles lifted, allowing him to dream for the first time that she really could be his after all. Then he had put his shoulder to the wheel and converted that dream to reality. It had been pure heaven - his hitherto unreachable nirvana - and he'd given himself completely and absolutely to his new love. But soon, and so very recently, the doubts had crowded in. What had changed? Why was she pushing him away? What did she know?

This is a story of love and deception, romance and retribution.

Follow Oliver E. Cadam

You can follow Oliver E. Cadam via his website www.oliverecadam.com or via Twitter and facebook.

1 – February 2007

Sunday 4th

Sunday afternoon and bloody freezing. February! Kept engine running, pushed feet right under heater. Cold enough for North Face mittens inside the car.
So far so good – cool. They left for swimming on time. Could see figures flitting about on screen through sash window.
Made agency call – took drive out to check other end – neat!

2 – February 2007

Sunday 11th

Ridiculous...but should be worth it.
Cold again. Pub at the end of the road had the fire on. Risky I suppose, but not if things work out. At one point thought a boy was going to come over to me – sweet, but he got distracted by his mates – phew, close call – don't need the extra hassle at this stage in the game.
Michael back to London earlier. Great weekend!

3 – March 2007

Sunday 4th

Went out to see old Grandad. I know I don't tick his boxes, but he's family. In fact since Mum died he's the only blood relative I have – not counting my real father, whoever and wherever he is – and why should I count him at all? The old boy's a canny old stick, I'll give him that, but I can't help yanking his chain. He asked me outright if I had a job yet. He can't understand how I survive on benefits – he has no idea. He thinks I'm a bit of a waster – just waiting to meet the right partner – one with money. I'll show the grumpy old sod.

Michael came down again – fantastic! Brought some fabulous new 'ecsies', little pink ones, wow what a high. He knows how to reach me, but he would. He's been through the same pain as me. He knows. He understands. I can feel his support for what I'm doing. Must be careful not to screw it up.

The yard was easy. Same entry point as last year. Still can't believe what I stumbled over that time. Makes the whole thing work.

Checked their movements again. All worked just the same. Fixtures, teams – check it out.

4 – April 2007

Sunday 1st

Getting closer, so close. Only about a month to run. Only once have they not been in the right places at the right time. That swimming club must run like a sewing machine. Still... they can carry on doing that even after daddy's been banged up. Serve that smug bastard right for stealing the best dad I ever had.

Checked the yard again. All good to go – so easy. Amazed at just how wide open that place really is. Will look so real on camera. Someone there on the day? – chill, just delay.

5 – *what goes around...*

The A12 around Woodbridge was always busy, but by late afternoon on a sunny Sunday in early May the artery was clogged with slow and surging traffic. Lots of City folk were heading back to London from their weekend retreats on the Suffolk coast.

She only needed to make a couple of junctions down the road before turning off into the lush and greening countryside. She cursed her luck – or was it her own misjudgement – that had prompted her to take the dual-carriageway instead of the back lanes down by the river Deben to the sleepy lanes of Compton-by-Westonfield. As she sat there, with the soft-top down for the first time in the promising summer season, her thoughts drifted back through her relentless double shift – Saturday and Sunday no less – in the office of a local estate agent. It was that time of year again. The property market had just exploded over the Easter break in early April and now the City slickers, with all their rude arrogance and bloated wallets, were out in force in search of that rural escape: perhaps a converted mill in Gainsborough country or a cute little cottage tucked away in the shallow folds of the gorgeous Suffolk landscape – something, anything on which to splash their easy cash. Properties near the celebrated Suffolk coast or close to a river or tidal inlet were always particularly sought after locations.

Right now she was just relieved to be out of the firing line and on her way home with the pleasing prospect of the Monday off in lieu of the weekend grind.

Her wayward concentration was interrupted just in time – by the mindless thump, thump, thump of a bass rap-signature booming out of a passing BMW – and she realised that she'd reached the first roundabout and a possible exit from the dense stream of vehicles. She swung the car off the by-pass and ducked back into the town centre, emerging just a few minutes later onto the narrow but much quieter lanes with their low hedges and pleasing floral expression. She smiled inwardly at the simple pleasures of life, assimilating the noisy hedgerow chatter as she drifted along, the sun warming the back of her neck and relaxing her shoulders.

She glided past a pretty little farm complex, one of her favourites in the area, and one she'd known all her life. At one stage she gave way to an on-coming tractor acknowledging the driver's grateful wave with a cheerful smile and the casual lift of an index finger from the steering wheel.

As she neared home – with mounting excitement at the thought of the evening's frivolities ahead of them – she unwittingly checked her optimistic mood with a sudden pang of doubt, or was it anxiety, about what her man might have been up to all day in her absence. Most pointedly she hoped that he hadn't been down the pub for the afternoon. Turning up at a friend's barbecue on the other side of the village with Lee already the worse for wear was not a prospect she entertained with any relish. It wouldn't be the first time either, she reminded herself. In her heart she would forgive him – again – for not having trimmed that damned hedge or painted out the spare room, if only he hadn't already over-indulged. After all, there were certainly enough jobs about the place to keep her less than diligent partner busy at a weekend.

However, she knew he'd have earmarked the live football on the TV: the only question was whether or not he'd have watched it at home or allowed himself – despite recent heated discussions on the subject – to once again slope off down to the Midshipman to watch it there. She feared the latter, and she counselled herself to try not to over-react if he were already well oiled. He could be argumentative at the best of times, but the notion of him being unleashed in cantankerous mood on an otherwise harmonious social gathering was more than she cared to consider.

In no time at all, or so it seemed, she turned gently into the short drive crunching lightly on the granite chippings. She pulled to a stop adjacent to the neat, pretty little front porch. She checked herself over in the rear-view mirror – not bad at all, with her hair still up and barely a few strands escaping behind pendulous earrings. Then feeling vaguely uplifted by her anticipation of the evening excursion, she tripped in past the delightful hanging baskets.

She ditched her bag, local newspaper and car keys in the hall and called out to Lee just hoping he was at home. Greeted only by silence she poked her head enquiringly into the lounge and then went through to the kitchen to check the garden, but only then did she hear the water running upstairs and turned on her heel to perhaps surprise him in the bath, to exchange tales of the day and to tee things up for the barbecue a little later. She rounded the corner returning to the hallway and fairly bounced up the staircase. Leaning hard on the crotchety old door handle she pushed the bathroom door open in mock surprise and with a firm grip on the door frame she pivoted into the room while grinning her warmest smile, and halted abruptly.

Her body tensed. She gave an ugly guttural gasp and as she exhaled she coughed and choked at one and the same time. Her left hand came instinctively to her face as if to contain her own reactions. Gripping the door frame, the fingers of her right hand whitened at the knuckles as the desperate search for stability – mental and physical – coursed through her system. She yawed to one side as her head swam with disbelief, all of her senses submitting to a welling nausea in response to the gruesome scene before her. She cried out, but the sound was instantly drowned in the tears and sputum of her desperation. Her breathing came short and sharp in her chest – her eyes first closing momentarily and then blinking erratically in exaggerated fashion as her brain attempted to verify and at once to eradicate the image in view.

Her balance shifted imperceptibly forward as her knees buckled. Her stiffened right arm, still fixed rigidly to the frame of the door, hinged her into the room, and her own radial momentum threw her to the floor where she scrambled for the rim of the toilet and heaved her innards into the bowl. She wretched and spewed uncontrollably at first and then sporadically, hacking and snivelling, until aching exhaustion demanded a momentary pause. Only then did she dare steal herself, while drawing her sleeveless forearm across her drooling chin, to glance again in his direction hoping, yearning against all rational thought that normality would have been restored – that the last dreadful moments had somehow been imaginary – only to look directly into that deathly pale countenance and to know that it truly was him. Racked by heaving, heart-broken sobs, crying out to herself in stifled confusion, she pushed against the ceramic oval, raising her shaking frame. She staggered backwards colliding with the open door and ricocheting out to the landing, and there she gripped the banister rail to steady herself. Looking back into the bathroom the grisly image seen from range rolled the shock wave back over her once again. She stumbled blindly down the stairs. Finding her voice at last as she clattered through the porch and out to the drive, she propelled herself forward, wailing with grief and pity against the inexplicable, towards the side gate and the sanctuary of her neighbours beyond.

The body lay in a curious position – as if propped up in the corner, supported by the heated towel rail where it met the floor and the side panel of the bath. The dull dark eyes – fixed in lifeless accusation – stared up at the vacant door frame. The head tilted oddly forward almost compromising the deathly line of sight. The fatal aperture in the forehead (just above the right eye) glistened in the pink fringes of traumatised flesh that contrasted sharply with pallid skin tones and the darkness of the wound itself where the bullet had penetrated the skull. Behind and above him the warm subtle shades of the room and the shredded, blood-stained shower curtain were awash in crimson profusion. The projectile had exited the cranium somewhere above and behind the left ear removing most of the upper half of the back of the head with the sheer ballistic force of the assault. The legs were splayed loosely across the tiled floor towards the door and the feet sagged openly to either side. The right arm lay slumped to the floor close to the wash basin pedestal, whereas the left arm reached along the edge of the bath. In the reflex moment of death the fingers of the left hand had seized the recessed chrome bath handle, and there they steadfastly remained – as if in a futile attempt to retain the last vestiges of life itself.

Above him and to his right the cold tap of the wash basin gushed noisily and unimpeded down the drain.

6 – May 2007

Sunday 6th

All done – he's a gonner! Couldn't believe the look on his face as he turned towards me in the bathroom. Not sure he even recognised me – bit of shame. I really wanted him to know me – that way he'd know why. The old thing took the back of his head away in less than a second. Solid piece of hardware. Must have built them well in those days – just like old grandad...same era I guess. Not so pathetic now, eh old man? Bet you never thought I had it in me, but your daughter is avenged and my broken heart can stop bleeding.

And I've got his surrogate son slap bang in the frame...and there won't be any escaping from that little trap either.

Michael will be so impressed with that smart little extra to the overall plot. He's going to love me even more when I tell him.

7 – on the right foot

The Orwell looked particularly grey that Monday morning as the Suffolk Police task force, under the guiding hand of DCI David Lehrer, began to assemble for the first time. The damp chill hanging over the water was a real disappointment after such a gloriously sunny weekend. The swirling silvery-grey current continued its relentless journey south towards the North Sea as they began to arrive in dribs and drabs – via stop-overs at the coffee machine in the corridor – to the top floor incident room of the Constabulary block overlooking the Ipswich waterfront.

Lehrer had purposefully re-arranged the layout of the room some months ago so as to deny his charges the opportunity to drift during any planning or de-briefing meetings by gazing out at the boats on the river – but today he needn't have worried. A sea fret was in and visibility was limited. Of course most of the officers and technicians present were familiar with the routine adopted at the start of any investigation – especially a murder investigation – but Lehrer sensed an atmosphere a little more charged than usual and he was encouraged by the concentration on show as soon as the meeting was called to order. Clearly the word was out. The fact that this was no ordinary dockside drugs bust gone wrong, or just another gangland confrontation with terminal overtones, was evidently already understood. The very unusual nature and circumstances of this new case had attracted a lot of attention within the team and around the station in general, and all that within comfortably less than twenty four hours since the incident had first been reported.

DC Adrian Hughes gave the brief. He was clipped and to the point. Information at this early stage remained sketchy. The victim, Lee Phillipson, had been hitherto unknown to the police. There was no police record. The man hadn't even recorded a parking fine as far as they could tell. He had been in his early-fifties, shared a cottage with Lynsey Bastion, his partner for the last five years: a local woman who was well known in the village and surrounding area.

He had worked in a small accountancy firm in Ipswich and had been there for about three years. The couple's lifestyle appeared unremarkable: there were no early indications of any external pressures such as bad debts, employment problems or family feuds. They all appreciated that sometimes some of the incomers might find themselves financially over-stretched in terms of holiday home acquisition and related financials. They knew too that some of those coming out to East Anglia to escape the more frenetic existence of the sprawling metropolis close by were not just looking to escape the chaotic pace of life in London. Some had good reason to hide in the sticks from past misdemeanours best left buried – but such cases were mercifully rare. None of that seemed to fit here. Outwardly this had been simply an ordinary bloke living a fairly mundane life in pleasant rural circumstances.

They knew that he hadn't been from their neck of the woods, but somewhere across country, and probably via London at some earlier stage in his life: such details were not unusual in this part of the world, and officers had already picked up from a quick sweep through the neighbours in the village that Phillipson had been previously married to another local girl for some ten years or more before divorcing and then later teaming up with Ms Bastion.

The first draft SOCO report was not yet in, forensic feedback was still due, and on-site inspections by an army of technicians had, as yet, revealed only scant information with which to work. More would come down the line soon and, as was typical of these investigations, the pace of development would accelerate quickly in the coming few days.

As the briefing progressed, Hughes crashed quickly through the essential framework and outline of the case. Questions were fired in quickly and pointedly. Interruptions were frequent. Options and possibilities were openly considered and short exchanges pursued before Hughes would summarise each parcel of data and then dole out relevant assignments to meet the needs of the job at this fact-find stage of the process. The session rattled on at a pace, the cohesion and sense of purpose of the group building steadily such that individual detectives, task teams and sub-units within the group – technical specialists, plain clothed and uniformed police officers – all readily appreciated that their strategy was beginning to take shape. Their next tactical steps at ground level would soon add real substance to the investigative framework under construction.

DCI Lehrer, like many of his equally experienced colleagues, knew this routine inside out, but he recognised too that this initial planning session was absolutely vital to the ultimate success of their anticipated investigation, and there were fewer more accomplished practitioners in this day-one scenario than Adi Hughes. With the exercise well underway – but still facing another couple of hours of rigorous preparation ahead of them – Lehrer nodded appreciatively to Hughes from the back of the room and slipped quietly out into the corridor beyond.

8 – the long view

He strained to see through the smear of the wiper blades as they fought, double-quick, to clear his screen of the deluge that had been threatening since he'd left the office half an hour earlier. He drummed his fingers on the steering wheel with impatience attributable to stationary Monday-morning traffic in an early summer downpour. He wasn't used to this – either the traffic or the weather. He knew his patch to represent one of the driest regions of the entire country, and as for traffic congestion, well... he could hardly consider himself a commuter. On office days he would be in well before the busying masses hit the road, in fact long before most of them had even rolled out of bed, and as for returning home later in the day... typically it would be middle evening or even later such were the demands of the job.

Strange, he considered in distraction, that the supposedly peaceful sanctuary of his Suffolk stretch would have need of such commitment. Perhaps it was the more pertinent threat of the Essex reaches with that unavoidable London overspill – Constable country maybe, but not many cosy references to yesteryear to lean on down there – and these days the sheer pace and activity in and around the docks at Felixstowe and Harwich signified only assorted headaches for Lehrer and his crew.

Maybe he was just inefficient and disorganised: maybe too slow with the paperwork. He'd never been comfortable with their administrative procedures, but he couldn't deny their essential nature. Perhaps it was his own misguided approach to the kind of selfless commitment he believed the role required, to be done properly that is – no Poirot here, of course, but he had succeeded over the years – he thought – by applying himself to the task more intensely than many he had worked alongside.

At the same time he'd honed his perceptive skills and his simple attention to detail after those few early howlers which luckily hadn't undermined future opportunities to any significant extent – or so it appeared now. He conceded in the same moment that the same independence of spirit, his determination to succeed in his policing career, had undoubtedly translated into a very selfish addiction to the thrill of the professional chase over and above the perceived pleasures of any domestic harmony he had once imagined. He had lived a fairly solitary life after the marriage had slowly dissolved. He couldn't blame her. If he were honest with himself, it had been the lure of the investigation and his own inability to control it that had subverted his somewhat feeble attempts at home making.

Having already visited the crime scene the previous evening there was little more to take from there before forensics came back with some workable details, so he thought he'd try for an early interview with the deceased's partner, Lynsey Bastion. When eventually the traffic developed some momentum he was able to reach the ring road and then – pushing out through Kesgrave and Martlesham – he avoided the A14 and chugged on down to Compton with minimal interference.

With the house cordoned off, Lehrer knew that she'd be billeting elsewhere and he guessed correctly that she would have returned to her father's place in Westonfield itself. Lehrer wondered idly – as he cruised slowly along the road peering at house names – how the name of the village had come about. Was it Compton or was it Westonfield? It looked like one and the same place, but perhaps it had been two smaller settlements which had grown and merged over time. Did they, then, just change the name to Compton–by–Westonfield simply to connect them? He supressed a smirk as he imagined a series of normally stuffy parish council meetings erupting in territorial dispute as representatives of each half of the village pushed to veto the claims of their opponents in favour of promoting their own identity onto the embossed signs at each end of the village. Clearly compromise had won the day – if indeed that's what had really happened, way back whenever – and compromise could only ever be a good thing he considered, but it was one hell of a mouthful for a place the size of a postage stamp. It was all a little too contrived, pompous even, in his view…but a pretty little escape down by the water's edge, for all that.

He'd also noticed that despite its limited boundaries the village sported not one, but two pubs. The Midshipman – down by the boat slip and right on the waterfront – had clearly been in Westonfield for many many years, whereas the Punch & Plough might just about claim to have been Compton's own watering hole before the merger. In a hamlet of this scale it seemed to him to make little difference bearing in mind their proximity to one another, and he wondered how the two establishments managed to survive in this era of declining pub popularity.

There it was. Yes. Hornby Cottage. That's the one.

Unfortunately – but not entirely surprisingly – Lynsey Bastion was under heavy sedation and fast asleep. Her aged father, gruff and clipped, left Lehrer in no doubt as to his chances of interviewing the woman. He also made particular reference to the doctor's instructions banning intrusions of any kind, most notably – even in difficult times such as these – those of inquisitive and typically demanding police officers. However, the older man softened in the course of their brief doorstep exchange, and while the two men arranged a suitable time for the detective's visit the following day, Lehrer was urged to drop down the road to the river and to pay a call on the landlord of the Midshipman.

"If you're trying to build a picture of what goes on around 'ere," muttered old Ric Bastion, "Jimmy's your man. There's not much he doesn't know about the comings and goings of local folk, that's for sure – and he's been observing us all for something like twenty five years I reckon."

"But what about you, Mr Bastion... I'll need to get your own statement too you know, so why not now, while your daughter is resting?" prompted Lehrer.

"I'm not up to it now – it's all so raw, if you know what I mean – but we'll give you our undivided attention tomorrow," the old boy offered with a toss of the head to include his grieving daughter recovering upstairs.

With that Lehrer climbed back into his robust Volvo estate and drifted a few hundred yards in the direction of masts and halyards visible at the end of the tarmac. He pulled up in the pub car park, right under the creaking sign which purported to show a young mariner aboard an old vessel of the line, telescope to the eye in earnest examination of a distant sail on a bright horizon.

"That's right Inspector, one of our regulars... yes, you could easily say that about Lee. At one time he used to spend a lot of time 'ere, right there in fact," and he pointed at the bar stool at the far end of the bar, still turned with its short back-rest to the wall so that an occupant might look along the bar or out at the wider lounge. There was a range of tables and chairs, and then the 'oche' and the dart board at the far end of the room.

It was a spacious area by traditional standards, more a bar and lounge combined and quite unusual in that regard. The place seemed homely enough – certainly neat and clean. The furnishings had been recently upgraded. The clean-cut cream-clad walls no longer struggled for their lustre against the chemical attack of nicotine from those cigarette-fuelled smog-filled evenings of earlier, less considerate times. Lehrer took his cue and angled himself up onto a stool in the middle of the row. The landlord, Jimmy Judge, continued with his chores behind the bar, casually fielding Lehrer's enquiries in an easy and yet reflective mood.

Sipping a refreshing orange and soda the detective prodded and poked his way delicately through almost three decades of personal observations and experiences of one of the local community's most central and best informed figures.

Jimmy Judge slipped straight into a local social history lesson, and Lehrer concentrated hard to recall the basics of the dead man's earlier connections and attachments. He at least remembered that he'd been married to a local girl before shacking up with Lynsey Bastion more recently.

The landlord had known Lee Phillipson for about fifteen years: ever since his appearance in Janice Swinton's life, and he'd known Janice for ten years more from the time she had appeared on the arm old Jeff Swinton. At that time – in Judge's own opinion – Swinton had been preciously close to spending the rest of his natural as a shy and lonely misfit despite the sobering fact that he was probably only about mid-forties by then. By some Jeff Swinton had been seen as a bit aloof – not all that good a mixer in the social sense – a quiet, sensitive type who, nevertheless, had achieved a position of some elevation in the eyes of the locals for his architectural imprint on some of the more imposing properties in the area. The local tradesmen, some of whom had worked on a few of his barn restorations and especially his old mill refurbishment projects, had grown to admire the man's contemporary designs and the tasteful style with which these were integrated into the traditional fabric of those older buildings. They had also come to respect his strict attention to detail on site – something that had cost one or two of them the odd retainer on occasions – but while he was not to be trifled with in a professional capacity, he remained fairly reclusive, didn't seem to enjoy any lasting relationships and was something of a mystery to many.

"You see Inspector," Jimmy continued, "he was 'ere when I got 'ere – been 'ere a while too as I remember – but this place wasn't really his cup of tea or pint o' bitter, if you see what I mean," nodding with a smile. "He lived up at the old farmhouse where Janice lives now – well at least when she's at home that is – and he didn't venture down here too often until she arrived.

"Then, well..." he paused, "what a transformation. She's still a real firebrand now – as you'll find out for yourself soon enough I shouldn't wonder – but then... well... then she was dynamite... so full of energy and always organising folk and getting things going. You know," he hesitated, "my little business here wouldn't have done nearly so well without her jump starting the village like that. Jeez, when I look back..." and he trailed off, lost in thought as he stacked a fresh tray of J2Os into the fridge.

"You know, they'd come down the road for a few drinks of a Friday evening, or bring that nipper down for a Sunday lunch, even when she was about to pop with their youngest, what's his name...Josh, yes Josh, of course, and they were here quite a bit and she really brought Jeff out of himself and they were good times," and then he quieted for a moment, looking rueful, and then added simply, "and when he dropped dead it just pulled the rug out from under them really. It hit us all, what can I say? And now this...," he exclaimed, "...terrible business. What's the world coming to, eh Inspector?"

"Well I can't deny that for a tiny little hideaway like this, it does appear as if Compton, or is it Westonfield, has had more than its fair share of drama," Lehrer submitted. Anxious to keep the conversation flowing he pushed on, "And Phillipson, Lee Phillipson, was he about at this time, was he local I mean, or did he appear a bit later?"

"Oh later perhaps, but not much later...twelve to eighteen months tops," the landlord threw back into the discussion quickly. "He seemed much more her type I suppose... you know, more outgoing like her, perhaps a little pushy on occasions, but generally sociable and it looked like he was getting along with the people around them here in the village. He was a keen angler and he joined the Fisherman's Friends – that's the local fishing group," he added by way of explanation. "The chaps convene regularly here at the Midshipman, and on top of that Lee came down here a lot for quiz nights, darts matches, New Year's Eve bashes, that sort of thing – bit of a party animal you might say. He could shift a pint or two as well I should say, not to mention the odd Bacardi."

"In what way pushy, Mr Judge?"

"Aw, nothing too unpleasant, if you understand me, but he was quite an opinionated bloke, about many things – in fact most things, truth be told – and I could sense early on that some folk didn't like to have their wings clipped on occasions by an incomer sat at the end of the bar. It wasn't a big deal Inspector, honestly, but when the beer was flowing he could sail pretty close to the wind sometimes and you know what – funny now looking back at it – but I spotted it quite early on: not always my strongest suit Inspector, despite everyone's expectation that the pub landlord never misses a trick. In his case I remember thinking that I should watch out in case there should be a need for damage limitation tactics. Ha, if only I'd realised", he ended bluntly.

"How do you mean?" Lehrer prompted.

"Well Inspector, if you offered me the chance to rewind the tape ten or fifteen years I'd jump at the opportunity to put things back the way they were. Compare the mood here in my pub now with those heady days and it's miserable by contrast. Don't let me mislead you. I'm not saying business isn't good, well... okay at best," he corrected, "but we have a good clientele in this vicinity and good passing trade for lunches and dinners – so no complaints on that score. But back then things were really hoppin'," he said with a reflective grin, "until... that is...Lee Phillipson drove a wedge into this community through a lot of silly nonsense and carry on that we could all have done without."

"Go on, Mr Judge, please."

"Jimmy, please Inspector, you make me sound like a Suffolk Magistrate," he laughed hoarsely. He shifted his attention to bottled German beer and threw fists-full up into the cool store shelves, talking both to the detective and to the rows of bottles as he turned back and forth with the task.

"You see, he misjudged Janice's popularity in these parts. She'd already been here ten years or so. No... more than that even. In Jeff's time she'd not only made some great friends here, but she'd practically lifted the atmosphere – you know, the sense of togetherness as a local community – on her own. We had endless summer events and festivities: fetes, gymkhanas, cricket matches between the footballers and the cricketers... you know the sort of thing Inspector: all the wives and girlfriends turned up and we had hundreds of kids running about. And then in the winter naturally the teams would reconvene in the wet and the cold for the annual footy match. Of course there were fantastic Christmas parties and New Year's Eve booze ups – Christ, we had the roof lifting off 'ere loads o' times – and in all of this Janice played a pivotal role. People liked her. She worked hard, played hard, helped out and got stuck in. Maybe Lee missed the point or perhaps just overlooked the obvious, but it proved to be a serious miscalculation in my view".

Lehrer interrupted. "Hang on a minute. It looks like Janice Swinton has a fine reputation. That says nothing about Lee Phillipson, so what manner of silly nonsense and carry on are you referring to? Are you saying that you think his recent demise could be traced back to events at that time: rubbing people up the wrong way, stepping on toes too often, botched relationships, you now Jimmy, people stuff?"

"No Inspector, that's not what I'm trying to say. It must take a lot of abuse for someone to harbour a grudge so big that he deliberately sets out to settle some old scores once and for all, if you're with me," he intoned. "No... I meant that he did rub some people up the wrong way to use your phrase, but equally, some folk really liked him. That's pretty much normal in my book. In here I see all sorts, as you can imagine, but I think I'm trying to say that those two camps became separated relatively quickly once he'd arrived and found his feet and started to be himself."

"And the miscalculation?"

"Inspector, being himself in Lee Phillipson's eyes basically meant looking after himself and his own interests as he saw them. He may have been quite an extrovert you might say – odd for a bloke who could sit all day by a riverbank with his fishing rod just resting on its stand – but inwardly, I have no doubt, he was only really interested in his own wants and needs. When things started to go wrong he didn't seem to be aware that he was hurting some of those closest to him... more likely, I just don't think he cared.

"Inspector, when you have a man propping up your bar for longer periods than is either healthy or welcome, in a very odd schedule too – sometimes all afternoon and evening on a weekday, other times all day at the weekend but on his own – you get to know more about that man than you ever wanted to. You see how he works the crowd, who he's comfortable with, what attracts his attention, who he likes to challenge or to avoid. In any event, he certainly miss-read the strength of feeling and some of the reactions he generated in Janice's circle of friends. He made a right mess of her social set-up and he drove that coach and horses through her life, more often than not, right here in my pub. God knows what it must have been like living with him at that time."

Lehrer drained his glass and offered it up to be replenished. The landlord did so efficiently with the practiced moves of an old hand and thus, having signalled his extended time horizon, the detective eased back into the interview without missing a beat.

"When did things start to go wrong, Jimmy, and what things exactly?"

"Oh dear, that's a long story," the landlord responded with a sigh, but he made no effort to check the clock behind him or to indicate a need to withdraw. It was still mid-morning and he probably had another half an hour or so before he would have to move up a gear. "Like I said, he was very opinionated, too opinionated for me and for many. It was as if he enjoyed the banter – the cut and thrust – and it didn't really matter what subject was under the spotlight. He could wax lyrical about almost anything in the sporting line. On politics he could be very persuasive. He seemed very comfortable with local issues and gossip, and he could stretch the conversation internationally at a whim. However, his ideas and his manner often appeared to exaggerate his case – to emphasise the facts as he saw them, naturally in his favour – with a surety that all too often translated as arrogance, conceit perhaps, even disdain sometimes. That's hard for anyone either to manage or to forgive, especially if over time it becomes typical.

"There were a few confrontations early doors – nothing serious, but you know how it is when someone just over-plays his hand at someone else's expense, in public of course right here in the bar and you can see the victim smarting with the put-down. It could be almost anything: a bit of gloating gone just a tad too far after an unexpected football result, or perhaps a few very sharp, quick-witted remarks about some political event of the day. It really is an open book Inspector, and Lee always had the confidence in his own views to push home any advantage. But honestly Inspector, his radar was bust. He just didn't see how things were going and he never knew when to back off. A minor point scored would become a major headline in no time and that could sometimes descend into a complete bloodbath – excuse the pun, please – if some smarter folk didn't intervene."

"In what sense?"

"Inspector, the number of times I've had to chip in to such exchanges to rescue some kind of sanity…well… you'd be amazed. Look, it's normal in this line of work, but it's obviously not normal for one of my regulars to get himself shot dead in his own bathroom, and that kind of thing definitely concentrates the mind I can tell you. Lee Phillipson was a decent enough guy, but he had a nasty edge to him that pissed a lot of people off, no question," Judge affirmed with confidence. "Many's the time I butted in to ask one of the bunch to maybe do something for me like pass over a load of glasses from a nearby table. It was just to shove some kind of distraction into the heat of things: asking if so-and-so's mate was coming down tonight or how had the missus got on with that job interview, or was it time for another round gentlemen… I mean anything really Inspector, anything that would break the flow or the trend of something going decidedly downhill. It seems remarkable to me now – looking back over all these years – to recognise how often he'd be at the centre of the brewing storm so to speak."

"But Jimmy, you just said that you couldn't see any of this stuff resulting in quite such a terminal outcome, so where are you going with this? What did you mean earlier when you mentioned a lot of daft carry on and nonsense?"

"Inspector I feel bad about this. Lee spent many happy hours propping up my bar and we had some good old chats about all sorts of odds and ends, so to be slagging him off now seems out of order somehow. Do you know what I mean?"

Lehrer looked him right in the eye, held his gaze momentarily and said with real sincerity, "Mr Judge, if you want me to catch the killer I need you to offload the last twenty years right here, right now," and then, after the slightest pause, "assuming you're not a murderer."

"Jeez Inspector, do me a favour will you," Jimmy retorted, and he looked genuinely shaken with the very idea.

"Well go on then," Lehrer encouraged, "tell me about the bust ups."

"Okay, okay," Jimmy replied with a withered expression, "but let's try to keep this on an even keel. I don't want to do the guy down, but that said it does look as if he's just wound up some poor sod just that bit too far and something's snapped."

He hesitated, as if gathering up history and trying to get the sequence of events roughly right in his head. "The earliest landmines, at least as I remember it Inspector, were a couple of clashes with blokes who had been good friends of poor old Jeff and – it follows, of course – good friends of Janice too. We're talking about business people: the sorts of chaps who'd been round the block a few times and made a few quid in the process, a bit like Jeff himself I suppose. You know the types: a local stockbroker with a bit of a regional empire hereabouts in East Anglia and a shipping agent from down Felixstowe way, both solid characters and good socialisers. But there was something in Lee Phillipson's past that had taken him into the financial world in some way – fairly small beer by comparison – but I think he'd had his nose put out of joint and he was still carrying a chip on each shoulder for balance, if you follow me?" he queried of his listener, just to check that the copper was paying attention

Lehrer nodded affirmation with a wry smile.

"On a couple of occasions he just went too far. He obviously knew a little bit about the world of money, the City and all that stuff. He could lord it over the lads in the cricket team and some of my other regulars without thinking about it – not that they delved too deeply into that murky world all that often when you could talk about the Ashes series or the latest bit of totty on Strictly Come Dancing – oh...yes... and we should come back to the ladies in a minute," he hedged, "but he certainly resented anyone who had done well enough to be financially comfortable. That, in Lee's eyes, meant better off than him. He had a disdain – a disgust even – for anyone who registered as successful and 'rich' by his own standards," and saying this he raised his hands and twitched his index fingers to signal the inverted commas. "Of course the problem with that was simply that the same category included many of my regulars and, equally, many of Janice's own friends. He just got in too deep a few times and the Adnams started to do the talking. Before I knew it I had a couple of my best customers tugging on jackets in a right paddy and making a hasty exit far too early for a Friday night. You know the score Inspector: heated exchanges, one or two personal pointers, all a bit over the top and regretted the next morning no doubt, but not by Lee Phillipson. He couldn't rationalise that stuff the next day or in fact at any time afterwards. He gave no ground once the lines had been crossed. He never saw his own failings. He harboured grudges and I guess it was inevitable that relationships were bound to deteriorate after those kinds of head-to-head confrontation had taken place."

"And the ladies?" enquired Lehrer with a perky lift of the eyebrows.

"Ah yes... the ladies, so many lovely ladies," Jimmy reflected out loud. "Do you know Inspector," he said with an apparently accelerating pace commensurate with his own interest, "the first time he ever came into my pub..." he halted briefly as if to corroborate his story... "he was with Janice, and she was all flushed with a touch of excitement and hint of anxiety because this was her new man on show for the first time and she wanted it to go well, and…well, they came in here and they perched themselves on the two end stools there. Blow me over, he'd even shifted it around with its back to the wall so he could see everything going on. We chatted a bit and different people came and went with their drinks and it was all very cute as they looked very 'together'," the same index fingers again, "and the whole afternoon he gave every female within twenty feet the once over. Yes… and all the bumps in the right places, thank you very much," and as he played the cameo Jimmy tilted his head first to one side and then the other as if feasting on a host of imaginary girls. "He didn't miss a single move.

"Hey… Inspector, the day I stop ogling the girls will be the day I'm in my box, and I'd wager you might say the same thing, but there is such a thing as discretion. Janice just didn't seem to notice. She was facing the bar most of the time, but I knew right there and then that this was a true ladies' man in every sense of the term. Not surprising therefore to catch a whiff of gossip every now and again that he'd been seen with so-and-so at the Wheatsheaf in Woodbridge or spotted in the woods along the water with an unidentified 'companion'," and those index fingers yet again, "but we could hardly miss the uproar here one night when a geezer turned up at a darts game.

"Midshipman versus Three Tuns from Ipswich I think it was, and when Lee's name was called out for his darts in a throw-off to settle a knock-out tie, this bloke steps forward – only a little guy too I should say, but as broad as he was tall – and he belted Lee right in the mouth and laid 'im out. He leaned over 'im down on the oche floor and balled at 'im, "Next time you so much as lay eyes on my girl let alone yer filthy mitts, I'll break your balls and your legs," and then he stomped out. Wow, Inspector…talk about a hush over the crowd or what. Lee pulled himself up, wiped his split lip with the back of his hand and then rattled in a twenty, treble twenty, double sixteen to win the leg and clinch the match. Unbelievable! My God, did they shift some booze that night."

The policeman nodded his acknowledgment at that rasping comeback in the face of such adversity, but in the same moment he said simply, "Jimmy, at some stage you're going to have to point me in the direction of our local prize-fighter, if you can." And then he added, "How did Janice react when she heard about it?"

"Inspector, as far as I could tell she never knew about it. Amazing really, but then folk round here would protect her from that kind of deceit I'm sure – I hope so anyway. I'd hate to think that even then she was tormented by such things and that she kept them locked away to save face. I don't know Inspector, to be truthful."

And then drifting off on another recollection Jimmy added, "He told me himself once that he'd been married before and that he'd met his first wife on a train – in the sense that he'd just brushed past her in the aisle – and thought to himself, wow, she was tasty, must go back and find her...which he did. He chatted her up from scratch right there and they were married within a few months. It didn't last long, all sorts of issues apparently... crazy bastard, what kind of bloke does that kind of thing..." It wasn't a question, more a statement.

"Jimmy you mentioned that Lee spent some strange hours here in the pub. How did that work? Was it like that from the outset?"

"No, no...not at all. At first they would come down for the odd beer of an evening and that progressed to a longer night on Saturday sometimes. Then that was dropped in favour of Sunday lunch in the main, but they were together and they looked the part. Then one afternoon he turned up about three-ish I suppose and stayed till last orders at eleven. He told me he was changing jobs and had a bit of free time for a little while, but the visits just multiplied. In a month or two he was down here an awful lot. He was on his own during the day of course, Janice working and all that, but then she started working away up in Hertfordshire or Bedford or somewhere like that at one of those big private nursing homes and she was hardly ever home. I'd see her maybe once a month at best, but the less I saw of Janice the more I saw of him. He was just about camped out here in my bar. I must say, it started to create some difficulties for me because, like I said, he wasn't everybody's best mate and I could sense that the two camps were polarising in a way – and the better clientele chose to avoid him – or at least that's how it looked to me. Maybe I was getting paranoid, but I know there was an atmosphere in the place that some found quite intimidating."

"What about her kids"?

"Well Josh was at school, but he usually stayed with his grandmother during the week. That's Janice's mother – nice lady I'd say. His big sister…er…Laura," he produced with a satisfactory nod, "she was away at weekly boarding school up Norwich way. No love lost there – with either of them – as far as I could tell."

"Oh…what do you mean exactly"?

"Oh, by the time Josh started to grow up, I think he had him measured up pretty well – saw through him basically. I always got along with Josh I think, but even when he came of drinking age he rarely came down here because he half expected Lee to be here at all times of day and night – and more often than not he'd have been right," he concluded with a sigh.

"And Janice, how did she come across to you? You'd known her quite a long time by then."

"Janice just looked more and more tired, more stressed, more anxious, more fretful. I really felt for her. I could see it in her eyes. There was a sense of quiet desperation about her, a form of panic, a sort of muted cry for help, but we just didn't know enough to know where to start. The months ticked by. She was away a lot and would come back sporadically and try to put a brave face on things. He'd been bullshitting us about different job opportunities, and then about his creative art phase which petered out no sooner than it had been mentioned. In any event it appeared to require a degree of alcoholic sustenance each lunch time which suggested a deep afternoon snooze was to follow in preference to a few hours at the canvas or spinning the potter's wheel. The whole situation just looked a right mess.

"Then one sunny afternoon – ooh… I'd guess about ten years ago now, a young couple pitched up here and she sat on that very stool where you are now Inspector, and they ordered drinks and a bar snack. It didn't take long to discover that they were new to the area. I think he'd come in for a job at BT over in that big complex, Martlesham way. They said they'd just bought a neat little apartment over the old post office in Martlesham high street. Well…I had to check myself and think pretty hard. I could have sworn that that was one of Janice's rental properties that she used to put out to summer visitors with a pretty full calendar most of the time. I'm sure it had been a nice little earner for her and Jeff in the past. They'd worked hard and spent a fair bit – time and money – doing them up. I think it had been part of Janice's idea for Jeff's early retirement, you know, a substitute income stream of sorts to allow him to wind down the day job a bit. We used to see lots of holiday folk in here who were staying over there. To learn that the place had been sold was, to me, a really sad indication of the true turmoil going on in Janice's life. A couple of years passed and then her other rental was sold. It was a lovely seaside retreat up on the coast by Orford. Things must have been desperate I reckon.

"I don't think he turned his hand to work for the best part of a decade and I can only assume that she had to sell those houses off to cover their costs all the while. How she managed to hang on to the farmhouse itself God only knows."

"How and when did it all end for them?" the Inspector quizzed, looking fleetingly at his watch and realising that his time was almost up.

"Ha... that's an easy one," quipped the landlord without hesitation. "He had a fling with one of my bar girls," and, looking rather shiftily to either side of the bar to check for eavesdroppers, he added, "they didn't call her the Village Bike for nothing, if you follow, but it was so blatant that Janice just called time on the whole thing and chucked him out. That was it, done and dusted."

"How long ago?"

"Oh... I'd say about five years ago, maybe six. You'd have to ask her if you want it exactly," he answered pointedly.

"And Lynsey Bastion?" Lehrer threw at him quickly.

Judge took a slow breath, adjusted his stance, pondered a little and then replied, "Nice girl, local lass – had her own problems in days gone by – but I don't know her all that well. Too good for him, but they did seem to hit it off. I can't deny that. Mind you," he cautioned quietly, "her old man was never all that impressed with Lee and if you asked me to put my money where my mouth is I'd say he refused to let Lee move into his home when he and Lynsey started to get it on. She had returned to live at home when her previous relationship had collapsed, but I don't know any of the details. I know they were just renting that cottage over yonder and I'm sure cash was always tight. Every time they came in here for a meal she would always pay, never Lee. You can make of that what you will, Inspector, but now I must crack on."

"Jimmy you have been most helpful, thank you. I hope you won't mind if we call on you again. A man of your standing here in the village will be able to help us with all sorts of information, even bits and pieces that you thought you'd forgotten, so I'll say goodbye for now and maybe catch up with you again sometime soon."

"I understand Inspector, no problem. Let's hope you nail this nutter whoever he is."

With that David Lehrer slipped down from his perch, waved a cheerio back to the landlord on his way out, but then halted abruptly and turning back towards the bar he enquired, "One last thing Jimmy: how did you know about Lee Phillipson's death? I didn't say why I was here, but you were already way ahead of me, and it happened only yesterday. How come?"

"One of my kitchen staff is the daughter of Lee and Lynsey's neighbours. She knew almost as soon as Lynsey did herself. Thinking about it, I guess she knew before you fellas did. The bush telegraph waits for no man, Inspector."

With that Lehrer lifted the heavy iron latch on the main door and crunched out across the grit to his waiting car.

9 – knock-on effects

He'd waited for some time – and had rung the bell three times – before he heard the shuffling approach of an apparently elderly frame to the other side of the door. Then, for a second or two, he began to expect a desperate and desolate version of the young woman, Lynsey herself, depressed with grief and unable to motivate herself even to respond to a caller at the house. However, as the door locks were fumbled free and the door swung back there stood old Mr Bastion once again.

He moved unsteadily aside and gestured the Inspector through the door and then through into the living room where Lehrer – looking in expectantly for the man's daughter – avoided the well-worn, comfy arm chair knowing immediately that this was certainly the owner's favourite. He switched across to the adjacent parlour chair which appeared to offer an altogether firmer seat.

Bastion wasted no time in letting the Inspector know that his daughter was still very shaken and was, as yet, not able to concentrate on the details of, "This terrible business". It was still savage he considered with a pained expression, and he'd spent much of yesterday evening trying to calm his girl down enough to answer just some of his own questions. But she was improving now apparently. She'd just popped out the back into the copse behind the house for a breath of fresh air and promised to be back in ten or fifteen minutes – and no more, unless she wanted her old dad to fret about her mental state. She'd be back soon enough was his reassuring message, although he couldn't vouch for her reaction to finding a police detective sitting in her old dad's front room. No…he hadn't had the heart to warn her of Lehrer's anticipated return.

The detective worked carefully to settle the old boy's mood before inching toward some of the more sensitive material he wanted to examine more closely. It was a Godsend that he'd caught him alone. He didn't want to force the conversation too aggressively, but he was anxious to get an unadulterated version of the old man's views before Lynsey returned. He wanted to elicit as much of the softer background information as he could without exposing the man to any potential intimidation or interference – intentional or otherwise – from his daughter, whose nerves were bound still to be in a state of high tension.

He needn't have worried. Bastion pitched in almost without a prompt. He had liked Lee Phillipson, but not trusted him. He had seen the happiness the man had brought into his daughter's life after the failure of her earlier marriage and the emptiness that had persisted for too long afterwards. But he had also recognised her own reticence in some areas of her relationship with her new man: difficulties represented by long spells without much communication between father and daughter at home – immersed, as they were, in a somewhat awkward and unsettling domestic atmosphere which nurtured unease, some friction and even a little suspicion on some occasions.

Bastion had lived in these parts all his life. He knew the who's who of the local social landscape as if the chapter and verse of it all were etched on his mind – lest his failing memory should let him down. However, he'd known little of Phillipson before the man had walked across his daughter's path. In fact his only firm recollection was that Phillipson had married Janice Swinton, more's the pity for her, and left her a little worse off for the privilege by all accounts. Janice had worked ferociously – and not for the first time in her topsy-turvy life – after the drifter had moved on, and she'd had some ground to recover then, and no mistake.

With a little gentle cajoling from Lehrer, Bastion confided that he had still been active enough in the community then to catch the drift of what had happened at Janice Swinton's old farmhouse after poor Jeff had passed on – to her properties and her land, and how the guy had seemingly done not a lot for many years as the whole thing crumbled around them. He remembered hearing once down at the Midshipman, that Phillipson had become an artist, a creative artist no less, although how a bloke could be an artist and not be creative Bastion couldn't hope to guess. It hadn't reduced his beer intake any, and as far as anyone could discern there had never been any creative things created. The man appeared to spend an awful lot of time propping up Jimmy Judge's bar or sitting on a little fold-away stool on the river bank with his fishing rod reaching out across the water from one day to the next.

But no… for a man who seemed to have drifted around so much in his life and achieved so little, Bastion hadn't been able to say that he was overjoyed when his own daughter took up with Phillipson. She was surely better than that, even though, he smiled as much to himself as to Lehrer, such an opinion was naturally biased in her favour. He thought his little girl just as pretty as her late Mum had been at the same age, bless 'er, and he wondered how his old gal would have reacted to all this horrible nonsense now – what a palaver.

Phillipson had apparently offered opinions on just about everything, whether or not he knew anything about the subject in discussion. He seemed to get quite agitated over some recurring themes: certainly those with money, aspects of politics, royalty and what he called the patronage system. Yes, he was a right little Bolshi when he wanted to be, and it all got that much more acute after a few glasses of wine or few pints of Jimmy's best ale. Aye… those were definitely recurring themes.

At first he seemed very different to the sort of blokes Lynsey had dated in the past, and certainly not like her ex-husband who had been a very odd fish. There, he'd known with certainty, was a marriage doomed to failure, but she wouldn't be told and sure enough it all just dried up through a combination of mutual boredom and disinterest. Lee, on the other hand, seemed to have a lot more spark and he quickly brightened things up in the early days. Then with familiarity came a creeping contempt. It became rather repetitive, then dull, and eventually just damned irritating. At one stage after she'd sold her own place and paid off the ex, she'd wanted him to move into this house, the family home, but the old boy hadn't been interested in that and it was then that Phillipson's resentment began to show. Sometimes it was just an edge, at other times quite a sullen, almost intimidating disaffection. Of course that only hardened Bastion's resolve not to give way even if that put his familial relationship at risk, but with all that mess down at the Swintons' farmhouse and Phillipson's own abortive attempts at property ownership many years earlier, Bastion really was in no position to get it wrong just because this unctuous fellow had schmoozed his way into his daughter's life.

Actually that last point clanged a few bells for Ric Bastion. What was it? Oh yes, that was it... something about Phillipson having been duped out of his house in Church Ivy. He, Bastion himself, had never quite got to grips with the point and Lord knows he'd heard it enough times. Perhaps he was just dim or something, but it was all about having been forced off the housing ladder at that time, when he was with Janice Swinton. Yes... that was it. Hadn't seemed right to Bastion and still didn't. Why had he sold up then anyway if he really hadn't wanted to? He could just as easily have kept that going providing he had paid the mortgage. He'd have got a lot more for it years later, naturally. Maybe he and Janice had needed the cash at the time.

"Jeepers Inspector, to look back at how things had deteriorated for them from then on, well...what a tale of near ruination that now seems to represent. They may well have needed some cash, but surely they couldn't have been that desperate. They were both working. They had jobs and income. I mean... what could have been so difficult for them that he had to sell his little place over yonder? It was the way he always talked about it from a victim's perspective. That was what came across every time – like he'd had no say in the matter. In any event, it certainly made me very wary about embroiling myself with him in the context of my own home," and as he spoke he cast a glance around his own sitting room as if to secure the importance of the point he was making. "I must say to you though, Inspector, my reluctance to let them move in here did drive something of a wedge between me and my girl, Lynsey, and I resented him for that."

At that moment the muffled sound of the back door, first opening and then closing, interrupted the old man's dissertation and they both inwardly braced themselves for Lynsey's imminent appearance and anticipated surprise. Shuffling steps approached along the hallway, the lounge door eased open and just as she began to report her return to her father her diffident, softly-spoken announcement trailed off into silence as her eyes met Lehrer's. Unable to conceal her disappointment, she sat, a worn, dejected figure, on the very edge of the sofa facing the two men before her.

"A policeman, Dad," she ventured gently, more in statement than inquisition.

"Aye lass," he observed by way of response, "and you know you're going to have to get through this now no matter how frayed your nerves might be. This is Detective Chief Inspector Lehrer. He's heading up the whole investigation and he's going to need your help love – you can appreciate that I'm sure. Let me put the kettle on and you two can get started. I'll be back in a jiffy," and with that Ric Bastion hoisted himself up pulling hard on the crook of his cane and pottered away through the same door retracing his daughter's steps back to the kitchen.

She looked wrecked, pale and drawn, with unkempt wisps of strawberry blonde hair plastered to her feverish, translucent brow. Her lips were almost grey, her dull gaze staring out from lifeless grey-green eyes partially obscured by swollen, reddened lids. She said nothing for some minutes. She clasped and then released her hands continuously, entwining her fingers, arching then liberating them interminably as if pursuing an entirely subconscious ritual born only from wretched anguish. Then she placed her hands flatly on her knees as if signifying that a decisive moment had passed – that she had encountered a formidable psychological hurdle and surmounted that obstacle – and she turned towards the policeman purposefully and asked him how she might help.

First and foremost his investigation would need a list of friends and neighbours – regular visitors to the house – which would allow the forensic team to identify and to eliminate potentially misleading traces left at the crime scene. She nodded her understanding, supressing a welling disbelief that she was indeed immersed in the harsh reality of real life-and-death murder enquiry. TV detectives this was not...somewhere out there was a brutal, heartless killer who had deliberately invaded her own home, their home...and she only just held herself together at the thought of it all.

Lehrer then explained that it was paramount at this stage that Miss Bastion lead him through as much background detail as possible in order to fill in as many of the missing pieces to this puzzle as she could. He outlined his need for more information about Lee's family background, about her understanding of his working life, about his previous relationships especially that with Janice Swinton. He also pressed home – while the going looked favourable – his need to understand her own relationship with the late Lee Phillipson. It wasn't just down to some of the more intimate aspects of that relationship – how they got along together, and whether there were any causes of difficulty or tension between them – but also with regard to things apparently routine or seemingly mundane. What about his comings and goings to and from work for example? Did he have any regular commitments to outside interests like his fishing or other pastimes? Could she describe any of his traits and habits, however innocuous, which may help Lehrer and his team to better understand the nature and character of the man such that they could apply themselves in the right areas during the next few critically important days?

She nodded mutely and pushed herself into the back of the seat, shifting a little to get more comfortable while pondering her initial focus on what appeared to be a fairly broad and yet detailed canvass. She made to speak and then hesitated, sighed and looked up at the detective with a quizzical, almost confused expression on her face.

"Let me help you if I can," Lehrer offered. "You've been through a very harrowing experience Ms Bastion…"

"Lynsey, please," she returned by way of interruption. "This dreadful business is bad enough, but sticking to formalities will not make it easier."

"I understand," he complied with evident compassion, "so let's keep it at Lynsey and David shall we?"

She accepted the proposal with a relieved nod.

"Lynsey, I know you were interviewed in your neighbour's home not long after you had made your terrible discovery at home on Sunday evening, so I don't need to drag you back through all of that – I have read the notes and I think I have a clear understanding of the essentials. What I'm more interested in is your own grasp of why this has happened – knowing already that you will not have any clear-cut answers. What I'm getting at are those hidden signs and pointers, those little flags and signals that currently sit within your subconscious – you're probably barely aware of them or indeed completely unaware – but there will be something lurking in the back of your mind that might just be sufficiently unusual or strange that we might be able to latch on to and develop as a lead within our investigation. That's assuming, of course, that there is nothing blindingly obvious," and he opened his hands to her plaintively seeking her response.

"No, Inspector…sorry, David… there is nothing obvious, nothing at all, and I think that's part of the shock of it all. I mean… who would do such a thing, and why?"

"There had been no recent difficulties or problems for you at home, or for Lee at work?

"No. None…well, I mean…none that I am aware of."

"And nothing unusual in Lee's movements and activities of late: no new names or characters mentioned in conversation, nothing of that sort?"

"Honestly David, nothing that comes to mind. Actually, I'd say it was quite the contrary. We were just trundling along in auto-pilot and everything seemed very normal, perhaps even a little boring to be frank."

"But you two were getting long well enough together?"

"Well, yes…at least I think so."

"Has there been anyone else in your lives of an amorous or overtly amicable nature – especially in the last few months?"

"Absolutely not," she fielded indignantly. He held his hands up in apology for the intrusion, but she understood the need for the question, and he pushed on.

"Not even on the periphery…you know…a name here or a casual reference there?"

"No. No, really, I think we were doing all right."

Lehrer didn't doubt the woman's sincerity, and he tried not to allow the pub landlord's version of history to sway his own judgement, but he decided at this point that she wouldn't be able to help him any further along his current line of enquiry. If Lee Phillipson had been involved elsewhere she was simply in the dark about it, for sure.

"Okay Lynsey, let's talk about work for a moment or two. You work in the property sector, don't you?"

"Yes. I'm with Dunstons up in Woodbridge".

"And Lee was an accountant with a local firm, isn't that so?"

"Yes, at Smallings..." and she halted momentarily and checked her contribution, "that's Smalling and Sedgwick. As you say, it's a small regional firm with half a dozen offices in East Anglia. It's one of the few I'm aware of that have retained their independence from the clutches of some of the bigger national firms."

"How was he getting on there do you think? In fact, how long had he been there?"

"Ah...well, two different answers there. Let's do them back to front. He'd been at the Ipswich office for about three years. I have to tell you though that he wasn't happy. I don't think he got on with his boss all that well."

"In what way? How did that manifest itself?"

"Oh..." she sighed. "Simply put, he was always whingeing and complaining about the guy, about the work, about the office, about a lot of things...but I really can't connect any of that with what happened here. I mean...it's one thing being unhappy at work – he thought the hours were ridiculous, and he always resented the pay and the lack of promotion for a bloke of his years and experience – but how does any of that result in someone getting..." and she trailed off tearfully, shaking her head in disbelief of the enormity of what had happened in her own home so very recently.

Lehrer concurred: friction at work was, per se, hardly unusual. He knew that the other side of that particular story might prove more revealing and he remembered that one of the team – McLennan perhaps – was due out to Smalling and Sedgwick shortly.

"How did you and Lee first meet?" He asked, switching tack.

She dried her eyes and blew her nose gently into the same tissue. "We met at the Midshipman actually."

"When was that?"

"Oh, about six or seven years ago I suppose." Her focus shifted a little as she lapsed into recollections of that earlier time, and a faint smile came and went in a moment. "It was one of those pub quiz nights, and the two of us got stuck on the same team."

"That must have been with Janice Swinton, surely," he challenged in deliberately unguarded fashion.

She appeared to bristle with resentment as if some scurrilous suggestion had been made, but then she quickly regained some composure and explained that Janice had not been there at that time.

"But you knew Janice then?" he tested.

"Oh, yes...and I still do, although not as closely nowadays, not since me and Lee started to live together. That's natural I suppose," she concluded defensively.

"But you and Lee had been together for what...about five years. Is that right?"

"Yes."

"Although you knew him from about six or seven years back?"

And again the unavoidable thrust of the unspoken insinuation piqued her indignation, but she held her nerve.

"Forgive this next question Lynsey, but what can you tell me about Lee's relationship with Janice Swinton?"

Her eyes widened at the audacity of the interrogation, and she swallowed hard.

"I'm not sure how much I can tell you about that," she rebounded defiantly. "No doubt you'll be hearing a lot of gossip about that period from a lot of busy-bodies around here, but if I were you I'd take it all with a pinch of salt. Janice was always a strong character, and she needed to be when she lost her husband like that..." and then she stopped abruptly, and a wracking sob erupted from behind her hand as she tried to contain her emotions as the terrible reality dawned on her. The same heart-wrenching upheaval that Janice Swinton must have endured all those years ago was now here at her own door, breaking her own heart. She crumpled under the pressure and wept uncontrollably, rescued only by her father's shuffling return armed with tea and biscuits on a small round metal tray.

Old Ric sat by his girl and patted her hand, soothing her back into a more subdued state. She looked up again at the detective and carried on.

"Like I said, Janice was always well thought of...always very involved, very active in the village and all that. But she was – still is – no angel. You can't be that tough, that influential, controlling even, and be nice all the time, if you get my drift. Lee thought he came out of that relationship with his reputation badly tarnished because of her stature within the community, and he considered that very unfair."

"What sorts of things are you referring to?" asked Lehrer innocently.

"Oh, Inspector," she lapsed, "these are long and, I'd wager, very tall stories and I really don't know the half of it. However, I would say that the business of Janice's rented properties getting sold off, and a lot of nonsense about why Lee sold his little house over in Church Ivy to move in with Janice...well...he always maintained that he felt somehow pressurised into doing those things very much against his natural inclinations."

"And you think these things have been misrepresented in the village?" he suggested.

"Well...yes, actually. Or perhaps more accurately I should say that Lee certainly felt that way. The worst of it came from further afield unfortunately. Apparently his mother and sister turned up a couple of times to pay them a visit. It appeared very obvious to Lee – at least that was his view – that Janice had called them down under the pretence of a holiday break of some sort. All along the three had been in cahoots and spent several days tearing into him about his lackustre contribution to the household."

"Really?" begged Lehrer in mock surprise. "What were they driving at?"

"Well...Lee had to go through a few job changes around then and he wasn't always earning, so it was difficult for him to chip in during those periods. I think he saw their criticism as something unjust and born of their own ignorance of his circumstances. He got really annoyed about it – then, at the time, and later in the telling – but that wasn't the end of it by any means. They also said that his behaviours and his moods – no idea what they might have been referring to – were causing the holiday traffic to the flats to dwindle – especially to the place up the coast. In effect, they blamed him in some way for those apartments being sold off. He was absolutely furious, and I can't help but think it was all grossly unfair."

At that the older man looked at his official visitor and raised his eyebrows in clear contradiction to his daughter's assessment of that apparently painful period in recent history.

The detective altered his angle of attack again and probed the dead man's earlier background.

"Lynsey, what do you know about any of Lee's earlier relationships...you know, not just before your time but even before his time with Janice Swinton?"

Again she swallowed hard. He could tell that she sensed a negative expectation – not just from his stated interest in years gone by – but in the suspicion that his curiosity had been fuelled by neighbourly tittle-tattle close at hand.

"Again Inspector, not much. He was married years ago... the first time around – we're not married by the way...sorry, we weren't married," she corrected timidly. "He had a son, but the marital relationship collapsed when the child was still quite young. Despite years and years of trying to maintain a link with the boy as he grew, the whole thing apparently faded, and Lee was bitter about his ex-wife's deliberately obstructive stance throughout the boy's early years."

"What do you think he meant by that?"

"Oh, simple things, like trying to reach him on the phone or trying to get birthday presents and cards through to the lad without her intercepting them. But you know, Inspector...sorry, David...out of the blue, after years and years, suddenly we got an email from the lad. He wasn't a lad any more – all grown up and living and working in London – and he wanted to come out to Suffolk to see his Dad. Well...what can I say? Lee was delighted. The lad – young man should I say – was a treat. I really liked him, but Lee seemed quite subdued about the whole thing. It didn't go especially well. They just didn't seem to hit it off. I couldn't see why, but Lee seemed reluctant to talk about it afterwards. I suggested that it was perhaps that his son – Dan, Daniel was his name... is his name," she confirmed, "was maybe trying too hard. I pointed out that it must have been incredibly brave of him and probably quite traumatic too, to be connecting with the father he had never met."

"And how did Lee react to that?" quizzed the policeman.

"You know...he just seemed to shrug it off as if it were hardly consequential. It was very odd I must say. I even suggested that their relationship might mellow with the next few meets, but again Lee just hunched his shoulders as if he wasn't convinced that he would see the boy again."

"Did you meet this young man Mr Bastion?" asked Lehrer, turning to his host.

"No, Inspector. I never saw him. He was here one minute and gone the next. I thought he was staying the weekend, but on the Sunday morning my lass here tells me he went back to London the night before. It was all a bit of an anti-climax I can tell you."

The detective knew he'd probably had the best of their time and concentration. He also recognised that he had a number of new and potentially rewarding connections to work with, so he hurried through some closing questions while sipping his tea, and then offered his hosts his grateful thanks, with due sincerity and compassion, and took his leave.

10 – hero to charlatan

The place was almost entirely clad in rich green ivy from ground to gutters, with each rectangular window of the main building providing a regular pattern of apertures – within the dense green mass – for its entire length. Lehrer considered the view from any one of those windows to be rewarding, especially to anyone with a gardener's eye. The lawns and flower beds were resplendent – two-tone mown stripes bordered by the cascading colours of a rich variety of spring bulbs, and flowering shrubs – with a fulsome backdrop of mature hedging to one side. To the southerly aspect, an impressive old red-brick wall supported the trained and disciplined branches of a range of fruit trees, and behind stood a vast swathe of mature trees in all their verdant spring-time glory. He thought of the elderly folk within, looking out at this delightful scene, and he felt sure that the changing seasons would continually alter and refresh this fresco for their consumption and to their benefit. He also thought it not a bad way to spend the quieter days of one's life, but then who was he to make such judgements for others?

His visit had been unannounced, and quite deliberately so. Park Green Residential Home (for the elderly) nestled into a leafy spot on the outskirts of Bedford, a two hour drive from the Suffolk coast. It would have scant need for a detective chief inspector in the normal course of events – or at least he hoped so – but he wanted, if at all possible, to catch her while she remained ignorant of her ex-husband's demise. It was more than likely that news had filtered out from Suffolk already – Jimmy Judge's bush telegraph or was it his social grapevine, he couldn't recall – but if her recent absence from home due to her working commitments had protected her from such depressing tidings, then Lehrer thought that he would have an infinitely better chance to glean something significant from Janice Swinton's earliest reactions. That assumed, of course, that there was something to discover which might assist him in his purpose, and that was by no means a given.

He was shown straight through to her office and asked to wait. He wondered if that were indicative of customary protocol, or whether indeed she would be annoyed with the young girl on reception who had been so helpful. Sitting there quietly – a potential imposter in the woman's inner sanctum – left him feeling a little uneasy. However, he reasoned that if it were to prove problematic, then it would surely undermine her sense of control more so than his, and that might work in his favour.

The office was extremely neat. Clearly this was the lair either of someone who had little to do – unlikely for a manager of such a large and outwardly impressive institution – or, and more likely, of someone terrifyingly organised and super-efficient.

On the corner of her desk stood two framed photographs, images in the stark contrasts of the monochrome print. The first and slightly larger of the two showed a curious old farm house of stone walls and tiled slate construction. He recognised the style immediately. It was somewhere in the English Lake District, an area he loved and where he'd spent many a holiday in rain and shine – more rain than shine he conceded silently. There he'd trudged the wild landscapes of the open fells and enjoyed some of England's loftiest peaks and the fabulous Lakeland views to be had from their slopes. He took a casual punt at identifying the rugged mountain rising up behind the old house in the background of the picture. Was it the Old Man of Coniston? Could be, and that would locate the building in Coniston village from that angle and perspective. He smiled to himself as the memories filtered through his professional concentration.

The second and smaller frame defined a young man so very clearly kitted out in the uniform of a British regiment of the Great War. Reaching out to grasp the picture, Lehrer drew it closer for a better look. The boy appeared pale and thin and that, suspected Lehrer, was before he'd seen any fighting for his combats remained pressed, his puttees spotless and his boots shone with the gloss of spit and polish. More conclusively however, he was smiling happily in a slightly self-conscious manner with, presumably, not the faintest idea of the carnage and devastation soon to confront him. Lehrer wondered if he had survived, and indeed who he had been. As he returned the photo to its place, the door flew open and in marched a bustling figure clutching an armful of files and papers.

Janice Swinton stretched out a hand and gripped his very firmly as she introduced herself.

"I'm so sorry Detective Chief Inspector," she offered with a concerned expression etched into her features. "I do hate to be kept waiting and I assume that any of my visitors feel the same way, so to have you dumped here unattended is quite unforgiveable...but please forgive me anyway," she beseeched him with a gentle smile.

"No need," he responded deferentially. "I've only been here for five minutes or so."

"Oh...not so awful then," she exhaled as her apparent stress receded. "And how can I help you – it's not the Meakins again is it?" she queried as she retreated around the desk and offloaded her paperwork. "Do you know," she continued regardless of his perplexed countenance, "I think that family ought to be certified. They should just leave the poor old girl alone. She's perfectly happy here and she's not about to dish out her considerable wealth to that money-grabbing clutch of lightweights for some years to come." But then she stopped, realising the missing wavelength and the potential indiscretion she had just committed. "It's not the Meakins at all, is it, Detective Chief Inspector?"

"Never heard of them ma'am," he returned with a smile, and they shared the good humour of her miscalculation. She laughed, perhaps a little nervously, but it seemed to help her to relax as she settled into her leather chair, elbows planted on the desk and ready to grant him her undivided attention.

He liked her. She had a sparkle in her eye – hazel with a pale grey fleck – and she came across as welcoming, engaged now, keen almost, and he imagined her as a formidable but eminently reliable and trustworthy manager. Her dark hair – showing with the peppered intrusion of greying strands – was gathered to a knot at the back which fielded a garish crimson clasp. She wore no discernible make-up. Her finger nails were clipped, short and functional. She wore a sensible, business-like day dress which accentuated her firm and shapely figure. He thought her to look about fifty, maybe a little younger, but he knew her to be closer to sixty.

"Fascinating photos," he floated into the conversation, pointing to them as he did so. "Lake District... surely, it must be," he suggested.

"Spot on Detective Chief Inspector...oh, Lordy," she sighed, "that's quite a label you're carrying around with you, isn't it? Would you mind first names? It would be so much easier," she proposed.

He agreed immediately. "It's David," he said simply, smiling back at her.

"And Janice," she affirmed in exaggerated fashion, grinning across at him as she leaned across the desk to shake his hand again, as if starting from scratch. Again he admired the strength in her hand. He concluded that this was a woman who had got through some physical graft in her time.

As she settled back in her chair she returned immediately to the Lakes. "Yes, you're right, David. It is the Lake District. I suspect I'm in the presence of an expert of mountain and fell, lake and forest – and I'll be no match for you in identifying any and every calendar photograph of the region – but I did used to own the old place up there once upon a time, and the area holds some very special memories for me."

"Oh, I'm the same," he said in positive mood. "I never had a place up there, but I just love that little corner of the country and I've spent many a vacation up there in my time. I may not be the expert you think I am, but I took a guess at Coniston," he challenged, with eyebrows raised in anticipation.

"Ah ha," she responded, clasping her hands together in appreciation. "How right you are indeed...amazing...well done," she congratulated warmly.

"And what took you up there?" he probed.

"Oh, my husband and I bought the place – my late husband I should say – and we had some great breaks up there when the kids were younger. Sadly I don't get up north so often these days, and the old house was sold off a few years back, but that's another story," she hedged.

Lehrer made a mental note to get back to that at some stage if he could engineer it, but he deftly switched direction and went back to the other photograph on the desk. He reckoned that the shift in time zones would maintain the convivial atmosphere without the intrusion of anything too emotive or too personal at this early stage.

"Now that..." she stalled for effect, "is my Grandfather, Walter," she explained. "He went to war with the Suffolks in nineteen fourteen. He was seventeen and he'd just enlisted when that was taken. I think they were garrisoned at Sedan initially, but they were moved around a lot in the horrors of the trenches. Just look at him," she urged, "so young and handsome, and yet so completely ignorant of the hell he was about to experience."

"The obvious question, if I may, is did he get through it all? Did he survive?" Lehrer interjected.

"Oh yes. He must have been indestructible – more like very lucky, to hear his own tales – but for us in the family he was something of a real-life hero – and as much for his second world war exploits as for his emergence unscathed from the trenches."

"But surely he would have been too old to be conscripted the second time around," asked the detective looking a little confused.

"Not quite," she confirmed, "but his injuries kept him out of the fray the second time around until the army found itself on the beaches at Dunkirk. My Granddad, like so many other unsung heroes, just felt a desperate need to do something, to help in some way. He sailed his old shrimper down from the Suffolk coast, across the Thames estuary and round the corner of Kent to join up with the flotilla of boats setting off to rescue the troops. I'm not sure how your maritime knowledge stacks up against Lakeland terrain, David, but a shrimper is a small boat indeed for an open sea voyage. They are coastal craft really. And I think men in their forties then were perhaps not so physically fit or even as athletic as some guys of that age now. It was just that era I suppose – a sense of middle-age by that age, if you see what I mean – but it didn't deter him. He faced Messerschmitts strafing the beaches, Stuka dive-bombers, encroaching German artillery...unbelievable really," she mused, "but still he came back with a boatful of lads in various states of health. I know he stayed in touch with many of them for years afterwards – until his dying day in fact. My son would have loved him, I'm sure of that."

"Why do you say that?" he pressed.

"Because he's boat mad, that's why," she laughed. "He had me repeat the old boy's tales so many times as he was growing up and messing about with boats on the river. I'm certain he and his mates used to re-enact that Dunkirk history over and over again at one time. But, of course, my son hadn't been born when my grandfather passed away."

"When was that? How old was he?"

"Nineteen seventy. He was in his seventies by then, but you know..." and she drifted as she reminisced, "strangely he still had the most incredible head of thick silvery hair. He used to brag about having to have his hair cut every two weeks because it was so vigorous. I can remember him very clearly. He looked quite dashing as an elderly gent, I must say, not unlike some of the fine old chaps we have here."

And with that connection she was immediately brought back to the present. She sat up in her chair rather abruptly and eyed him more warily.

"David, why are you here?" she demanded pointedly.

He smiled the smile of an interrogator who had hoped to learn a little more before being unmasked. He steadied himself and prepared for the impact his revelations might have upon his newest confidante.

"Janice you live-in here don't you? You don't go home every night, do you?"

"No. That would be an impossible commute. I stay here on site for many weeks at a time sometimes. The in-house nature of the job here is such that it's difficult for me to get away with any regularity, so I don't get back to my home in Suffolk save for the odd long weekend or for a holiday break."

"And you are the chief administrator here at Park Green?"

"Yes, the manager," she insisted, "of the entire complex," now getting a little more irritable.

"You haven't heard from friends or family back home in the last couple of days then?" he asked, feeling immediately grateful that their news embargo appeared to have worked in this case at least.

"For Christ's sake Chief Inspector," frustration and anger visibly rising now, "what has happened? Is it my son, or his family? Is it my daughter...have you had some dreadful news from Brazil?"

But he motioned her to calm herself. He had news, but nothing to threaten her immediate family.

"Janice, I must apologise for this rather unorthodox approach, but I believed you were in a better position to assist me with my current task if you were not alerted to the specific nature of the investigation in which I am presently engaged. To be blunt, I'm sorry to have to inform you that I'm heading a murder enquiry. Lee Phillipson was shot dead in his own home on Sunday afternoon at some time, we think, around 5.00 pm. He was discovered by his partner, Ms Lynsey Bastion, at about 5.30 pm."

She stared out mutely from her chair, and then nervously cleared her throat with a slightly higher note than her normal register. Then she closed her eyes as if seeking privacy.

"I realise that this will have been a great shock for you", he went on, "but I am here to ask for your help. Statistics tell us that homicides of this type are usually the result of localised factors, banal arguments and disagreements, financial problems, marital and relationship issues even personal slights and criticisms. By definition, the perpetrators of acts such as these are often hidden within the victim's immediate circle of family, friends and acquaintances. I must ask you Janice, can you think of anyone who might have the motivation and the capacity to do something like this?"

Her mind swam with so many thoughts that she couldn't easily control and order them.

She swivelled in her chair, effectively turning her back on her inquisitor. Then she stood and walked slowly away towards the full-length window at the rear of the office. She felt blank, void, empty. So much sadness, so much bitterness bottled up these last five or six years. She returned and slumped into her chair – which now obscured her almost entirely from the detective's searching gaze – and simply stared out at the descending rain as a fresh shower pummelled the greenery beyond the glass.

Discreetly she wiped away a solitary tear with the back of her index finger as a myriad of living images kaleidoscoped through the cinema of her past. She saw dreamy boat trips out from the Deben and up the coast to Aldeburgh and Southwold. She warmed to romantic walks along the winter sands of the river in brilliant sunlight, all wrapped up against the chill sea air, their wispy breath trailing behind them as they skimmed stones across the estuary where the river oozed into the salty foam. She smiled within herself at the many fond reviews of those happier early months, when she thought she'd found a friend and a lover and that the children had found a father worthy of Jeff's hallowed reputation.

But quickly the contradictions crowded in. How soon had she begun to have doubts? The mood swings had been awkward at first, the overt selfishness, even loutish aggression after one too many pints of bitter or shots of Bacardi, and sometimes both. Even at the Midshipman he'd begun to raise a few eyebrows and a few hackles quite early on. And then when he just jacked in that job – and the weeks of soul searching and way-finding turned into months of idleness punctuated by those sporadic, lighter moments of hope – only to descend once again into the abyss of rank disappointment. She had failed to overcome those serious and threatening spells of real depression. This had been a withering time for her and, she was sure, for the kids. Laura, already pushing into independence – had made her views plain for all to see. But she had the approaching outlet of university into which she could escape. Not so Josh. He too had seen through the wretch remarkably quickly. As a teenager he had been growing up fast and was no longer too young to miss the point. She ran the tape a moment longer knowing that the tale didn't have a happy ending.

Composing herself she propelled the chair around to face him once again.

"In answer to your question Inspector, no, I can't think of anyone who would want to see Lee Phillipson dead, at least not enough to go out and actually do the deed. That's not to say he didn't have enemies. Unbridled arrogance and opinionated tactless point scoring, these were some of his better traits and he cost me many good friends at that time. He seemed to revel in – or was it default to – a sort of careless or fickle approach to life's relationships and opportunities. It's true that he racked up a long line of aggrieved parties from many different quarters, but for someone to deliberately set out to end his days, well… that beggars belief, frankly."

She slowly leaned forward to buzz through to her assistant and to instruct that the management meeting she had arranged should start without her and that she'd be along shortly.

Her mind suddenly raced off on another tangent. A delayed shock impacted her thinking with the sudden realisation that maybe, just maybe, she had miscalculated the tensions of that time and she knew that some of those closest to her had responded to Lee's blundering conceit in very different ways. She'd seen her daughter explode with anger on occasions and worried too about the sullen distance that had developed between her and her only son. All this as a result – she was certain – of the destructive effects that interloper had forced upon them as a family. She cast the net a little more widely and remembered the splintered left-overs of his own immediate family. His own sister had, to all intents and purposes, disowned him. His mother, her former mother-in-law, despite desperate attempts to intercede in their failing relationship, had been callously shunned. That rogue had reduced her to a greyer, thinner figure than the confident elegant woman she had known earlier, before the pathetic truth of her own son's dishonest life had been laid bare.

As she forced her way through these disturbing memories she offered a muttered commentary to her visitor, who felt as if he were listening to a strange radio documentary.

"You're describing a rather unpleasant character, Janice, if I may make that observation," he prompted.

"Yes indeed," she admitted, "but he was also a great charmer, on occasions a truly wonderful lover and he really knew how to let his hair down and have a good time – something that all of us around him found quite infectious. Even so," she countered, "unpleasant would be a lenient criticism, but to take somebody's life for some personal slight or perceived injustice seems – in the grander scheme of things – an outrageous idea. Heavens Chief Inspector, we're talking about rural Suffolk not the Bronx."

And then her mind raced off in another direction: to his first wife, abandoned with their baby son and to the many affairs he had pursued apparently without thought or care for the hurt he would inevitably inflict. In that moment, it seemed to her that his entire adult life had been a tragic tapestry of sorry episodes and casual deceptions. His wanton self-gratification had produced that seeping, corrosive fall-out from which his victims simply hadn't been able to protect themselves. Was there the whiff of revenge somewhere in all of this?

"He was a dreadful philanderer you know David," she commented tersely, "and I say this as someone personally scarred by some of his more crass antics in that regard. I often thought it distinctly plausible, based on the many heart-breaks I suffered, that somewhere in his murky past he may simply have upset one too many jealous and jilted lovers. To think now, however, that these things might ultimately have had terminal consequences seems rather extravagant. On the other hand, how can you tell? Who knows?"

"Well...clearly someone does," he said stiffly. "We have already ruled out suicide."

"Ha, suicide," she blurted. "Lee Phillipson hasn't – or should I say hadn't – the courage to take his own life, and anyway," she said with contempt, "he couldn't get passed his own ego to get the job done."

And then it dawned on her.

"Christ Inspector, you didn't come here thinking I did it, did you? Is that why you're here?"

He confessed to having had some initial doubts when he'd first scanned some of the comments from the neighbours in the village, but he explained that these had dissipated pretty quickly and been put to bed finally at the outset of this conversation. He wouldn't expand further, but he had to ask that rather predictable question, just to keep the records straight.

"Nevertheless, I should ask where you were last Sunday afternoon?"

"I was here, and yes, Inspector, there is a veritable army of people who can vouch for me."

And at that they smiled at one another acknowledging a sense of good nature and good humour amidst what could have been a much more difficult session for the two of them in their own different ways.

"Look Inspector... er... David, sorry...I hear your cry for help. I appreciate that the sooner you can pull all the threads of the story together the sooner you will be able to make progress in finding who has done this awful thing. However, your visit is entirely unannounced, and – providing you're not going to arrest me and cart me back to Ipswich in chains – I do need to press ahead with my management team. I'm already late for that meeting. Is there some way we can talk again: a little longer perhaps next time? There is a lot to say about Lee Phillipson. I really don't know if it will help, but I'm willing to give you the time. What do you say?"

He rose to leave and thanked her for her time. Then he threw in a couple of departing questions.

"Brazil. You mentioned Brazil earlier?"

"Yes, my daughter Laura works out there…for the IMF actually, in Sao Paolo."

"And what about your son, what does he do?"

"He works at one of the boatyards in Woodbridge. He's a boat builder and a properly apprenticed craftsman in that regard. Like I said, he's boat mad."

"Thanks again Janice. You've been most helpful. We'll reconvene soon then," he finished confidently.

"Yes that will be fine David, but I'll come to you next time. The tongues will already be wagging at this end and the very idea of another visit from the police, doubtless accompanied by a WPC next time," she hinted rather pointedly, "will bring this office to a complete stop and we can't allow that, now can we? And now I really must get to that meeting."

11 – turning stones

Adi Hughes had left the door-to-door reports on Lehrer's desk and the DCI skimmed through them with Hughes's attached summary note dominating his thinking. He was right. Some of the neighbours' comments really had grabbed Adi's attention – sufficiently, in fact, for him to have reviewed and sorted the different statements, broadly speaking, into two piles. He'd picked out a couple in particular and conferred with two of the foot soldiers who had participated in the earlier canvassing exercise. He'd been left in no doubt that Lee Phillipson had not been universally popular in the little village of Compton, not by any means. Both sheaves of formatted notes seemed to confer a real sense of shock at the events of last Sunday and that was hopefully to be expected from folk living cheek by jowl with the victim in the most tranquil of countryside settings. However, one list appeared to exhibit a genuine degree of distress, even sadness and a scattered dose of outrage that things of this nature could be allowed to happen in rural Suffolk, whereas the other was suffused with a vague, and in many ways subdued but nevertheless tangible air of acceptance. Within this group there was a smug undercurrent of quiet satisfaction, unstated of course, but seemingly lurking there just under the surface. It seemed the case that Lee Phillipson had been either liked or loathed leaving little in between.

Lehrer poked his head out of the door and invited his senior team to join him for a quick status update. Hughes and McLellan shuffled in and grabbed the only two free chairs. DS Addison perched her compact frame on the corner of a low filing cabinet and DS Barnes closed the door before turning his back on it to play sentry, standing at ease and facing the group.

"Okay, what have we got?" Lehrer demanded abruptly, and then continued. "Adi, I agree with you on the door knocking reports – mainly black and white with very little grey. Can you cut your cloth accordingly and get back to some of those more opinionated types just to see how far it takes you?"

"Already happening, Chief."

"Mac have you been out to the accountancy firm yet?"

"I have Chief, and a fairly bland response I had too. The head man in the local office here was less than enamoured with the late Mr Phillipson. Apparently our victim hadn't been there all that long – about three years, or slightly less – but he'd been a real handful throughout that time."

"In what way?"

"Well...it transpires that he'd been out of work for some time before he joined Smallings. Evidently he was mightily relieved at getting back into gainful employment, but the firm – led by the head honcho and senior partner, Jed Waring – had taken the opportunity to knock him down on salary and benefits. That all seemed fine until Phillipson realised the discrepancies which existed between his own take and those of some of his colleagues. At the same time, as the older bloke, he considered himself more experienced than some of their younger employees, but he appeared very keen to overlook his relatively low level qualifications and an apparently woeful work rate when consistently pushing for more dosh and even a position as a partner at the firm. In short, he just got more and more shirty about his status, and Waring had long regretted his recruitment. The guy seemed to absorb a lot of managerial time. High maintenance really doesn't cut it. He looked shocked at the news when I told him, but he quickly got over that disappointment I can tell you."

"Fair enough. That ties in with some of Lynsey Bastion's reflections. Any other relevant feedback?" asked Lehrer. "Was there enough for us to take a closer look, would you say?"

"No. Any vaguely potential protagonists have solid alibis. There is nothing alarming about any of their reactions. To put it bluntly, the man was just a bit lazy, and a right pain in the arse by the sounds of it, but you don't go shooting people for reasons like that. They did say that Phillipson was quite gregarious and could be a bit of a rabble rouser round at the pub after work. Waring also suspected some interesting liaisons with a couple of the girls in the office – nothing substantiated, but certainly distracting within the unit there."

"Right... fine...thanks. Adders...what about nearest and dearest?" Lehrer pushed on.

"His mother and sister have been informed by our Hampshire colleagues, and very upset they were too by all accounts," answered

Amy Addison. "Our friends in Southampton reported a degree of distress and a heavy dose of remorse over some of the earlier chapters in Phillipson's life. It's easy to make superficial judgements, but by all accounts there had been some sort of family rift there. His father, on the other hand, was quite defensive – very upset about his son's passing, and fairly liberal with his comments and criticisms in all sorts of directions. His ex-wife and his own daughter took the brunt of his anger. Janice Swinton copped a lot of stick too. She certainly wasn't one of his favourites. That seems very clear.

"We've also had feedback from the Met," she continued, "regarding Phillipson's estranged son Daniel, together with some details on his mother – Phillipson's first wife, Katherine – now Kate Crighton. The son adopted his step-dad's surname when his mother remarried. It sounds like Kate Crighton was fairly ambivalent to the news about her former husband, although a little taken aback by the violent nature of his death, but Daniel was apparently distraught. He had recently tried to make a connection with Phillipson – his natural father –and had actually travelled out here to meet him for the first time since he was just an infant. However, that reunion did not go too well. He had hoped to nurture some kind of familial bond over time, but that's beyond his reach now, obviously."

"Again that ties in with Lynsey Bastion's statement, but there is a suggestion of something else at play there between father and son, some wariness on Phillipson's part that she couldn't really decipher," recounted Lehrer.

"We have DNA swabs from the two of them being sent down to our forensic team here," she confirmed, "but each – mother and son – can account for their movements on the day in question, and I'm not sure what else we can get from that quarter."

Lehrer remained unsettled by that abortive reunion, but just as he was about to turn to forensic data Amy Addison interrupted him to say, "Oh, yes...nearly forgot, Chief. There was mention from the son of an affair between his father and a neighbour many years ago, when he was just a baby. It seems likely that Phillipson had a bit of a fling with a girl across the corridor in the same apartment block in south London somewhere. The boy... well, I say boy, but he's late twenties now," she threw in with a hunch of her shoulders, "seems to know a lot about those days despite his own age at the time. He apparently stated that his mother and late grandmother had made him very much aware – as he was growing up – of shifty episodes and murky tales of that nature."

"All of which makes it potentially odd, doubly so," Lehrer mused out loud, "that he wanted to make up with the old man having been abandoned at such a very young age."

"Yeah, but you can't really tell how those stories may have affected him," cautioned Tommy Barnes. "It might just be down to maturity, you know… growing up and adopting a different perspective as an adult."

"Blood is thicker than…" imposed Ken McLellan, and Lehrer nodded with the sentiment.

"Right then…" commanded the boss. "Adders, I want you to get down to the Met and get along to see mother and son. I assume they live separately these days, but one way or another we need to know a lot more about those little stories. In particular I want you to test the young man's loyalties. Find out what he really thinks: you know what I'm saying."

"No problem Chief," she responded. "Kate Crighton lives in some sort of extravagant penthouse – top floor, overlooking the river – in Shad Thames. Sounds like a bit of a Grand Designs project by all accounts. It'll give me some ideas for future reference," she suggested with a cheeky grin. In response to her visibly cynical all-male audience she implored, "Well…I can dream, can't I?"

"Forensics?" tested Lehrer next. "Tommy, what do you have?"

"So…" he commenced in the scientific vernacular, "what I haven't got is either a bullet casing or a slug as yet."

"Eh, are they finished over there?" asked Adi Hughes.

"They were, but they're going back with some more sophisticated kit. There is the long-shot, if you'll excuse the pun, that the killer actually collected his own shell before hot-footing it out of there, but the slug itself must surely be lodged in the stonework somewhere."

Lehrer's frustration edged up a notch and he shook his head in despair.

"Will someone tell our techy brethren to check the plug hole in the bath and to take a look down the pan?"

"Fear not Chief," Barnes reassured him, "we do at least have some interesting info' to think about."

A bit of eyebrow raising and anticipatory shuffling greeted this announcement.

"I think we can skip the pathology details," he continued. "I don't suppose there is much point in spending a lot of time on cause of death bearing in mind the poor bastard lost most of the back of his head – and we've all seen the mess it made – but we have an estimated nine millimetre calibre weapon. That estimation was taken from the entry wound, obviously. That's a very common calibre, as you know."

"Typically a Beretta PX4 or maybe a Glock of some sort, any one in a range in fact," chipped in Hughes casually. He had some experience of the weaponry toted by some of the more colourful characters involved in a surprisingly fertile drugs scene in and around the docks and ports of Felixstowe and Harwich.

"Please," Lehrer pleaded in mock despair, "you make it sound as if the country lanes are crawling with Chicago hoods and mafia hit-men."

"Not exactly Chief", countered Addison, "but we know that the stats for gun crimes – and especially gun trafficking through the ports – are on the up, and these are the brands and models we're coming across more and more often."

"And it doesn't stop there," Hughes added. "Even the people traffickers are turning up armed these days. Just look at those truck drivers who were deported last month – turned up again last week and every one of them packing something…and not just African migrants and veggie pickers from Bulgaria either."

Lehrer interceded. "Okay, okay…let's get back to the point. Tommy, what were you saying about some useful info'?"

"Powder traces taken from the cranial examination suggest some very old ordnance indeed. Whatever killed him, it achieved the end result with just one shot. We know that. But the bullet has been dated – in terms of its manufacture, if you like – at sometime around the

Second World War. It's hard to be any more precise than that, without the slug I mean, but of course that's very unusual."

Ken McLellan gave out a soft low whistle, but their collective surprise left them all stumped and silent, bereft of any immediate ideas.

"Wow, where does that take us?" pondered Amy Addison.

"Almost certainly not back to Adi's gun runners and drug smugglers I'd suggest," said Lehrer emphatically. "They'll be equipped with very modern tools for their particular trade. No. There is...how should I say... something very left-field about that little statistic, and we need to get our thinking caps on.

Meanwhile...anything else Tommy?"

"Only to confirm that we are sifting through Lynsey Bastion's list of people and we've already eliminated some of the more obvious locals. We do still have a number of unidentified trace elements including one clear finger print and several strands of hair and clothing fibre. There is still a lot to do in the lab with all of this," he admitted in conclusion.

"Understood," said Lehrer, half lost in thought. But then, thinking about practicalities, he dished out a series of tasks. "Adi, you've got the locals to get back to. Be careful not to ignore the pro-Phillipson set. I think we need a visual from the day. Someone must have seen something out of the ordinary. Remember, this was a murder committed in daylight hours.

"Amy, you're off to London to plan you're executive suite for when you've won the lottery. Make sure you come back with some work related ideas too, that's all," and she frowned in mock disgust.

"Tommy, you stick with the forensics – we need more."

"Ken, I want you to get back down to Compton and firm up those leads through Jimmy Judge, you know ...the pub landlord. We could do with tracing that bloke who took a pop at Phillipson during that darts match. There may be more than one lead of that nature." McLellan nodded.

"I'm off to field a press conference," he sighed reluctantly. "Needless to say the press embargo has been lifted: the Chief Superintendent left us no option. I've nothing to tell them, and all of us must keep this matter of the old bullet very much to ourselves. Is that clear?" he insisted, and they all acknowledged the instruction. "Tomorrow morning I have Janice Swinton coming in to see me here. Tommy, while I'm in that meeting I want you to get out to see Janice Swinton's son, Josh, in Woodbridge. I've heard enough already to suspect some very strong feelings there when it comes to Lee Phillipson. Make sure we have DNA from him soon, if it's not in already."

12 - lazy days

The press conference had been thoroughly embarrassing. To make things worse he had predicted as much to the boss, but the Chief Superintendent would have none of it and he had avoided Lehrer's gaze during their extremely short and less than useful de-brief in the corridor afterwards.

Those hounds had openly ridiculed him and his team for their apparent lack of progress to date, but he counselled himself – in the absence of any supportive reassurance from a higher authority – that it was still very early days, and also that they had something to concentrate on now that they understood the unusual nature of the ballistics they were dealing with. He grunted a self-congratulatory acceptance under his breath that neither the press nor the big boss had prised that little pearl from his grasp.

Janice Swinton once again looked impeccable. Modest make-up and adornments, neat but very feminine shoes and a superbly tailored pin-striped lady's suit gave her all the allure of a mature and successful business woman. In a way that's just what she was, but David Lehrer soon discovered that the rich trappings of wealth and sophistication he would normally have ascribed to a lady of her obviously high standards had eluded her for reasons largely beyond her control: all of that despite a formidable pace of work which would have put many younger professionals to shame.

Lehrer tried to settle his visitor before she tackled the emotional challenge of regurgitating all she could remember about her former husband, Lee Phillipson. He even had a young assistant run across the road to Costa to get a couple of Americanos to order – anything was better than the muck dispensed by those machines in the corridors. Janice Swinton seemed to appreciate it and she headed off into that treacherous minefield that was her own story with little need of encouragement.

She described her early days as working mother, when she had precious little save for her adorable little girl, no marital support from a husband who went out to work one day and simply never game back, and a near manic desire to extend her education and vocational learning so as to be able to lift herself out of the ordinary and into something more rewarding and exciting. Those had been tough times. She knew – and remembered very clearly – what it was like to have no spare money. Her baby daughter wore second-hand clothes and the mortgage payments drained a huge majority of her inadequate monthly salary. Juggling child care and extensive out-of-hours study commitments had been draining.

Then a ray of light, a chance encounter, a lucky break, whatever you might call it…something turned to her advantage when she met a lovely, lovely man who was soon to become not only her second husband, but the real and only love of her life. He had been a bit older than her, a quiet affable character whose gentle exterior disguised a steely determination to get on, to win through come what may. In that unexpected moment her life had seemingly changed forever. He brought stability and direction to their lives as well as love and affection – through him they built a proper family unit within that prized traditional framework – and they all blossomed as one. Jeffrey, her Jeff, had been an architect, a successful professional for many years here in East Anglia. Through the rewards of his achievements he took them through an entirely new range of experiences extending their joys and pleasures though new activities, foreign trips and lots of quiet family time together. Little Laura grew to love him as her own father and he had given Janice another great joy in her life – her second child, her son Joshua.

They re-developed the old farmhouse he had owned in a local village for some years and that was when she came to know Compton as home. Then they took on a rather run-down flat above the old Martlesham post office and they slaved for a few months late into too many evenings to bring it up to a rentable standard. They had considered it a holiday rental and thought it might generate a little extra income as Jeff began to incrementally reduce his contractual commitments prior to retiring.

The early indications had been so encouraging that they dipped into more of his capital and doubled-up with a renovation project on a charming old stone-built cottage which they transformed into a wonderful coastal escape not far from Orford.

They worked hard – physically hard – and Janice continued her studies in the wee small hours too. They travelled in the wilder corners of the country: the Lakes, the Highlands and Islands, and even across to Ireland and they loved all of them. They trucked around continental Europe trying always to balance their own hunger for the cultural excitement of new places against the playtime needs of young and growing children, and in time they became familiar with those spots they really liked – where they felt most comfortable and at home. Eventually they splashed out again on a beautiful but run-down old farmhouse on the edges of Coniston village in the Lake District. There they subsequently spent many a demanding holiday break bashing down walls, repairing window frames, tearing up worm ridden floor boards and replacing missing tiles on the roof – and at every opportunity they tried to develop relationships with their rather stand-offish Cumbrian neighbours who looked on and wondered whether the incomers would tough it out for the long term or not. That was the house in the picture frame which Lehrer had seen on Janice Swinton's desk in Bedford.

Those had been great days, wonderful times, which had nurtured the family in every respect. Catastrophic then had been the day when poor Jeff collapsed and died, alone and unattended in the garden in Compton, to be discovered by Laura, Janice's eldest, when she got back from school. Despite no previous signs of illness or weakness, he'd had a thumping great heart attack and had died almost immediately according the coroner, later. The trauma had been utterly destructive, the abject sense of loss truly miserable for them all. Yes, even today he was sorely missed and Janice only thanked her lucky stars that this dear man had allowed her and her daughter to share their lives with him, and in Joshua, she had a living reminder of the real prime of her life.

"And since then David, there have been some ups and downs, some fun days and the odd light hearted moment here and there, but equally there have been some bleak, empty periods in my life when I despaired of human nature. My kids have kept me going of course, but they've been through the mill as well. It seems as if I've been working flat out since about nineteen seventy and here we are in two thousand and seven. Throughout that long period I consider myself lucky to have spent eleven wonderful years with Jeff Swinton, but either side of that very happy time it sometimes appears – to me I mean, and hopefully only to me – that I have wallowed in so much unfairness and injustice that I wonder sometimes how I've kept going. I suppose the kids have kept me going really. You can't just give up on your kids when you're a bit down in the mouth."

"Oh I'd say that you just aren't the quitting sort…if someone were to ask my opinion that is," he offered with a glint of admiration in those pale blue eyes. "But somewhere in that considerable time-span you spent quite a few years with our dearly departed Mr Phillipson. Can you tell me how that came about?"

"It was quite simple really," she replied. "Lee Phillipson had worked for…oh," she hesitated, "a couple of years at least as Jeff's accountant. He used to do the books and the basic submissions to the Revenue and so on, so I'd known him through his various visits to the house during that period. When poor Jeff passed away I needed quite a bit of advice and guidance regarding his estate and our joint finances. I mean…the holiday lettings business was still running of course, and I wondered at one stage whether or not to stop working in order concentrate just on the cottages. I had no real feel for the way the holiday market was developing and I wasn't confident in making my own business projections, so I was… well…let's say unsure about what was best. It seemed obvious to call on Lee for his professional opinion. True, he had only been accountable for Jeff's architectural business, but we'd talked before about wider considerations…you know…business planning, investments…that kind of thing…so it seemed rather obvious at the time."

And then she sighed and looked down at her hands and her tightly twisted fingers as they writhed with the anxiety of the memories. She shook her head gently, and when she looked up he saw the glassy sheen to her eyes as she fought to steady herself.

"David, if, in the course of your work, you ever need to refer to a near lethal dose of naivety – or was it simply crass stupidity – you have my express permission to quote my example as your case study."

Lehrer couldn't determine whether it was pure anger or the shame of self-loathing – or a combination of the two – against which she railed.

"Lee was a handsome and engaging guy in those days. Tall, blonde, quite rugged I suppose. I'm sure he could have charmed his way into almost any girl's life if he'd a mind to, but I know now – to my absolute remorse and abject cost – that my position as a widow at the age of forty was, of itself, hardly a compelling attraction. I wasn't especially attractive," to which Lehrer raised a questioning eyebrow, "and I had two growing kids, one eleven and the other sixteen, to poison the cup so to speak, and, well…I hardly presented myself as a stunningly good catch, now did I? But if you threw in a reasonable bank balance, a lovely old farmhouse, a couple of holiday lets, a holiday home up north and a steady job then yes, of course, I could probably have given Nicole Kidman or Scarlet Johansson a decent run for their money," and they both laughed at the comparisons.

"And it really was as simple and as uncomplicated as that. I can see him now sat in his office in Ipswich pawing through my financial affairs and thinking to himself, wow, just look at this lot. She's not a bad old girl – he was a few years younger than me you see – and I could probably milk this situation for many a year to come. Then he activated the charm gene and set about buttering me up."

Lehrer cut in. "Are you telling me that his intentions were that transparent?"

"No, no…not by any means, not then…and that really is my point. I just didn't see it for what it was. I must have been walking around with a bag on my head or something." And then she started a little in her chair as another important reflection crossed her mind. "Do you know, I think the kids saw it all so much earlier than me. Laura really didn't take to him from the outset, but then I argued – inwardly, with myself – that she was at that very delicate age for girls. Middle-teens can be pretty unpleasant for a girl, and just as horrible for those around her, so I didn't apply too much thought to it in that context. Josh seemed to warm to him early on, but then they both loved sports – Josh and Lee I mean – and before I knew it, there they were, the two of them, kicking a football around or throwing a cricket ball about. You see, he wooed me off my feet – quite literally, if you get my drift – and that was an experience I can tell you," she laughed rather self-consciously, "and he'd moved in within a year of Jeff's passing. Christ do I feel guilty about that now, but I guess I can't undo what's done, can I?"

"Well...it sounds as if his contribution had...er, shall we say...certain compensations," stuttered the detective in a distinctly embarrassed tone.

"Indeed so," she responded with a smile, "but I promise you David," turning immediately more serious, "such pleasures soon lose their edge when you realise that your lover is a complete charlatan who has eyes for every bit of skirt in the local pub and who sets about systematically dismantling everything you have worked for while draining your cash for his own benefit at the same time."

"But how? What happened? I mean...how did he get away with it?" he demanded.

"Oh man, you have no idea...no idea of just how gullible I was and not the faintest clue about how slippery smooth that total shit really could be." She held up an apologetic hand and said, "Sorry David – excuse my French."

He waved it off and she pressed on.

"In no time at all he'd sold his own house over by Shottisham, Church Ivy to be precise. I doubted the wisdom of that move, but he gave me some soft soap argument about how difficult it might be to look after the farmhouse and *our* holiday lets as well as his little new-build over there. He whined on – I can see it now for what it was – about being closer to me, spending time with me, actually living together, and like a dreamy girl I swallowed the entire pitch in a haze of lovey-dovey aspirations. The harsh reality was that he had a massive mortgage on the place and for him that signified just one thing...work, work and more work...to pay the mortgage off over time, you see. Later, and much to my dismay, he actually accused me of actively persuading him to sell that little house only to find himself off the housing ladder and missing out on the capital appreciation that the property had enjoyed. I was speechless I can tell you, but that dubious step, back then you understand, had certainly been part of his overall plan.

"The next step in his execution of that plan was a real shock. It took the wind right out of my sails."

"What happened?" asked a rapt and attentive policeman.

"He came home one evening and just said he'd resigned from his job – walked out. Did I not tell you about this the other day in Bedford? Forgive me if I'm repeating myself, but I guess it helps with the chronology.

"He was working in the accounts department of a local firm, a small book-keeping outfit on the outskirts of Ipswich. He'd just had enough. The boss was a pain. People in the office were a bunch of back-stabbers... you can imagine the line he took. But when I asked him if he had lined up an alternative he just shrugged his shoulders and said "naw". He pulled a cold beer out of the fridge and went out to the stoop and slumped in his favourite chair. He opened up his tackle box...he was a keen fisherman you see...and he picked out a particularly garish fly, you know, a lure for the fish, and he started to wind the fine twine around it and the hook he was trying to attach. My God," she recalled with some chagrin, "the countless hours he spent in that chair making up those pretty little flies, well...it became synonymous with everything that man stood for, or should I say lounged about for.

"He didn't work for the best part of ten years. He went through a quite ridiculous so-called creative art phase – we even decked out the smallest bedroom as his artiste's studio, bought him a range of brand new kit... you know, easel, canvasses, brushes, tubes and tubes of oils and acrylics...but I never saw a single artistic offering come out of that room save for a great rash of yellow post-it notes which covered every surface reminding him of all those important tasks he never got round to.

"Then the next phase of his clandestine scheme quietly kicked into action. There was no fanfare you understand. Oh no, that would have blown the lid off the whole strategy. He simply set about a systematic process of insulting some of our most reliable and supportive holiday makers, those who had stayed with us for years every summer or Easter – or even Christmas in some cases. He could be an abrasive sod when he wanted to. There weren't many subjects he didn't have strong opinions about and it didn't take him long to wind people up – especially when it was intentional. A couple of years ticked by and our bookings had slipped significantly. Of course, I didn't see all of this for what it was. He metered his activities so carefully – and most often when I was away with work and the kids were at school during the day. It didn't take him all that long to propose that we should start selling off the holiday lets to release the capital they represented. It seemed a cogent philosophy bearing in mind the disappointing slump in the levels of income we were receiving, but I really hadn't been aware of the malicious under-current he had set in motion. Selling the first one just broke my heart. I felt I'd dishonoured Jeff and all that he'd achieved.

"By now the wheels were falling off our personal relationship. I tried to enlist the help of his mother and sister who came down a few times and tried to cajole him into something more constructive, but he was dismissive. In fact I'd say their efforts only pushed him closer to his father and that just exacerbated all my problems. The old boy was a miserable, nasty piece of work. The family unit had imploded many years before, and Lee's sister Pippa had clung steadfastly to her mother's apron strings as the spoils had been divided. They're good people. They tried their best for me, but Lee's old man thought the sun shone out of his only son's *wotsit* and, do you know…I think he actually encouraged him to strip me and my family to the bone. I think the old bastard saw it as some form of reward for all his wayward son's unfulfilled promise and failed attempts at making something of himself."

"Janice I already know that the cottages were eventually sold, both of them, but how bad did it get? What was happening on the day-to-day treadmill and how were people reacting around you?"

"I'd already lost so many good friends – actually quite quickly in the scheme of things. Like I said when you and I first met the other day over in Bedford, he could be a thoroughly obnoxious sod when he wanted to be, and he didn't have to try very hard. People seemed to polarise into two groups: a small band of true mates who really put themselves in the firing line and a bigger bunch of former friends and acquaintances who just didn't know what to do and who, like so many people in life, were just terrified of the very notion of confrontation."

"So he was aggressive you mean?"

"Oh he certainly could be. It never came to blows at home – although he shook me violently and pushed me around a few times – but he seemed to revel in the cut and thrust of the heated exchange. That was just too much for many folk.

"Then another bombshell exploded just as we were selling the second rental. I took a call one Saturday morning from a chap from the Child Support Agency. It threw me for a minute and I got a bit confused fearing that there might be something wrong with Josh at school or something."

"Why Josh?"

"Well…to be frank…he had begun to see the light – the same illumination his stupid mother had been blinded by. He had drifted away from our unwelcome intruder and his behaviour was becoming something of a concern at home and at school. Anyway…it took me a minute or so to realise that the guy on the phone was actually searching for a Lee Phillipson. He asked me if Lee was at home and to my relief I was able to say that he wasn't. He was actually away on a fishing day out with some of his drinking buddies, wasn't he! And then you could have knocked me down with a feather. The bloke said it was to do with Lee's son and the consideration of missing maintenance payments going back twelve years or so. Words don't cover it, David. I just didn't know what to say or think or do."

"You must have challenged Phillipson about it?" he prompted.

"Dead right I did! I was stunned, aghast, the very idea that he had a son and I knew nothing about it. The sheer panic that if Lee had been unearthed and was about to be served with a maintenance order, guess whose cash would be covering that little outlay…time to rustle up some more readies from somewhere perhaps?" she seethed.

"Hell's teeth, is there any end to this? How did he react when you cornered him?"

"He just shrugged his shoulders, reached for another beer and sloped off to the stoop again. I screamed at him expecting a massive row, but he just smiled that slippery grin and padded off to catch up on the sports news."

"It sounds for all the world like he just didn't give a damn about anything, or more accurately, he didn't care a jot for anyone or anything except for money. It's all about money, and someone else's, definitely not his own."

"Indirectly you're right David, but it took me several years to realise the true nature of the man's reckless approach to life. Ironically it was a conversation with his own sister – not all that long ago actually – which made me appreciate the real driver in his life. You could say he was a philanderer for sure. You could call him selfish in the extreme and brutal in his callous dismissal of many good people around him, including his own kith and kin. You could argue that all that deceit and deception had, at its roots, the craving for money and the comforts it can provide, but I have come to know with certainty that Lee Phillipson's greatest weakness was pure unadulterated sloth. He was bone idle. He would cut any corner to avoid having to put his nose to the grindstone. If he could make a fast easy buck he would jump at the chance. If he couldn't, he'd happily, wilfully stick his dirty mitt into someone else's pocket...and on a grand scale if my case is anything to go by. He would run away from every responsibility in life if it brought with it a financial commitment which, in turn, demanded some hard work. He never sought to better himself. He never studied: he had the bare minimum of vocational qualifications and he probably hadn't tried in that regard since his days at school. He watched professional people go streaming past him in life's fast lane – he could see why they were doing so much better than him – but he just couldn't break free of his natural indolence. He was mind-numbingly lazy, and that was the root cause of all the heart ache he visited upon me and mine."

As she finished a single tear trickled over her cheek bone and ran headlong down to her jawline before taking the plunge on to her wringing hands, clasped firmly in her lap.

Lehrer was rescued by the small but arresting sound of a military klaxon close to his chest. He reminded himself that he must change that ringtone. Then, whipping his mobile from his jacket pocket, he excused himself and stepped nimbly out into the corridor.

"DCI Lehrer..."
"It's me Chief."
"Ah, Ken. What've you got?"

"I think we're getting closer Chief. That bar room brawler...you know, the bloke who threw a punch at our man during the darts match..."

"Yeah, yeah...what about him?"

"Turns out he works in forestry over at Rendlesham, but he also runs a very active side-line in wartime memorabilia, and...wait for it..."

"Firearms?"

"In one boss! He trades in firearms – hand guns and pistols a speciality. I'm on my way to see him now."

"Are you accompanied?" demanded the DCI.

"Yes. Don't worry boss. I'll get back to you shortly. Out."

Lehrer felt a surge of optimism. Perhaps they were beginning to close in on the perpetrator after all.

The call had reminded him that however enthralling – and seriously depressing – Janice Swinton's story might be, he really had to steer her back through those dark days with the hope that she would be able to apply a different perspective. He needed something of an external view, if she could manage that, in order to pick out hitherto random figures from her ugly tale, those who might just be worth a little more attention.

He straightened his tie and re-entered the interview room. Janice Swinton had recovered her composure.

"Janice we need to re-examine this frightful mess from a slightly different angle. I know that sounds onerous, but you will understand that somewhere hidden away in all of this dreadful history is a clue, or perhaps clues, to who killed Lee Phillipson. But look..." he paused, "let's finish this sorry tale first and then we'll try to pick our way back through some of the salient peripherals, shall we? Just tell me how it all ended...the personal relationship I mean."

"Oh that's very straightforward," she replied. "I said he was a bit of a playboy, well...I couldn't produce a definitive list you understand, but I'd swear he must have had a handful of flings and extra-marital affairs during our ten years together. In the end – and much to the delight of some observers in the village I've no doubt –

he had a very public...er shall we say coming together... with one Loose Lucy, the rather vacuous barmaid at the Midshipman. She was better known as the Village Bike, for the want of clarity," she offered with a terse chuckle. "I actually caught them snogging in the churchyard of all places – unbelievable. I went home and emptied his clothes onto the drive. I had the locks changed the very next morning. That was it."

"And a simple severance based on his conduct I assume?" asked Lehrer.

"Ha," she coughed out with derision, "I wish! Even then I couldn't see through his idle deceptions. He convinced me that we didn't need to use solicitors. It would only drain our coffers – and this time he knew that I'd only be paying for my brief and certainly not his – so it seemed reasonable. To be frank, and again naïve in the extreme, I reasoned that I would just be happy to see the back of the conniving bastard, but he caught me again. At the eleventh hour I received a full legal deposition from his lawyer. It really shocked me, although you might be wondering why I'm such a slow learner.

"The legal chappie was smart. He'd cobbled together a clever attack based on a statute originally designed to protect vulnerable women who had been forced out of their homes by violent and dangerous husbands. Under the terms of that legislation I was threatened with the liquidation of my entire remaining assets in order to split the proceeds fifty/fifty with my poor disadvantaged husband. Well David...you can imagine my consternation. The heartless wretch had also named my Lake District holiday home quite specifically, and instructed me to sell it as part of the sharing process.

"Lee Phillipson had barely lifted a finger in ten years. Am I repeating myself?" she said for extra emphasis. "He'd been unemployed all that time, by design. He stripped us of two rental properties and spent big chunks of that money on outrageous holidays in the likes of Italy, France and even Asia attending art classes and getting up to God knows what. There he was instructing me to sell our place in the Lakes, a place he'd enjoyed, a place where, again, he'd hardly lifted a screw driver or paint brush in anger.

"My own solicitor was powerless. We managed to drop the Lakes house out of the final agreement, so I managed to retain it for a little while, but I ended up paying that selfish lout a seventy five grand settlement and I copped a charge on our family home. Even that wasn't sacrosanct."

"What kind of charge? How did it work?"

"Simple: if the house were ever sold he – or his estate – would take eighteen percent of the proceeds. More importantly, upon my death, if that were the first chargeable event, the house would have to be sold outright to facilitate the realisation of his share in the form of liquid cash. In one go my kids had lost their inheritance for good. Even if he were to die first – as is now the case – his rights would pass through his estate to his abandoned son. It's a disgusting travesty, but that's where we stand."

"But that's outrageous," exclaimed David Lehrer.

"That's right, but we're stuffed. There is nothing we can do about that, although..." she stalled, thinking out loud..."I did hear from my lawyer only a few weeks ago that Lee had tried to make some sort of alteration to that arrangement with reference to his son. I really don't know where that got to, but I'll certainly be finding out a soon as possible."

Lehrer was troubled by the inequity of such an arrangement, but more important to his investigation was the extent to which Janice Swinton's adult children understood those legal arrangements. A monumental injustice it might be, but that little nugget – the charge on the house – applied a lot more scrutiny to Janice's son Josh and also to Phillipson's estranged son. He knew that her daughter was and remained abroad and therefore beyond suspicion, but he wondered about Josh. If Josh was entirely familiar with those legal arrangements he would presumably be less likely to pop his hated step-father knowing, amongst other things, that it would force the sale of their family home. Of course the lad's loathing of the dead man may have simply carried him beyond anything rational – a crime of passion, well...of sorts. However, assuming at least some emotional control, knowledge of the details of that guillotine clause would almost certainly have been enough to restrain him. But the flip side of the same argument would look a lot more suspicious if the lad wasn't aware of the legal trip wire in place or just didn't really understand its significance.

Lehrer knew he had to make sure of Josh's understanding of that invidious legal instrument. Despite its obvious sensitivity, he thought the opportunity simply too good to miss and so he floated the question to the lad's mother.

"Janice, how well do you think your own children understand the mechanics of the legal charge?

"Oh barely I'd say. I've tried to shield them from that ultimate disappointment."

He stalled for a moment looking thoughtful.

"Look...er, we already know your whereabouts and those of your daughter when Phillipson went to meet his maker, but what about your son Josh? What was he doing that day?"

She looked at once shocked and guarded.

"No Inspector," she responded, reverting to the formal, "you can't really suspect Josh of taking things that far, surely?"

"Janice, he has been described as angry and disaffected in terms of his relationship with his step-father, has he not? Is it not also the case that he and his mates were once cleared from the pub car park where they waited for Phillipson with sticks and cricket bats with the intention to give him a bit of a going-over?"

"Well...yes, but...hang on...they were just lads at the time, just macho teenagers trying to stretch the boundaries a little. You can't be serious, surely?"

"I think I can," he answered bluntly. "We have to exhaust every avenue, and until I hear a sensible alibi for Josh he will remain a suspect in this investigation. I know you understand that."

"Well, yes, of course," she flustered, "but I know my own son. He might have hated that manipulative monster with every fibre, but he would never stoop to such depths. I'm sure of it."

"Let's hope so," the detective soothed. "Hey look," he prompted, "why don't we nip over the road for another coffee. We could probably use the change of scene and we can carry on over there fairly discreetly I would suggest. We do need to look around the edges, so to speak, if we are to uncover some pertinent leads for my boys and girls to get their teeth into.

They adjourned, weary for the telling of the tale and relieved for the change of atmosphere a new venue would provide. As they descended in the lift DCI Lehrer made a casual attempt to cross-check one other little detail in his mind.

"So you managed to keep the Lakes hideaway for a little while then: that must have been some consolation at least?"

"Sadly not David," she confirmed glumly. "I kept it clear of the agreement just so he wouldn't get his hands on that too, but I was forced to borrow to pay him that insulting level of severance. In the end I simply couldn't keep the payments going. I sold it a couple of years later to pay back the loan. So you see David, no consolation at all. That creep really did clean us out completely. I'm not sorry he's gone. I just want to be able to banish him from my mind. The real victims in all of this have been my kids. They will never forgive me, and I can hardly blame them."

As they crossed the street and ducked in to the coffee shop, DCI Lehrer felt the most sickening twinge about one of those kids. Josh Swinton really did demand some very close scrutiny, and Lehrer wondered how DS Tommy Barnes had fared on that particular errand a little earlier. At the same time, Daniel Crighton, Phillipson's abandoned son, loomed a lot larger in the frame and Lehrer hoped that DS Addison was closing in on him at that very moment in London.

They slipped into a quiet booth, the high-backed bench seats providing a fairly private space in which they could try to pick over any tangential connections that her sorry story had unearthed. But the mood had indeed shifted. Perhaps it was the cosy cubicle in which they sat stirring their cappuccinos while mentally rummaging through the incongruous backdrop provided by her life spent with a bad and now dead man. They pushed their way half-heartedly through some of the detail, but the tenacity had left them.

He wondered to what extent his earlier doubts about her son were now gnawing at her spirit. The discourse wandered off track a little, and after several attempts to realign the conversation he let things slip and allowed her to ramble freely. He watched her as she looked up at him to make a point and then looked back soulfully into the steadily disappearing foam in her giant-sized cup. She was an attractive woman, no doubt, he reaffirmed silently to himself. Her bright eyes and engaging manner settled warmly upon him. Her fulsome breasts rose and fell with the variable insistence of her delivery. She had a quick mind and a rare wit, even in these difficult times. He felt comfortable with her. He readily understood why Phillipson had been so keen to shack up with her, and it wasn't just about the money; of that he was certain. Was there an escape here from his loneliness, a safe way out of this for the two of them? Could there be something for them after this ghastly investigation was finished? He couldn't tell, but he reprimanded himself earnestly within about the professional risks associated with any relationships which might develop with suspects or witnesses during the torturous unravelling of a capital crime, indeed any crime. He'd been there before, many years before, and he wasn't going to repeat that mistake. Even so, as he relaxed in the honesty and sincerity of her company, he felt himself being drawn in ever closer by the evident charms of a mature and very desirable woman.

She recognised a softening of his approach as she admitted to herself that she was probably talking too much. She liked him. She thought that perhaps she had liked him from the off when she had first and only quite recently discovered him waiting in her office at work. He seemed interesting; at least he had other interests besides policing, or so it appeared. Clearly a smart thinker, this man looked and behaved as if he were confident in his own strengths, and that he had long since come to terms with some of his natural weaknesses. She felt comfortable with him. She could see herself with him, this handsome chap who, it seemed likely, never lost his temper and always had a firm hand on the tiller. If only she had met someone like him instead of that waster now dead. Oh if only, she mused silently as the measured discussion ebbed back and forth across the table. And that glint in those pale blue eyes, the gentle smile…the unusual name; Lehrer – German or Germanic surely, hence those captivating eyes perhaps? Then abruptly she readjusted back into line, to the here and now, to the impact of that bastard's death on her, on her family and on the family home, to the dreadful nagging anxiety that somehow somewhere in all of this her son just might have done something truly stupid. God she prayed not, but the stricture in her gut tensed at the mere thought of it.

As they left she thanked him. He sensed that she meant more than just the coffee. They stood there on the pavement outside the coffee shop and she stretched up on her tip-toes to kiss him lightly on the cheek. Each flushed with embarrassment as she turned on her heel and marched quickly away without looking back.

13 - messing about on the river

Barrington's Boatyard looked a bit ramshackle as he turned in from the road and parked at the end of a line of cars and vans. The automated sliding gate appeared to be the most sophisticated piece of equipment on show, although as it yawned permanently open to the street it gave little reassurance as to the security consciousness of the firm behind the fence and its small band of maritime minions within.

DS Barnes climbed out of the car, stood and stretched, and scanned the mixed collection of buildings before him. There was a series of what looked like big sheds running away from him, all uniformly aligned with the waterfront suggesting open access to the river, although those elevations remained hidden to him from his position by the car. The biggest structure stood at the far end and appeared lofty, vaulted in some way, and he could see a heavy external crane gantry running off from its façade in the direction of the water – a boat-lift the obvious conclusion. Littered around the smaller sheds were numerous dry-standing small craft of various descriptions and a variety of boat-slip trailers and pulling tractors. There were drums and reels scattered here and there, and as he crossed the yard – heading for the corner of the nearest office block – he saw a wide stretch of water to his left with many boats moored at small floating jetties or to bouys a little further out into the river. Further left he saw some low-lying red-brick buildings with flat rooves which offered the prospect of workshops, offices and perhaps a machine shed. Overall the site was bigger than he'd expected and certainly more extensive than it appeared from the road outside.

Tripping up a rather rusty metal staircase he reached a heavy metal door, and beyond that he encountered the sullen features of a greying middle-aged man who looked blandly and silently towards him.

"Josh Swinton about?" he asked with an apparently light-hearted cheerfulness.

"Who's asking?" scowled his newest gate-keeper.

"I just want to ask him a few questions."

"You haven't answered mine yet."

"Give it a rest," sighed Barnes as he flipped out his badge and ID waiting for the visual impact to impress a change of mood on the man before him. "Detective Sergeant Barnes, Suffolk CID," he added. "Now answer mine."

"Okay, okay, keep your hair on young fella – not a bloody mind reader – why didn't you say?" Then he turned his head to one side and bellowed, "Eric...can you get young Josh up 'ere pronto – important visitor to see 'im?"

Barnes could hear no obvious or immediate response, but when he heard a different door bang shut in the breeze he assumed that someone had run out to locate the lad and bring him up to the office. Instead the heavy door behind him creaked open and another old-ish chap poked his head in and beckoned Barnes to accompany him.

They descended the metal steps together and headed out through the yard.

"He's in the ferro shed," explained Barnes's newest companion. "It's the second from the end, next to the big one."

"What's a ferro shed, if you don't mind me asking?"

"It's where we do the concrete builds and the odd cement repair job."

"Eh? Sorry...forgive the sarcasm, but I thought this was a boatyard."

"Nice try," Eric responded with a smile. But then seeing that the detective was genuinely perplexed he added, "You really don't know anything about ferro-hulled boats then – cast concrete bottoms?"

"You're kidding. Why don't they just sink – must be as heavy as...well...concrete I suppose."

"You obviously haven't heard of Archimedes either then, you know...upthrust and all that...weight of water displaced?"

"Another language mate, sorry," offered Barnes lamely.

"They've been making concrete hulled boats for about a hundred and fifty years. They're very popular mainly because they are usually very stable at sea due to the low centre of gravity afforded by the low-slung concrete-cast hull. It's not solid concrete – that probably would be too heavy, even for Archimedes. We mould a thick skin of special cement over a metal or fibre frame to create the required shape of the underside of the vessel. It's cheap, durable...it works really well. A French idea originally I think – respected mariners, the Frogs, and rightly so in my view. We make new designs here and we do some ferro repair work too when boats have been bumped or snagged. They can lose the odd chunk of the stuff every now and then, and the fixtures – you know...concrete hull to rest of boat – need regular checks."

With that the two men ducked under a low metal door frame and simultaneously stepped over a high metal threshold into a cavernous open space inside the building.

The cool waterfront air blasted him as soon as he stood up inside the wide span of the boat house. He thought immediately that busy little workers here, inside the shed and out of the sun, must have to keep moving just to stay warm. Of those, he could see not one.

He could see numerous craft of various types dotted about the waterborne reaches of the open hangar. They were mainly tied to pontoon jetties or floating at buoys out in the river. Inside and protected from the worst of any inclement weather were a couple of sleek yachts propped up on trestles. One appeared to have no keel at all, the other no mast. In addition, another boat – much older – appeared to be similarly supported, but this time in the depths of a drained dry-dock. He could barely make out the form and profile of the hull such was the limited light down in the dank, dark basin, but just then a wild blue flash illuminated its slippery sides and etched a racy silhouette of streamlined perfection. No sooner had the arc welder revealed the impressive lines of the Bermudan ketch she was once again lost in darkness. But again the crackling, fizzing discharge erupted in staccato bursts and the two onlookers could make out the sympathetic lines of the caulked teak decking so typical of fine older craft. They looked on for a moment, both spellbound by the purity of the light and its surreal effects.

Barnes looked to his right, to the farthest corner at the back of the building. His face adopted a confused expression.

"What's that then?" he asked bluntly.

"Oh that's a Caribbean racer. She belongs to one of our American clients who just happens to be over this side of the pond for most of the year, so..."

"No, no. What's that over there in the far corner?"

"Oh sorry, yes…er, that's Josh Swinton's little marriage breaker."

"Come again," queried the detective.

"Only joking…but it is Josh's project and he does spend quite a bit of time on her. Well…", he hesitated, "he used to. I mean there was a time when he would put in several nights a week on that old tub, but since he got married and then had the little girl he's certainly curtailed his exploits in that regard. Can't say I blame him. Have you met his wife?"

Barnes threw the man a questioning glance with raised eyebrows. Eric carried on by way of explanation.

"Cute little thing she is. No wonder he spends more time at home these days rather than freezing to death down here on that boat renovation."

The boat repair in question looked a very odd affair indeed. Barnes could just about make out the stern of the vessel in the gloom of the shed. He could see a heavy old propeller rusting silently beneath the aft end of the hull. The rest of the boat was hidden from view by what looked like rows of hay bales stacked up along both sides. There were no masts visible, and the cocoon effect was exaggerated by a heavy grey tarpaulin which stretched over the top of the bales and spanned the decking and cabin completely. Eric explained that the cold winter nights often encouraged young Josh to put a couple of heaters on under the boat just to fend off the chill. The make-shift structure with its canvas cover helped to retain the warmth while he was working.

"So what's he actually doing to it?"

"Well…since you're asking…it's a total re-fit. He's been at it for a few years off and on, and I'd say he has a few more years to go yet. I was surprised at the scale of the job, but even more by his commitment to it. And he has real skills as well; amazing attention to detail."

They looked on, each trying to imagine the personality of a young man so driven.

"Come on then, let's go and find him. He's the man you want to see, isn't he?"

With that Barnes nodded and headed off in the direction of the hay bales. Eric called him back.

"He's not over there now. He's in the drawing office down this way," he motioned with a flick of his hand, raised thumb indicating a run of pre-fabs close to the water's edge.

As they pushed in through the first doorway they entered a short corridor and Eric called out for his younger colleague. In response to a muted cry beyond the next door they continued through to the office where a studious young man pawed over an expansive board to which was clipped a huge and very detailed elevation of a Bermudan ketch.

Eric introduced his visitor quite formally.

Josh Swinton sighed an exasperated note of frustration as he reluctantly turned away from the drawing board and said, "'Bout bloody time too, if you ask me."

Eric sloped off quietly and headed back to the main office.

"So you're not surprised to see me then? offered the detective.

"Hardly!"

"And you know why I'm here?"

"Oh yes," he smiled, "in fact, I wondered what took you so long."

"Yes, I get your drift. So tell me, how did you know about it?"

"Well...you know what...it's all over the village," he said with a shrug of the shoulders.

"But you don't live in the village," the detective countered.

"Yeah...I guess...but it's still home, and I get down there all the time, you know, to see Mum, and my mates too...off and on, if you know what I mean? Last night the pub was just buzzing with it all," he confirmed.

"Oh, really! What's the craic there then?"

Josh Swinton smiled the smile of amusement, satisfaction almost. "It's open season if you ask me."

"But I am asking you," his inquisitor prompted.

"Well to be frank..." and he paused momentarily, "I think they're running a book behind the bar."

"You're having me on?"

"No...seriously. There are so many people who might have done it," and he shook his head in mock amazement. "I don't envy you lot having to sift through that bastard's life. If our experiences are anything to go by it's going to be a long list, and it'll take you ages to narrow it down to something workable."

"And should we put you on that list, Mr Swinton," came the expected challenge.

Josh shot him a brief but penetrating look before he clipped, "As you like, mate…no problem at this end."

"Are you sure? You don't seem particularly upset that your former step-father is dead. In fact you don't seem too bothered about much at all."

The young man chuckled, as if to himself. "Are you having a laugh?" he threw back. "Have you done any homework yet? Do you know anything about that idle fucker? Have you any idea how many lives he's ruined? Have you the faintest inkling as to how many wrecked human beings he's left trailing in his wake from one decade to the next, year after year after year?" the anger in his voice rising throughout.

"Enough to die for?"

"Oh yes…for sure…absolutely no doubt about it and not just in my view either. You'll be chatting to all sorts of people in the next few weeks who could very easily justify that level of response."

"Response? That's an odd term to use isn't, in circumstances like these?"

"No. No it's not. Call it cause and effect, call it human nature, call it what you like, but nothing is beyond the line for that shifty low-life," and he bristled with indignation as he spat out his evident hatred for a man who had so invaded his own life and the lives of those around him with such devastating consequences.

"So you're not sorry he's gone then?"

"Do I look sorry?"

"On the contrary, you look positively ecstatic."

"And why not?"

"Even to the extent of revelling in his passing?"

"Certainly!"

"And even though you might be a suspect in our eyes?"

"I'd be hugely disappointed if I weren't," he suggested with a smirk.

"Well that's something at least".

"What's that?"

"You are a suspect, of course, but you knew that already...right?"

"Makes sense – made sense as soon as I heard the good news actually – though it pains me to say that I can't hang that particular hat on my own peg."

"We could though," the copper injected with a hard stare to back it up.

"You could try, but I missed that boat some time ago, and I'm pretty clean...you know...alibi and all that..."

But his examiner interrupted his flow. "So tell us about the night you and a bunch of yobs waited for Phillipson in the pub car park – cricket bats was it, or pick axe handles?"

"Oh c'mon...you're not serious? We were just lads – not yobs, if you don't mind – just a bunch of lads with a few grievances to put right, that's all."

"Oh I see, so you're not alone on our list of suspects then?"

"Didn't I just make the same point?"

"Sure, but it's an easy way to throw in a decoy or two, wouldn't you agree?"

"Only if I had something to hide, wouldn't you say?"

"So you're comfortable with the notion that you lot could easily have bashed the guy's skull in after a few pints of cider and a couple of hours of lurking around in the shadows outside the Midshipman? What's more," he continued with a gathering pace, "if you've nothing to hide you'll be just as comfortable in checking back through your happy teenage memories to reveal the names of your would-be accomplices that night?"

"Just stick to the real-life narrative Sherlock," Swinton flashed back at him with barely masked disdain. "We were never out to kill him, just to rough him up a bit...well, a lot actually...and it would have pleased me no-end to see that twat hobbling around the village for years to come if we'd smashed his knees or busted his ankles. That would've been the least he deserved, but now...well...it's hardly relevant is it? Anyway," he hesitated, reflecting on the high tensions of that near fateful night, "Jimmy chased us off and that was that. As for my mates...you'll be all over them soon enough I shouldn't wonder."

"Sorry...Jimmy?" he quizzed.

"The landlord at the pub – he's still there these days, so you'll be getting to him too."

"Actually I think my governor has already put in a visit, now that you mention the name. Jimmy as in Jimmy Judge, right?"

"Yeah, that's him. He's a good bloke when all's said and done."

"And if only it were...all said and done, I mean. But you did mention the 'a' word," he pushed, with eyebrows raised in questioning mode."

"That's easy," Swinton replied. "Sunday afternoon is footy afternoon – rarely miss a Premier League game – and on that happy occasion the Gunners managed to hold Chelsea to a draw at home, which meant that the Russian Blues would fall short of their final push for the title," he nodded with a wry smile. "I took it as two wins that day, myself."

"Two wins, how's that?"

"Yeah, don't you see? Arsenal stop Chelski from making up the gap to Man U – and then Phillipson cops his lot...two nil and no messin' about in my book."

"And there was I thinking you'd be a caring sharing Tractor Boy...you know, local lad, local team?"

"Oh, I do care for Ipswich Town – I look out for their results, go to the odd game at Portman Road, that sort of thing – but Arsenal is my passion...well, after family and boats that is... you know what I'm saying."

"Nice lead-in," the detective added, "I mean...I was curious about the boat you've got moth-balled in hay bales at the back there."

"Ah...a labour of love she is, but I have little spare time these days, what with the other two girls in my life – wife and daughter, I mean – but I'll get back to it in time. It's a renovation job: an old Suffolk shrimper, actually. She was a beauty once upon a time, and so she'll be again, mark my words," he finished with an air of confidence.

"And that alibi: who's to say you didn't just catch the scores afterwards...you know...after the event I mean, the main event?"

"Smart idea," Swinton acknowledged with an approving touch of the forelock, "but the girls at home will back me up on that score.

The football is our only source of domestic friction – if that's not over-doing it – but it's something I've ring-fenced as my only selfish, private time and my domestic Goddess allows me that little bit of space in gratitude for curtailing those previously long nights here on the boat."

"Okay, okay, let's leave it there for now. I will be checking out that alibi of course, you know that, but just answer me one important question, please."

"Go ahead."

"Why does everyone hate Phillipson so much? What did he do to collect enemies like antiques or tea-spoons? I haven't heard a good word for him yet, and I don't think any of my colleagues have fared any better either, at least not as yet."

"Oh Christ," sighed Swinton in exasperation. "That's just not something I can tell you in a couple of minutes, and I really haven't got much more time than that just now."

"Aw c'mon...this guy has a bit of a reputation – or had, should I say – and he's been playing away from home every now and again, and he seems to have been a bit light on some of his financial obligations over the years, but was he really so hideous as to attract a long list of possible killers...I mean, this is murder, cold-blooded, calculated murder...nothing less. Was he really so bad? Maybe it was a simple case of mistaken identity, you know...wrong face, wrong place, that sort of thing."

"Listen mate, you have no idea. When you get more of the story put together do, by all means, come back to see. I would even come in to see you, if that works better for you. We're ordinary folk running pretty ordinary lives when it comes down to it. Phillipson was no different, even if he was from the trashy end of the social spectrum, but he was an arch bastard of the worst kind. Affairs and spurious offspring are elements of his life story that barely line the inside cover. He conned my mother in every respect. I used to think she was no mug, but not only did he bleed her dry throughout his time in our house – her own hard sweat and way too many tears – but in addition he rifled her accounts, sold off nearly all of our properties and then – as he was sneaking off through the back door – he stung us with an escape fee through some fucking ridiculous legal loop hole. That cost her tens of thousands of pounds, and all supposedly to protect us from him coming back for a second bite at the cherry, so to speak. It just about broke my Mum, I can tell you. I heard many times that he had put out some pathetic yarn about how his life with my mother had simply deteriorated over time – a vague notion of incompatibility. He put it about that some of the more damaging outcomes occurred more by accident than design."

"But surely that's plausible," interjected Barnes lamely.

"Not on your life," retorted Swinton angrily. "If it were all so haphazard and unavoidable, how come we are carrying a legal charge on our family home, even now, after all these years? How come my mother is actually covenanted against developing any new personal relationships even within her own home while he's swanning around with every tart in the territory?"

"You're kidding…that just can't be right," said the detective, incredulous.

"You'd think not, but that's English law for you. That's the law you and your lot try to uphold every hour of every day, and for what? To protect selfish pariahs like Lee Phillipson, that's why. I mean…if there is a better definition of true spite in a single human being then I don't know of one."

The policeman looked a little crestfallen. Clearly his interviewee was doing his best to control some very turbulent emotions that swirled and eddied just below the surface threatening to suck the two of them into something less useful and less flattering. "Look…er, I know you're busy, but we'll get back to your missus if that's all right, and we may well ask you in for a bit more of that detail…that's if Jimmy Judge hasn't already given us chapter and verse on your mates with the big sticks," and he smiled in gentle good-humour in attempt to diffuse the rising tension. "Can I just take some dabs and a mouth swab for DNA before I go? It'll allow us to eliminate you fairly quickly I think."

"Sure, no problem, that's fine with me. Just don't be afraid to feed-back my utter joy at that man's untimely dispatch. I'm glad he's gone, and I hope he suffered."

"Untimely? What do you mean by that?" asked Barnes, as he busied himself with the finger prints.

"Only that it should've happened years ago: that may have rescued my mother from so much heartache, and it might just have saved her – and us as a family – an awful lot of money."

"Although I guess some of those terrible constraints you mentioned will be lifted now…you know, now that's he's dead, I mean?"

"You could be right. I really don't know. Perhaps his estate sticks its nose in at this point. Your guess would be as good as mine. I think he has a son – abandoned soon after he was born I believe – but that bloke, whoever and wherever he is – might find himself in line for a chunk of money at our expense. Shit, I'd happily resurrect that bastard Phillipson just to kill him all over again."

"I'll pretend I didn't hear that."

"You can say what you like, mate. I really don't give a flying fuck when it comes to that waster."

14 – risk and reward?

Henry Moston had rarely felt so relaxed. He leaned slightly forward in his chair, picked up the small spoon from the saucer and carefully folded the chocolate sprinkles into the creamy white foam of his cappuccino. Pushing his shades back up his nose, he eased himself back into a comfortable slouch and returned to watching the world drift by with an uncharacteristic and very gentle smile across his lips.

Henry – Harry to friends and enemies alike, for as long as he could remember – had been offered his favourite corner table of old by his trusty mate Toto, the proud owner of this, one of the most famous Italian coffee houses on the South Bank. This time however, Harry had declined…with all due courtesy, naturally…but he no longer felt the need to adopt a guarded vantage point from which he could see anyone approaching onto the open street-side terrace. This time he opted for a table close to the pavement from where he might peruse the hustle and bustle around the ever-popular Borough Market. He could take a sneaky peek at any passing lovelies or look out with amusement for the plethora of earnest joggers who panted past – heading east or west – through the narrow and truly ancient thoroughfares of Southwark.

Toto – Salvatore to his elderly and very proud mama – had seen his old acquaintance approaching from the Southwark Cathedral passage and had drawn in a short and rather tentative breath. How to react? What to say – if anything? It had been a long time, and relations with Harry had not always been rewarding – no surprises there considering the nicknames Harry had carried around for too many years. *Mad Mo* was an interesting one, and somewhat understated it had to be said. *Harry the Hands* was a lot more sinister, if only for the truth behind the rumour.

The two men had greeted one another warmly, the host welcoming his customer with a flourishing manly embrace that only Italians seemed able to carry off with style. Harry had smiled, nodded his appreciation and taken the open pew closer to the mainstream of life in south London.

Harry listened to the lilting cadence of passing conversations and cared not to register any of the details. He observed all manner of physical shapes and sizes as the busy human traffic came and went, but he paid little heed to who they were or what potential threats any of them might represent. He heard the excited incessant chirping of the birds as they flitted from leafy city branch to vacant stone sill and wondered how he hadn't noticed these things before, when last he had enjoyed the opportunity to absorb such pleasantries. But then Harry was also aware that the old city gaol, the original Clink itself (now a museum for ordinary folk to visit), was situated – quite literally – just round the corner, and that infused a touch of tension to his otherwise unusually carefree mood.

Harry Moston had spent most of his adult life in prison. In fact – hand on heart – he'd spent quite a bit of his teenage years behind bars as well, but now that was all in the past. He had been a tough south London boy who had indeed done some rum stuff in his time, but – the point was – now he'd served his time. The slate was clean. As far as he knew there lurked no more threats from the past. Scores had been settled. Honour among thieves – and villains of many kinds – had been satisfied. He was off the hook and not going back. He'd been tapped up after his last release – he'd expected that, of course – but no more, not for Harry Moston. Enough just had to be enough. He'd let the old gang down gently. He was too old for all that now anyway. By and large he'd played his cards right… …well… apart from that little trip, and what a cor-blimey shocker that had turned out to be, but he'd got away with it. He thought so, at least. Jesus, talk about a close call. Nice to know the bastard got his just deserts after all. Shit…what a long time. Too long for a scheister like that, but no matter – history now.

Harry sat there just enjoying the day. As he rummaged his way through the back streets and alleyways of his hitherto tawdry existence, he ran the index finger and thumb of his right hand (either side of his mouth) gently through his grey-white goatee, pulling the coarse hair to the point of his chin. He'd had plenty of time to master the delicate grooming procedures required by his new hirsute image. Spending time in front of the mirror required – at least in Harry's view – either a very big ego or lots of free time. The latter had been plentiful in Harry's recent past, banged up as he had been for that ridiculous GBH conviction. Harry thought his carefully sculpted facial addition made him look especially suave and sophisticated. Upon delivering a second cappuccino to his old mucker out there by the kerb, Toto just thought the damn thing added about ten years to its owner's already worn countenance. What was it about men in their sixties, he wondered?

A young blonde woman sidled up to an adjacent table, and – having planted her shoulder bag into the chair closest to Harry – she plonked herself down heavily into the chair opposite, facing Harry as she did so. As she ordered her latte she inadvertently caught Harry's casual glance in her direction. She tipped her head forward and smiled in acknowledgement before avidly studying her mobile phone for messages. Harry thought her quite cute… in a butch sort of a way – pretty features, and a neat bob illuminated by the bright sunlight, but quite a solid build… athletic perhaps…but hey, who the hell was he kidding? He could have been her father. He went back to people watching.

Suddenly the two chairs either side of him were scraped back from the table and two crumpled suits sat down at Harry's table.

"Well Detective," announced one of them looking at his opposite number, "just look who's enjoying a bit of rest and rehabilitation on a lovely warm day in his old south London manor. If it isn't Mad Mo Moston acting like an everyday law abiding citizen. Well now Harry, pray tell…how are you, my old mate?"

Moston's eyes glowed with pure rage. His knuckles whitened to the bone as he clung to the table's edge in a desperate attempt to control his ire.

"Who the fuck do you think you are, you bastards?" he hissed at his newly acquired and most unwelcome entourage. "This is intimidation, and you know it, you cunts, you fuckin' shit stirring cunts. Where do you get off on this stuff? What right have you got to be following me around like this? I'm clean. I've paid my dues. Just leave it out and leave me well alone or I'll have my lawyer onto you wankers faster than you can say police corruption."

But as he made to rise and move off to pay his bill one of the plain clothes Met officers placed a firm hand on Harry's forearm and pressed him back into his seat.

"A little word in your shell-like, big man," he suggested.

"I'd rather you pissed into my ear-'ole than share a conversation with scum like you. Now back off. This isn't going to get messy...you'll be pleased to know...this aint the fuckin' old days, not anymore, so thank your lucky stars is all I can say...but you've already ruined my morning coffee, so let's just leave it at that shall we?"

"Harry, for a man who looks so old these days – what the hell is that thing on your chin – you do so easily present yourself as a juvenile and one who has an awful lot to learn. We know you better than that, Harry, and if you don't sit down and shut the fuck up we'll have you in an overnight cell for threatening not one but two police officers and for causing an affray."

"What sodding affray?" he pleaded. "I'm having a quiet cup of coffee, or at least I was, and minding my own sodding business, so what are you tossers talking about?"

"Don't wind me up Harry," the taller of the two detectives urged. "You know the form, and you know how easily we can make it look bad for you. All we want is a quiet word, so what do you say?"

"I'd sooner cut my own tongue out," he seethed. "You bastards 've stitched me up more than once. I owe you naffink," he stressed in his exaggerated Battersea twang, "and if you don't get off my case right now I'll swing for you, see if I don't."

The other detective chimed in.

"Harry, if you're so clean, what's the big issue: what could you possibly have to hide? What are you afraid of?"

"Naffink...I've been out just a couple 'o months, and I've been taking it very easy and," he emphasised, "on the straight and narra, that's the truth, no dramas, so what are you bastards trying to stiff me with this time?"

"No, no...it's nothing like that Harry, trust me..."

"Trust you! Would you just listen to yourself...trust you...yeah like the last time... and have another five years for your troubles 'Arry, me old mate. Fuckin' jokers the lot o' yer."

"Been out of town since you got out, Harry?" prompted the first detective.

"Nah! Why? What for? Why would I? This is my gaff. This is where I belong: where I got friends. I don't suppose you have any idea what I'm talking about, do ya? This is where I can come and go without being fingered by you lot, where Toto here," he flicked a nod in the direction of the coffee shop, "can shake my hand and get me a decent cuppa," but in maintaining his bravado he shifted a little in his chair and the officers sensed a tangible drop in the man's confidence as he looked past them at the blonde girl sitting at the nearby table.

At that very moment she stood and advanced upon the three men. She wrenched out the last vacant chair from under the table and sat directly opposite Harry Moston, offering her target a perplexing smile as she lowered herself into the seat.

Harry *the Hands* Moston looked at once crestfallen, then frightened for an imperceptible moment, then absolutely furious.

"You utter bastards," he raged under his breath. "What the fuck is going on? What kind of set up is this?"

Deadpan in response, the first detective introduced their newest participant.

"Harry, this is Detective Sergeant Addison from the Suffolk Constabulary. I'd like to be able to say that she's here in London to assist us on a special mission, but the truth of it is that we are actually assisting her with matters closer to home in her neck of the woods. Now can you think of any reason why DS Addison would need our help all the way out there in Suffolk? In fact Harry, while we're at it, do you even know where Suffolk is?"

"Arrogant tosser…course I know where Suffolk is…" and then he hesitated momentarily, but then charged on, "but what the fuck has that got to do with me?"

"To be frank Harry…mate…we're really not sure, but we wondered if you knew anyone out there in the greenery? You know, friends, contacts, accomplices…that sort of thing?"

"Enough of this horse shit. I'm calling my lawyer right now," and he made for the phone in his inside pocket, but the lead detective staid his hand.

"That's not a shooter in there is it Harry? Don't suppose you picked one up shortly after you got yourself paroled, now did you?"

"Piss off you crazy bastards…" said Harry with abject disdain.

"Well, well…DS Addison, imagine Mad Mo Moston calling us crazy bastards. Have you any idea where his slightly nicer epithet came from?" he questioned his female colleague in mock interrogation. The merest inflection invited her colleague to enlighten her. "As an ambitious, aspiring young lad of the most dangerous kind, Mad Mo had a bit of a penchant for driving fast cars very fast and fast motorbikes even faster – usually, that is, when being pursued by Her Majesty's law enforcement officers. He had a nasty tendency to race the getaway car through pedestrian precincts at very high speeds – with not a lot of care and consideration for the innocents he bowled over on several occasions. One time we apprehended him when unconscious behind the wheel of a motor which he'd very kindly embedded in the front window of a jewellers shop. It wasn't a ram raid – he got to those a few years later – it was just a fast car out of control. In addition our 'Arry," he offered with maximum sarcasm, "was not beyond some fabulous motor bike stunts that even James Bond would have been proud of – but this was in real life, of course. Riding through a huge five foot diameter pipe at full throttle in order to escape a patrol car – down in the old East End docks a few years back – must have looked spectacular till he emerged out of the other end only to discover he was right at the quay side of KG5 dock."

"Wow, what happened? she asked, with genuine interest.

"He sailed a great fifty foot arc through the air and plunged into the water below with colossal force breaking both legs. How the hell he didn't drown I just don't know, but *Mad Mo* is a badge he had earned many times over before he reached the age of thirty."

Harry sat there quietly boiling at this humiliation as it was played out in front of him.

"And *Harry the Hands*?" she begged with some trepidation.

"Ah, yes...not a great story Detective Sergeant, but something characteristic of his later, shall we say more malicious period. Yes, our 'Arry here developed something of a scary reputation for crippling his nearest and strongest competitors and adversaries. He ran a lot of rackets...protection, petty drugs, booze... never much of a one for smuggling guns or people...but he got scarred early in the tale and resolved never to let an enemy come back at him ever again. And how did he do this? Simple: by breaking and mutilating their hands so that they literally couldn't fight, couldn't hold a weapon, couldn't do much except for paying for gangland hit men who came looking for him ...much to their cost, it has to be said. In short Harry is not – or at least hasn't always been – a very nice chap. Is that fair Harry?"

"Maybe so, maybe not," snarled Harry Moston resentfully, "but like I said, I'm clean: you can't treat me like this."

"Maybe not, maybe so, Harry. I guess that depends on what you've been up to of late doesn't it?"

"Are we going round in circles just for the fun of it? You pricks got nothing better to do with your time, or is it just your shit for brains that's making you hard of hearing? Let me spell it out for you just once more... I haven't been doing anything but taking it easy, and that's all there is to it. Now unless you're going to charge me with mass murder in a shopping mall or kidnapping Kate Middleton or something just as outrageous, might I suggest you sling your 'ooks right now and leave me in peace?"

"Love to Harry, but when we spoke to Kate this morning she confirmed that she was enjoying breakfast at the Palace with her prince charming and her future grandfather-in-law. Her biggest problem was handling the old dog's impressive range of expletives relating to getting a soft-boiled egg to be actually soft – but no...it was something a little more mundane. In fact... it was more to do with your recent travel arrangements."

"Jesus H Christ, is there any end to this bollocks?" Harry groaned, adopting the tortured twist of exasperation across his features.

"Tell us about Suffolk then Harry," said the bigger officer, directly.

"You looking for a travel guide or something Detective? I mean... what do you want...what is this all about?"

"It's about your recent trip to Suffolk, Harry...listening skills mate...are you following this?"

"I haven't been to Suffolk recently," Harry pushed back with as much bravado as he could muster.

At this point the two Met men sat back and smiled laconically to one another.

DS Amy Addison sat forward, planted her elbows on the table and looked Mad Mo Moston right in the eye.

"Okay Mr Moston, as you appear reluctant to talk about trips to the Suffolk coast, why don't we talk about something else?" she offered in mock appeasement.

Harry interrupted her sharply. "What... like nail varnish and lipstick colours, sweetheart."

"I was thinking more about Monique Leboutilliere," she suggested with a blank facial expression and a silent close.

Again Harry shifted uneasily in his chair. Warning lights flickered in his mind. The simplest most casual mention of her name induced two immediate reactions within, and Harry knew he had to quell his emotions and control any visible signs of alarm.

It had been so long ago...the best part of thirty years back, but she remained the one true love of his life, even to this day. His heart ached at the mere thought of her beguiling smile, her slim curvaceous form and her bewitching French accent – French Canadian to be accurate. He remembered the wild and exciting times they'd had in the dreamy world of the big city with all the distractions it offered two starry-eyed lovers who knew how to absorb its wonders. What a life they led. What times they enjoyed. God, if only he could travel back through some parallel dimension to recapture that idyllic period in their lives, that indescribable sense of true and lasting fulfilment. But then the painful recollections jostled their way back into his mental frame. He remembered the day she realised the true nature of his so-called profession. He remembered too the joy of acceptance, the warmth in her recognition that it really wasn't so bad and that her man could afford to keep her in a certain splendour which suitably compensated her for the elevated stresses and intermittent flash points his often dangerous activities could engender. She had even remained loyal when he found himself banged up on a feeble, trumped-up charge for assault and battery – even that hadn't been a problem so long as he kept her funds flowing through his clandestine network. No...even that extended separation had proven manageable...until that bastard across the hall started dipping his wick where it had no right to be. When that little bombshell had been fed back to him in Wandsworth he had just about exploded. He knew then that one day he'd find or engineer the opportunity to mark that fucker for life. It infuriated him to think that she'd not only run off, but actually flown back to Montreal only to find that the creep had chased her over there in a desperate attempt to prolong his filthy relationship with her on the other side of the pond...until, that is, her brothers had taken him out, metaphorically speaking, and left him in a mess on a plane back to London. For many years Harry had promised himself that revenge would indeed be very very sweet, but his extended commitments to Her Majesty's Prisons had persistently pushed that priority further and further down his action list.

As he momentarily reminisced the time lapse extracted some inquisitive glances from his audience.

"And what do you know about Monique Leboutilliere?" he spat in her direction, trying as he did not to yield anything of use to the blonde girl across the table.

"No, no...let's not get confused Mr Moston: this is about what you know about her, I'd only be guessing at best," pushed back Amy Addison.

"That's years ago, and none of your damned business, so keep your nose well out of it if you want to keep that pretty little face of yours."

"Take it easy Harry. Threatening a police officer is a serious offence as well you know," chipped in the taller of the two Met men.

"Oh piss off you daft buggers: we're talking twenty five years ago at least. I haven't seen her in all that time," and then he hesitated, acquiring a thoughtful pose, and simply concluded, "and as far as I know she went back to Canada."

Amy Addison carried on.

"And why did she go back to Canada?"

"How the hell should I know? I was under lock and key at the time. Never saw her again, more's the pity."

"Don't treat me like a fool Mr Moston, please," Addison persisted. "Your support network was perfectly capable of paying for her every whim whilst you were... unavoidably detained shall we say, and yet you seem to be asking us to believe that you had no active communication with her at that time."

"Correct," Harry offered bluntly, but Addison stepped up a gear.

"Tell us about Lee Phillipson," she demanded.

"Who?" he said, without so much as a flicker of reaction or recognition.

"You serious, Mr Moston? Are you really saying that you don't know of a Lee Phillipson in connection with your former girlfriend?" Addison demanded.

"Partner, not just girlfriend," he threw back contemptuously at his female interrogator.

"Who cares?" questioned Addison defiantly.

"I care," insisted Moston with some determination.

"All right, so you care," she sighed in frustration, "but where does Lee Phillipson fit in?"

"No idea. Like I said, I've never heard of him. What's all this about? Come on you lightweights, what are you trying to hang on my hook this time?" Harry pursued.

But then the leading Met officer interjected with a very different question.

"So... Harry...if you were driving out from London to Suffolk which route would you take?"

Harry just turned his head and smiled as if trying to humour the wayward course of their disjointed ramblings.

"What kind of a question is that? I have no idea. It's not what I do," but just then a sheaf of paperwork landed on the table just in front of his coffee cup. It was a rental agreement with a national car hire firm. The second Met detective nodded at the notes in front of them all.

"Harry, my snouts tell me that you took out a nice blue Merc hire car (soft-top/hard-top SLK) for a little spin to the country a little while back. That in itself is unusual for you Harry, but not – on its own – a cause for concern in our view. Anyone can pop out to East Anglia for a bit of a run about or maybe to view some holiday homes up for sale, you know the routine, but in this case you registered the car under an alias – David Tennant, no less – for which you would have needed a driving licence in that name and other supportive documentation."

He let the accusation sink in, and then he went on.

"Furthermore, our CCTV footage produces a very unusual route out to Suffolk. Not for you the A2 south of the river out to the M25 and through the Dartford tunnel heading north. Not even the Blackwall tunnel onto the north circ and then a right on to the A12 all the way out to Suffolk in a straight line. No... a very odd mix for you: over Tower Bridge from the south, then a right to follow the A13 along the old Commercial Road heading east all the way out to the M25 at Thurrock before heading north for a couple of junctions, and then joining the A12 at Brentwood in order to head north east into East Anglia. Any casual observer would think you were trying to camouflage your intentions," and with that another folder hit the table top spilling a couple of traffic shots taken from CCTV recordings.

Harry Moston appeared rattled for the first time in the entire exchange. He fingered the black and white images and checked the corporate logo on the letterhead of the supposed rental agreement.

The same detective began to draw the encounter to a close.

"I think we need to take a walk round to the station, Harry. We can nip round to Southwark, it's handier than Peckham."

"Oh no you sodding well don't," challenged Moston, indignation rising quickly now. "You have nothing to justify this aggravation. I know how you bastards work. You need a warrant or at least something before you can shove me around like this."

"Or we can just arrest you on suspicion of the murder of Lee Phillipson," the policeman threw back at him nonchalantly.

"What? Have you guys lost your marbles? I told you, I aint never 'eard of 'im. Where the hell is this going?"

"Well that's an easy one to answer – and you'll need to make it very clear when you make that call to your legal friend. Southwark nick it is."

Moston simply slumped in his chair. He stared from one of his oppressors to another and shook his head forlornly. Then he slowly pulled out his mobile phone and called his solicitor. All four of them suspected he'd reach an answer phone at best, bearing in mind that any self-respecting professional would have more than just Mad Mo Moston's concerns to worry about.

As he poked at the send button he sensed a new presence close at hand. Just behind him – one at each shoulder – stood two uniformed policemen. When the short call was concluded they each raised him by the arm out of his chair much to the fascination of a small but growing crowd of onlookers. Harry Moston wriggled free from their grasp and gathered himself as he walked off with the group, his head held high.

As they moved away the bigger of the two London-based detectives glanced surreptitiously towards the doorway of the coffee house where its owner, Toto Lentini, gave him a barely perceptible nod. He returned the acknowledgement in the same vein and stepped out behind his new charge.

15 – a close encounter

Harry Moston shuffled and fidgeted his discomfort in the hard-backed plastic chair he'd been dumped into in one of Southwark police station's bare, sanitised interview rooms. Behind him a lone uniformed policeman stood sentry by the door. Harry could make him out as a dull, blurred reflection in the one-way glass pane in front of him. From hard fought experience he knew that he was being observed from the other side of that glass, but he knew also that there was nothing he could do about it. When his legal beagle arrived, whoever was secretly watching him would then join them in the room and take up their seats on the other side of the table, with their backs to that window. To his left and at the end of the table, pushed up against the wall, the recording equipment emitted a barely audible electronic hum.

In the observation room Amy Addison and her recently acquired local colleagues looked in on him and silently acknowledged his disquiet.

"Well, well DS Addison, I didn't have you down as one for a bit of melodrama, but when you threw in that very suggestive French moniker I almost laughed out loud at Old Harry's rather lame attempts to stifle any reaction. So pray tell… who is, or was, the lovely lady and what on earth has she got to do with Harry the Hands?"

"Aw look…I'm really sorry about that chaps, but I had no way of passing that on to you before you guys arrived on the terrace there this morning. In fact, I'd already had a busy morning and an interesting interview with a woman just along the road from here in Shad Thames. What's more," she carried on, "I also had a fascinating discussion with that same woman's son, over at Limehouse Basin, yesterday evening."

The Met men were all ears.

"Wow, what a pad…what can I say?" she continued.

"Which one? Limehouse or Shad Thames?" came the reply.

"Oh…er…the one on the Thames. Well…," she adjusted, "the Limehouse place was very nice too, way beyond my price bracket and lifestyle that's for sure, but his mum's penthouse overlooking the river is really something," she considered in almost dreamy distraction.

"And the relevance of this well-to-do family connection is what, exactly?"

"Put very simply," and she stalled momentarily for the impact she knew it would have, "they are my murder victim's first wife and his only child."

"Really," was the keen response. "My, my… you have been busy up here in the big city. So how did they react? What did you find out, anything useful?"

"Chalk and cheese in terms of reactions," she said. "The son was pretty cut up about it all. I'd been tipped off as much by the uniforms who had been round to do the nearest and dearest visit. It transpired that he'd been trying to build some kind of relationship with his father despite the father having abandoned him as a baby. Apparently he'd travelled out to Suffolk quite recently for their first reunion, but it seems that the process stalled quite quickly and he'd returned home a bit confused and certainly feeling rejected. His mother, on the other hand, took the news of her ex-husband's demise in her stride…hardly a flicker of emotion first time around apparently, and no different with me: very controlled, almost subdued I'd say."

"But that's interesting in itself, isn't it? I mean…to have lived with someone, been married, born the man's child, well…you know…you'd think there might be the odd heart-string twanging away beneath the calm exterior. I mean…what did she actually say?"

"It wasn't so much what she said as the manner in which it was said, and it all seemed a little matter-of-fact, phlegmatic you might say, impassive.

"The lad, well…I say lad, but he's probably not much younger than me, was really quite distressed. He talked a lot about his mother and late grandmother filling him in regularly – as he was growing up – on the obviously thorny topic of the lightweight waster that had been his father. When the boy had been still just a kid he'd harboured a degree of animosity towards his absent father which developed into a real sense of hostility – his words not mine – which was only tested as he began to mature into his teens.

"Only then did he begin to question the one-sided nature of the character implanted in the back of his mind by the older matrons in his life. That reawakening, if I can put it like that, began to antagonise his mother as he began to question all those tales which had been so relentlessly imbued in his understanding of the past. Nevertheless, and despite the frictions of that phase, their relationship – mother and son that is – is a strong one. However, I suspect for a while in his late teens they must have had some seriously confrontational debates about the past and what may or may not have happened in reality way back then.

"Even so, they remain close. It's clear that he's had a female hand around and about him all his life – in the absence of the father figure, I mean. His apartment is not just neat and orderly, but the decor has that distinctly feminine touch in terms of colours and textures that only a girl's perspective can conjure." She hesitated, realising that her insensitive remarks had registered with her all male audience, and then she attempted to soften the barb by adding, "What I'm trying to say is simply that it looks like a combination of girlfriends' good tastes and his mother's ample financial support has furnished that young man's quarters to an admirable standard. And its location…well…how exciting must it be to be living just off Narrow Street, a two minute walk from The Grapes pub, only five minutes from Canary Wharf and just two stops on the DLR into the City? From his balcony he looks down over the sailing boats and narrow boats moored in the basin and the Thames is just across the road. Come on, I mean…most of us will never get that close to luxury-living even if we work till Domesday."

"Nice part of town these days," conferred one of the London detectives, "but did you get the sense that the boy's resentment of his old man's disappearance all those years ago may have tripped him into revenge mode?"

"No, not at all. He's either up for a Golden Globe for his emotional rendition of abject misery, or he really is desperately disappointed that his plan to build some kind of harmony with his estranged father has been thwarted forever. He really was very upset, and it took me half my time to comfort him and to alleviate his obvious tension before I could glean anything of any use.

"His mother – this morning – seemed a very different type altogether. Okay, let's face it, it is a long time ago, thirty years back to put a time line on it, but she was cold in her apathy. It took me quite a while to warm her up. Certainly when I iterated Phillipson's death to her it recorded barely a minor tremor on her emotional scale. It's worth saying though that once she did start talking it became pretty clear pretty quickly that she hadn't missed her first love from the day he walked out the door."

"And that's because...?" and he left the implied question hanging in the air.

"Because he turned out to be a shallow individual who could offer her nothing for the long term. Of course like all of us, as youngsters, we make snap judgements based on limited experience and sometimes those mistakes come back to haunt us. In her case she actually met this bloke on a train. It was literally just a casual passing in the corridor and before she knew it he'd turned round and followed her back to her seat where he proceeded to chat her up with such aplomb that they were married within six weeks.

"It had been a disaster, and she succumbed to that conclusion within about six months, but the relationship limped along for another year or so by which time Daniel was born. Sorry, yes...er, Daniel, that's the name of the son, you understand."

They nodded casually.

"But the child's arrival more or less convinced Phillipson to make a hasty exit, not least, in his wife's opinion, because he really didn't want to shoulder the burden of caring for the child. Apparently it wasn't so much a responsibility issue, more a financial one. He just didn't want to pay for the child's upbringing, nor did he contribute more than a handful of loose change, relatively speaking, for the next eighteen years."

"So he just dumped his family, just like that?" they prompted.

"Seems so," she confirmed.

"That must have been tough for a single parent starting a family like that from the beginning, or as near as damn it."

"My thoughts exactly, and yet Kate – the mother – just didn't see it that way. She was aware that the CSA was digging around in the background, but apparently Phillipson kept on moving around with some regularity in order to make it difficult for them to pin him down."

"CSA?" came the vague enquiry.

"Child Support Agency." she answered, and they remembered after all.

"They're supposed to bring absent fathers to heel even if it's only to force them to contribute to the anticipated costs of the child's development. Phillipson dodged that particular commitment for the best part of two decades."

"But they must have struggled something rotten. Where did all this take place?"

"Right here in south London actually...er, Tooting and Bermondsey for the most part, if I remember correctly."

"Phew, an expensive existence for a young mum with a baby, I shouldn't wonder. How did she manage? I mean...she must have been desperate for some of his cash in those early years when the bastard had just done a runner."

"You know, that's what I said to her – and it was the only time in the whole exchange that I saw a spark of warmth or excitement in her engagement – but she openly professed to missing not his money, but his prowess in the bedroom! It took me quite by surprise, and she talked for a few minutes about that particular aspect," she said with a grin. "It was as if we were in some kind of girly confession, this middle-aged woman spilling some of her inner-most secrets. She even dropped her voice a little in case her partner overheard the revelation. Then, to confound me completely, she admitted that she'd been with her new man for twenty five years or more and I wondered what could have been so sensitive to have threatened such a long standing relationship from quite so many years ago, but there you go...who knows what goes on behind closed doors?

"As for the money – or lack of it – she insisted that she wouldn't have accepted a bean from him anyway. Call it pride, call it what you like, she was absolutely determined to rid herself of any connection to that man from the minute he'd ditched her and the kid.

"Her parents helped out a lot in those early days. They ran a pub then, somewhere just off Tower Bridge Road. It was a bit of a rough old shop by all accounts, and Kate assured me that it attracted all sorts of clandestine huddles in the enclosed booths in the bar and poorly lit corners of the lounge, but...," and she was interrupted.

"That'll be the Red Knight I'd say... at a guess anyway. It had quite a reputation in those days for the likes of Harry the Hands and his cronies."

At this point they all turned to look through the grey glass where Harry looked at his watch and seemed irritated by his lawyer's delayed arrival.

"Very probably," Addison went on, "but Kate Crighton must have been a fiercely determined young woman at that time. She moved on very quickly. By that I mean that she moved up rapidly in terms of her social standing. She completed her veterinary studies even though she was dragging a little boy in her wake. I reckon her own mother must have spent a lot of time with little Daniel during that phase, but Kate didn't hold back. She started out professionally in a local vets' practice in Clapham. In no time she was a partner, and then a controlling partner. Within ten years she had joined forces with one of those partners, bought out the practice and extended into two more, the first in Battersea and the next in Wandsworth. Wind the clock forward another decade and she owns – or at least shares in the ownership of – a chain of about a dozen veterinary outfits spread right across south London and she's awash with dosh as Harry might say."

"Which presumably explains the plush roof top suite on the Thames?"

"Indirectly, yes," she nodded. "They were bought out by one of the big nationals, you know...Vets n Pets or Pooches n Paws...one of those anyway, and needless to say she'll never work again. She'll just never need to. It's amazing how much money people will spend on Fido and Tiddles," she said, gently shaking her head in disbelief.

"And that goes some way to explaining the lad's cosy little gaff over in Limehouse, wouldn't you say?"

"Possibly...and I'm sure he's been supported by his mother at all of the major twists and turns of his life to date, but young Daniel is something of a chip off the old dear and not off the old block, if you get my meaning. He's obviously got the same drive and work ethic as his mother."

"What does he do?"

"He's a pharmacist. He works with one of the smaller chains and is responsible for the dispensaries at a host of chemist outlets north and south of the river. I think it would be a safe bet to say he's doing pretty well, no thanks to his runaway father."

At that moment a disturbance in their peripheral vision attracted their otherwise engaged concentration and the detectives looked again through the one-way window to see a neatly suited and booted professional chap just closing the door of the interview room behind him. He nodded politely to the standing officer. Then he approached his client, shook him firmly by the hand before pulling out the adjacent chair and ditching his brief case on the floor beneath the desk. They fell into mute conversation glancing fitfully up at the glass with the obvious suspicion that they were indeed under surveillance from the next room.

The solicitor waved his hand in the air gesturing towards the glass. The taller of the two male detectives flicked the intercom switch to ask what was required. The legal man replied only that he needed at least ten minutes with his client and the officer acceded without hesitation. The solicitor then shared a little chuckle with his client feeling satisfied with the point they'd scored.

Turning back to his pretty blonde colleague from Suffolk, the same officer threw a new question into the ring. "All of this is an impressive study of the successes of the capitalist system, but we appear to have overlooked the French connection…you know… that clever little thrust from you this morning over coffee at Toto's."

"Ah yes, I was coming to that," she reassured him with wistful smile. "The cute and sexy Monique Leboutilliere is certainly not to be overlooked: perish the very idea," she added with mock emphasis. "In those early days and during that very brief period of not-so-wedded-bliss, Lee Phillipson had tagged himself to his young bride here in south London. They shared a modest flat in Bermondsey, and I'd suggest that it was indeed fairly basic. Bermondsey – at that time – would have had its sharper edges, of that there is little doubt, but for a young couple there would have been at least some opportunity to make a start in life.

"Lee Phillipson was doing some basic book-keeping and accountancy courses at the local poly, but it seems he didn't always apply himself either to his studies or to his day-to-day work commitments with all that much concentration. The charm offensive his wife had so enjoyed – on that train a year or so earlier – had not been put to bed along with their nuptials. On the contrary, it seems that he remained quite attached to his flirtatious approach to attractive young women, and he was an attractive young man by all accounts.

He went through his first period of unemployment around about that time and he found himself moping around the apartment with time to kill – this was before the baby came along, by the way. He must have bumped into a number of people coming and going, up and down the lifts and so on, but amongst his haphazard encounters was a young French beauty, who must have mesmerised him at first sight, and in so doing triggered a predictable rush of testosterone-fuelled adrenalin. That was Monique Leboutilliere – not a French temptress, but a French-Canadian lovely from Montreal. She lived not just in the same building, but across the hall on the same floor. Her man, a certain Henry Moston, was often away for long stretches on business contracts abroad, or so she had at first believed," and they all smiled at the deception knowing full well the truth behind the yarn. "Our man Phillipson happily bedded the wench to his heart's content until one afternoon he was caught in the act by one of Harry's trusty lieutenants, and then the game was up. We can only speculate as to the real drivers behind Phillipson's hasty exit, and his abandoning the family without an apparent care in the world, but it's safe to say that his card would have been marked behind bars in Wandsworth by our friend through the glass there."

"All of which suggests a motive for that circuitous little day-trip out to Suffolk a few days ago."

"Oh sure: that's going to be a tricky one to wriggle out of, if you ask me," said Addison. "You've got that journey recorded on the very same day that Phillipson was killed. That's a long way beyond suspicious. Mind you," she queried, "you'd have to wonder why it took him so long to get round to it. It's thirty years ago, don't forget."

"Yeah, but with the girl long gone by the time he came out of prison he probably just got side-tracked with so many other more pressing distractions to attend to in his growing and already vicious little south London empire. And the dead man did maintain a fairly mobile lifestyle, as we've heard, and it must have been difficult to track the sod down during those brief spells back on the street between sentences."

"Shall we go through and find out?" she proposed.

As they rounded the corner the uniformed sentinel – who had retreated to the corridor to give the solicitor and his client some privacy – turned sharply around and rapped hard on the door. He didn't wait, but opened the door with practiced authority and then stood aside as the three detectives passed through into the interview room.

The taller of the two London-based officers took station to one side standing and leaning casually back against the wall. The other, together with DS Addison, sat opposite Harry Moston and his legal counsel, and he leaned over to flick the recording gear into operation, delivering the essentials for the record before reclining in his chair.

They had agreed that Addison would begin proceedings. However, as she passed the CCTV copies and the hire car documents across to the solicitor, clearing her throat as if to commence the questioning, the legal man held up a polite hand of intervention.

"My client has outlined the details of his predicament. He tells me that he is in grave danger of being accused of murder. He maintains his innocence. He has also explained the circumstantial evidence that outwardly connects him to the crime – a crime which took place recently in the county of Suffolk, as I understand it. He wishes me to concede on his behalf that some aspects of the case you are building against him do look, well...how shall I put it...if not conclusive, then certainly damaging. Nevertheless, he maintains his innocence."

Addison interrupted the flow. "Which aspects does your client think are damaging?"

But the solicitor pleaded earnestly with her saying, "Please detective, just give me a moment longer to explain our position. I think you will find it a little testing, but we can cut to the chase very quickly and save us all a great deal of time. Hopefully you will see the sincerity in my client's contribution, such that you will not feel the need to remand him here pending further enquiries."

The taller man by the wall snorted with derision and shook his head slowly, incredulous, but he added nothing to the debate. The solicitor ignored him and continued unperturbed.

"My client has spent too much of his life in prison. He wishes never to be incarcerated again. He insists that some of his previous sentences have been unjust and therefore he harbours a natural distrust of the police and indeed of the legal system in general. However, he also admits that he has indeed killed a man…in the past, you understand…when he was just a teenager, but that was accidental and represents his only capital crime for which he has paid his dues through time served in various forms of detention. He did not kill your most recent victim, of that he is adamant, but he is about to tell you how close he got to that sorry event on the day in question. His story may appear…shall we say…far-fetched, but his plea to you is that the apparently incredible nature of his explanation is, or should be, enough to persuade you that another potential perpetrator requires your attention."

Before preparing to let Harry say his piece the solicitor added, "As officers of the law, familiar with all the aspects of a modern criminal investigation and the legal processes attached to it, you will readily understand that I am no expert in the realm of forensics and related sciences. However, I will predict here and now that you will find yourselves entirely unable to corroborate my client's involvement at the scene of the alleged murder. He simply wasn't there. Whether this becomes conclusive in proving his innocence or not, depends largely on your own perceptions of the validity of his account."

With that he turned to his client, and with a deft movement of the hand he motioned Harry into the imaginary spotlight. The detectives were silent and captivated.

Harry swivelled slowly in his chair and eyed the detective standing by the wall. He'd known him a long time. He said nothing. Just as slowly he turned back to his inquisitors on the other side of the table and he scanned their faces for any hint of mood or thought beyond doubt and suspicion. Then he began, and he addressed DS Addison directly.

"You're right my dear. You're right," he repeated, "to link me to Lee Phillipson through my girl Monique. She was the best thing that ever happened to me by a Country Mile. We had such a fabulous time together I can't begin to tell you..." and he trailed off in fond memories for just a moment or two. "But that bastard Phillipson ruined her. He ruined her for me, and I swore blind – when I heard from my boys what had being going on – that I'd have that low-life if it were the last thing I ever did. But you know," and he stopped abruptly as if trying to find the right words, "it wasn't just his filthy paws all over my girl – that was bad enough – it was the thought that she ran away from me: that she was actually so terrified of what I might do that she deserted me. That's what really hurt. That's what broke my heart."

"Do us a favour Harry, old son, we know you haven't got a heart," jibed one of the Met men, but Harry Moston spat out his venomous reaction.

"Shut it, you tosser! Will you ever learn? I'm telling you the truth 'ere and it'll save you an awful lot of time and energy. What's more," he insisted with utter disdain, "it'll stop you jerks from making complete twats of yourselves, as per fuckin' usual."

"Harry please," his lawyer soothed, "just stick to the plan and tell them what you know."

"Okay guvnor, okay." He breathed in a chest full of air and slowly exhaled as he regathered his thoughts. "As I was saying," he offered to DS Addison, "she broke my heart, that girl, when she left. I couldn't work out if it had been her own shame at bedding a guy across the hallway, a married man, and knowing the man's wife as she must have, surely," he petitioned, "or whether it was her fear of me and how I might react. Anyway...whichever...it was his fault, all of it. He was going to pay for it one way or another, one day or another. But I never intended to kill him...even from the earliest days...and I didn't kill him. I was just going to break him up a bit. I'm pretty good at that sort of thing, as you heard this morning darlin'.

"So, yes...you're right again, with your fancy CCTV images and all that clever stuff...I did take a little trip out to see if I could find the bastard. I'd done a little research, called in a few favours – you know the form – and I was fairly sure I could locate him, but to be honest I only went out there to case the joint...you know, to get the lie of the land and so forth. I'd waited all these years, I could wait a few more weeks and I wanted to get things right in my head as to how the job could be done. Okay I admit it, I did have a pick-axe handle in the boot and I would've bust more than just his hands if I'd 've chanced upon 'im like, but I didn't get that chance."

He paused to reflect for a second. His hosts looked at one another with a hint of intrigue floating across facial expressions.

"I was pretty sure I'd found the right place, but there was no way of knowing if he or anyone else was at home. I sat for a while in a little lane just opposite the house and little way up the road. I watched for any comings and goings and it all looked very quiet. It was a Sunday afternoon. I didn't want to leave the return trip too late. It sounds as if Sunday evening trips returning to the Smoke are just hellish, so I wanted to avoid that if I could. No need to be sat in a car on the A12 when it looks more like a car park now is there?" he reasoned with a soft smile.

"When I was happy that the place must've been empty I left the car and took a stroll down the road. I thought I'd put in a shufty round the back – check the layout, test the locks and windows, that kind of thing – but just as I was approaching the end of the hedge near the driveway I heard it."

"Heard what?"

"The shot! It was a gunshot, a single shot. I'd know a gunshot from a hundred yards and I was only twenty or so from the house. There was no doubt in my mind."

DS Addison silently registered the fact that to her certain knowledge neither she nor her colleagues had told this man the method by which the dead man had met his end. Here he was talking openly about a gunshot. This was either a fantastic double bluff, or he really was telling the truth. But then she considered the potential for Harry's network to have furnished him with this potentially implicating knowledge. Harry ploughed on.

"Jesus Christ," he hissed anxiously," I just didn't know what to do. I know what it's like to be genuinely afraid, trust me, but I was terrified. I just couldn't believe my luck – or bad luck as it turned out – to be standing outside that bastard's own house when he gets popped...at least that was my immediate assumption. I didn't really care that he'd been well-sorted...way overdue anyway in my book...but it was the immediate thought that I might very quickly end up in a room just like this talking to ugly buggers just like you." Then he looked at Amy Addison and smiled and said, "Sorry love, you excluded, of course."

She ignored the compliment and asked, "So what did you do next Harry?"

"I scarpered o' course... walked smartly back to the car racking my noggin as I went: just desperate to think through my next steps. As he said earlier," nodding across the table in the direction of Addison's colleague, "that hire car was as bright as a button – metallic blue, drop down hard top, the works – not exactly helpful in remaining incognito you might say. But nothing happened for a couple of minutes. I didn't hear any commotion from the house. There were no sirens wailing in the distance. The place just carried on ticking along on a quiet Sunday afternoon. Then I heard it."

"What? Another shot?"

"No. No, not another gunshot...nothing like that. It was an engine. Just a car or a van starting up somewhere just off to my left...maybe fifty yards or so...but it wasn't just the noise of the engine, it was the way the driver barely turned it over before he fairly raced out of his parking spot. There was a great rasping scourge of dirt or gravel or chippings...something like that...and the engine whined as it accelerated away."

"And?"

"Well...I followed 'im, didn't I. It just had to be connected to the sound of that shot. I was convinced he was linked to that shot."

"How did you know it was a he?"

"Aw c'mon...leave it out...I didn't know it was a he or a she. It's just a figure of speech. Even later, after I'd tailed him a while, the only glances I'd been able to get had revealed a grey hoody, and that's all. He could have been a she for all I know, but I must say he drove that van like a bloke if that's any help."

"Whoa...hang on a minute. Just hold it right there," Amy Addison complained. "Are you seriously asking us to accept that little Enid Blyton short story? I mean...how naïve do you think we are? There is nothing there for us to hang our hats on, nothing at all."

"Blimey love," Harry replied, "that's the whole point. It's so ridiculous you wouldn't really expect me to sit here and tell you something so pathetically shallow as that little yarn. But I just did, because it's the truth. I'd wager my next prison sentence on it, honest! If you think I couldn't 've fabricated something more convincing then I'm disappointed."

He looked at his persecutors with a blank expression and open hands, inviting their acceptance.

"But Harry there is nothing for us to run with. Looking at the paperwork there in front of you we have so much more to work with, and you've just confessed your own presence at the crime scene on the day."

"Listening skills love, listening skills...as the good lawyer here as already pointed out, I did not go into that house and you will not find any trace elements there to counter that claim. I don't know the specifics of that bastard's last moments, but they took place in that house and I wasn't there," he asserted forcefully.

"So you tailed this van along the country road out of the village and then what?" Addison persisted.

"Well what can I tell you? I mean...I lost him... in the end."

The male detectives openly derided the man's wandering diatribe.

"Well...I mean...I stuck with it for a bit on the way up to Woodbridge of course, but I couldn't allow myself to get too close. A shiny metallic blue sporty number is hardly inconspicuous in the country lanes of Suffolk, so I had to hang back. Fortunately those lanes have a fair bit of hedgerow cover for a low-slung two-seater with the roof down. It was a warm sunny day after all. They also have a few tight bends which gave me the opportunity to catch a quick profile through any gaps in the hedge as he was racing along the next straight stretch after a corner or a switch-back – if you follow – but when we got to town I got stuck at the lights and he just drifted away."

"Harry, you just said, "on the way up to Woodbridge", didn't you? How well do you know the area?"

"What? I don't. Never been there in my life."

"So were you following the road signs through the back lanes or what?"

"Nah, didn't see any, love. Actually I was too busy lurching around those bends and hoping that those bloody great big farm tractors have good brakes."

"So how did you know you were heading for Woodbridge?"

"Well I didn't, and even when I got closer to civilisation there was no big sign telling me the name of the place. It was a tiny little back lane after all. I just assumed we were going that way."

"Why?"

"Because the name of the place was plastered across the side of the van, that's why."

"Are you sure?"

"Yeah, I'm sure I'm sure...Jeez, what do you take me for...reminded me of my old uncle if you most know. He was a distant relation to one of England's best ever batsmen. Do you remember Ken Barrington? Nope, of course you don't," he said, to the vacant looks opposite. "You're just too young, but when I was a kid I used to love watching him at the crease."

"Sorry Harry," quizzed the big detective, stepping forward as he did so and placing his hands on the edge of the table, "you're losing me, mate. What has this got to do with our dead man in Suffolk?"

"Barrington's Boatyard...splashed all over the van it was, Barrington's Boatyard, Woodbridge."

16 – time well spent

She saw him strutting along towards the dining room from the far end of the corridor, doing his best to deny his reliance on two ivory-handled walking canes upon which his mobility was almost entirely dependent. She upped her own pace in order to reel him in. Previous discussions about wheel chairs flashed through her mind and she inwardly recoiled from the old man's resentment. She hadn't handled that particularly sensitive issue very effectively at all, and the man's pride had been severely dented – and in the public forum of the main lounge no less. It had taken several months to recover her ground with him. Her obvious regret had clung to her like a nasty smell, a niggling nagging feeling of shame that she should have acted so naively in the face of an elder statesman who had earned her respect many times over.

Now here he was pushing on in regimental style, head up, chin out and back ramrod straight as he disappeared round the corner to join his equally elderly entourage of largely female admirers at their territorial retreat – the window table in the central bay overlooking the main lawn.

"Ah, there you are Wing Commander, how lovely to catch up with you just before lunch. Can you spare me five minutes?" she asked as she gestured towards the dark leather armchairs in the adjacent alcove. "I just wanted your thoughts on a couple of new ideas for our entertainments agenda, and I suspect that you will, as ever, be cognisant of the collective views of the majority of our residents."

The flattery worked immediately. With a glint in his eye he smiled and gave a deferential nod to this woman: a younger specimen and a glowing example of attractive maturity. Despite recent disappointments she had long since won his admiration and his active support for the disciplined and very successful manner in which she ran Park Green. Had she been of his generation he felt sure that she would have acquitted herself with distinction amidst the organised determination of the war effort – perhaps in the War Office, or as a senior ranking WAAF. By Jove he thought, she'd got this lot knocked into shape very quickly after her arrival a few years ago. And a fine figure of a woman too he reminded himself as he changed direction and stepped out towards the comfort of firm, well-worn leather.

Janice Swinton knew only too well the tell-tale signs of one of her favourite inmates – as he had often urged her to call them – who might be feeling a little run down and peaky. The Wingco, as she and her team referred to him – but always in a good humoured fashion and with every due courtesy – had certainly had a difficult few months. He looked pale and drawn. Through the ruse of an extra quiz or two, or the addition of a chess competition at which he would doubtless excel, she hoped to get a quick review of just what had been gnawing away at him sufficiently to subdue him beyond his normally active and engaging self.

"Well, Wing Commander…this is a nice change. We don't seem to get the chance to chat as much as we once did. It must be my fault," she conceded, "but the administrative workload never seems to slacken off."

"Not at all, Ma'am. Not at all. It's a fine ship you're skippering here, if you ask me, and if that means we get a little less time to natter, then that's a decent price to pay I'd wager."

"How very kind of you, Wing Commander. I do appreciate your support even though I'm not always able to show it. But tell me, how are you these days? How are those knees holding up?"

"Oh, mustn't grumble Mrs Swinton. It's the left one really…you know, the one with shrapnel still in there…not a lot we can do with it these days, and it's been there nigh on sixty five years, so I assume it'll go the fires of hell with the rest of me in due course."

She'd heard these lines before and she half nodded and half smiled as he ran through his predictable responses with the nonchalance and charm of a war hero who retained modesty as a guiding principle in all things. "But what else is happening in your world at the minute," she prodded rather vaguely.

"Well my dear, I suppose much the same as in yours since we share the same world most of the time, do we not?"

"Indeed we do, and we're all the better for your acquaintance sir, If I may say so?"

"You may...of course you may...and I feel much the better for your compliments my dear, I must say."

"And yet you have appeared a little distant of late, perhaps a little distracted. Have you been ill...not telling my girls about it maybe...taking a sicky on the QT? I know you military chaps – stiff upper lip and never admit to any weakness. It's not always the best policy, you know," and she looked at him, searching for the reveal. However, he slipped into a moment of brooding consideration and she quickly assumed that she'd lost his interest: then he perked up again.

"You know Mrs S, it was a double anniversary recently, and not the happiest of reminders."

She cringed inside. Had she done it again? She waited.

"Yes, my old girl passed away at this time of year some years ago. I still find her absence very hard to bear, but the anniversary of my daughter's death, *our* daughter's death I should say, has troubled me greatly in recent years. Coming as they do, both quite close together, turns this month into something of a psychological minefield. I have to admit, and I am comfortable telling you this, that I am struggling to keep my thoughts on a positive track when these pressures seem to gang up on me like this."

She cursed herself silently. She had indeed done it again – hadn't got her ducks lined up, keen to check the old boy over, but not prepared properly for it, and now look what she'd done. The Wingco must think she's losing her grip. "But you must alert us to your difficulties when they arise, Wing Commander. That is what we're here for after all," she implored.

"Oh Mrs Swinton you are our Guardian Angel, I'm convinced of it, but you have so much on your plate. I tell you, this is just something that I have to get through as best I can. Worse things happened over the Ruhr in all that flack, that's a dead cert, and I can't burden you with these recurrent personal issues. However, I must hand it to you my dear. You are perceptive. I have been struggling and it obviously has been noticed. Hats off to you and your team, but look here...I'm an old war horse of sorts, a Pegasus of the RAF as you well know, and I can get through this. In fact I'd argue right now that just talking about it like this must surely ease the anxiety. How does it go, a problem shared and all that. Well...we're sharing, are we not?" he said plainly.

"And so we are Wing Commander, but I do worry about you bottling these things up. With no family to rely on you really ought to lean on us as your surrogates. I know, because we have discussed it before, that your daughter committed suicide. They say that it's terrible for parents to be pre-deceased by their own children, even adult children. There is something almost beyond the natural order of things in that regard – and I don't ever want to put that to the test – but suicide must be grievously difficult to cope with. I feel for you," and in saying this she laid her warm comforting hand on his bony knuckles. She made to continue, but he interrupted her.

"It's the futility of it all, the wastage, that rotten sense of failure that remains forever pervasive."

She saw the tears welling behind his eyes, but he fought them back and carried on. "She had a difficult time, my little girl. Of course she wasn't a little girl at all when she took her own life, but the root causes that drove her in that direction must, at least in some way, have been spawned at home."

"But you can't blame yourself, surely?" she begged.

"In part I must, as must her mother if we follow that thread logically, but our lassie made some bad choices both in life and in death. She never really applied herself when she was younger, and so she could never command a good job and thus create the lifestyle that comes with reliable earnings. In addition, she picked her men friends very badly indeed. By George, there were some rough diamonds floating around my girl at one time, and also a few fly-by-nights who just took advantage of her for months or years at a time before abandoning her. I warned her, but you know how stubborn young women can be sometimes. Now all I have left as family is my feckless grandson who could hardly find his way out of a very large bin liner with a commensurately large hole at one end. He's weak and he's lazy. There is no spark there at all. I don't how he gets away with it, but I'm sure he's just drifting through life like a modern-day tramp. I have no idea what to do with him or how to guide him appropriately. I have to admit that I have little time for him. I don't even like him, and it's a relief that I see him so rarely. Doesn't that sound truly dreadful?" he pleaded, downcast and consumed by self-loathing.

"Don't be so hard on yourself," she responded quickly. "We all have our limitations. We can't cover all of the bases all of the time, to use the Americanism."

"Ah yes, that's as maybe, but if my memory serves me correctly, those Yanks would give every single task their very best shot rather than turn their backs on the more testing missions in life. By God, when I think of those boys up there in broad daylight over Hamburg and Essen in those bloody great Fortresses, Dorniers and Fockers swarming all over them and ack-ack blasting them on every bombing run, those *guys*," delivered with deliberate emphasis on another Americanism, "just made us all so proud to be up there with them fighting the same enemy. There was never any question of them shirking their responsibilities, and yet have I followed their example in this somewhat sticky relationship with my grandson? He's my own flesh and blood and yet I can't find the key to unlock the boy's apathy – and I've given up trying, if I'm to be honest with you."

She mirrored his apparent depression as they slid into the backs of their chairs, lost for words and spent for the psychological examination. At least her hunch had been right, and now at least she would be able to re-visit the same subjects without having to broach them afresh each time. She made a mental note to include the Wingco on her management rota at the team briefing the following morning. Then, anxious not to keep her dapper admirer from his lunch for much longer, she shifted focus and mood with one simple word.

"Chess?" she hinted in the elevated lilt of an intended question. He looked confused for an instant, but then smiled in anticipation.

"The king and master of all games Ma'am," he conferred. "If you're asking about the levels of interest here among us inmates, then yes indeed my lady, consider it a winner already. There are a number of casual players – I include myself in that category – and I believe there is enough scope for us to introduce a formal competition of sorts, perhaps even with some decent prizes if some of us can get hold of some external sponsors. Time for some of our cohort to squeeze some younger and rather well-healed relatives methinks," he grinned. "There we were, fretting about my own sense of responsibility, and just see how quickly we've turned it around and grafted some predatory fangs onto the beast. Leave that with me. I think it will complement the bridge set very nicely...and a much purer sport in every sense...goes without saying – no luck of the draw or slight of the dealer's hand, if you follow."

"Wing Commander you are a wicked man, but even scurrilous tacticians need calories to drive their ambition, and if you don't get into that dining room now you'll be writing a letter of complaint to the management by tea time – about rations and impending malnutrition."

"But Mrs S," he whinged lamely, "aren't you the management?"

"That's me," she acknowledged, "but as I said earlier, my admin workload does not need any extra contributions to my in-tray. Be off with you," she commanded with a turn of the hand, and he pushed himself up briskly, grabbed his sticks and plotted a course to his waiting ladies by the window.

Janice Swinton remained buttressed in comforting old hide as she watched him plodding away. Her mind effortlessly scanned the long list of residents, all of whom she knew intimately, as she tried to pick out the likely chess protagonists among the extended household.

She smiled to herself as she acknowledged the broad diversity of humanity within her charge. She only wished there were more like the Wing Commander: largely good-humoured, alert and involved, and fundamentally in good health for a senior citizen. Sadly there were others, all of them just as dear to Janice Swinton, who were not so robust and yet still carried with them their own private disappointments, personal traumas and rumbling anxieties. How she marvelled at the way in which so many mature folk now lived their lives through the auspices of their children or grandchildren at a time of life when they might have expected to throw off the yoke of responsibility and niggling apprehension that appeared to torment them constantly.

For some it was a wonderfully fulfilling period in their lives, a time when they could enjoy their familial ties or long term friendships. Janice smiled again as she remembered old Mrs Hulme cavorting with her great-grandkids only last week in the common room as the little ones clambered over the large sofa, upon which she held court, and tried not very hard to wriggle out of her tickling fingers. The look of shear relief on the grinning face of her granddaughter, the children's mother, was reward enough. The girl looked like she needed a recuperative week at Park Green on her own such were the unending demands of the two little perishers.

And then there was Mr Kenton, a grey and stooped figure who looked to all intents and purposes like he might just tilt forward a degree or two too far and crash to the floor never again to get up. Put him at a coffee table in the comfortable lounge with his own son however, and he could talk all afternoon in the most eloquent terms on any subject matter he cared to consider. His son, himself already in late middle-age, seemed to relish the same cut and thrust and the two of them would arm themselves in preparation for their weekly encounters with all the latest current affairs, political news and sporting reaction. Janice had, on more than one occasion, taken fresh coffee or tea and cakes over to them just so as to be able to engage with the pair, but she soon had to beat a hasty retreat as the next hour on the clock seemed to disappear in just a few seconds, and anyway, she was hardly a match for their attention to detail and real depth of knowledge on so many issues of the day.

As for sporting enthusiasts, well...Mr Canning and Mrs Arkwright had to take that particular prize. She a Lancashire lass with a true passion for her rugby league, and he a West Country lad who wore the rugby union hoops of the Gloucester cherry and whites with the pride of a former player in his day. The intensity with which they supported each code of the game was matched only by the solidity of their companionship; a true bond which had blossomed after each had lost their lifelong partners to illness and tragedy. Their respective families had delighted in the new and blooming friendship of recent times and even they had been drawn into the light-hearted but deeply felt debate about all things rugby. What joy then to witness the two of them carted off together – not once, but twice – by adult children and grandchildren to watch England on the international stage. For Paula Arkwright to walk out at the highest level of the Old Trafford grandstand just as the crowd erupted in welcome (for the white shirts of England and the green and gold of Australia) was to fulfil a dream of a lifetime. To do so with her dearest best friend and rugby league convert beside her, surrounded by a clutch of both families, was indeed extra special. But then to have the tables turned and for her to stand at the top of a short flight of steps on the third tier at Twickenham, arm in arm with her good mate Dennis Canning, who wrapped a hand around hers and just beamed at her with all the excitement of a first-timer to the hallowed stadium, that too was something dreams are made of, especially when the All Blacks chanted the haka and the home crowd roared its defiance.

On reflection Janice thought she should consider herself lucky that her list of residents included many such encouraging examples of the kindness naturally prevalent in human nature. On the other hand, she knew only too well that their numbers were easily overwhelmed by the morass of spiteful, intrusive, pedantic relatives: leeches who maintained contact with her charges only in the twisted hope that they might benefit from the ultimate demise of the targets of their questionable affections.

How dear old Mrs Meakins managed to stave of the constant verbal battering given her by those cockroaches of nephews and nieces Janice simply couldn't fathom. She had little doubt that the cattery would get the lot eventually, and if asked, would she gainsay such a poetic outcome – not likely!

There were the Eden sisters; engaged in a psychological war of attrition with the husband of one of their daughters.

Then there was dear old Mr Mason who, not unlike the Wingco, had seen too much tragedy among his offspring and now found himself increasingly fretful over the rather listless, wayward life of his only grandchild. On the rare occasions she came to see him, the scrawny girl appeared incessantly absorbed by her mobile phone. It appeared unlikely that she could construct more than half a sentence at a time and her monosyllabic grizzling only helped persuade her elderly trustee that the she remained unemployed and that she flitted from one weedy young man to another in order to sustain her casual drug habit.

Janice Swinton then quietly and inwardly recoiled as she tumbled across her recollections of Mrs Yates' obnoxious snake of a son-in-law, and Janice herself felt confident in spotting such urban wild life after her own extensive exposure to the creepy crawlies of human existence. She conjured pictures of wrinkled chain-smoking middle-aged hags as they pressed home their desperate needs upon their own sickly parents. Then there were the slippery souls brim full of goodness and well-meaning as they dragged in their reluctant solicitors in feeble attempts to have wills changed and signed-over for their own eventual benefit.

Oh, the list was certainly a long one. If only she had more Wing Commander Lionels to chew the fat with...now that would make day-to-day life so much more bearable, but even he had his own personal labyrinth to navigate as she had only just rediscovered. Worrying about that boy wasn't going to bring his own poor daughter back.

Note to self she thought: must pay attention and then not forget what you've learned!

The forensic team back in Ipswich had made a bit of a breakthrough, or so it appeared to their newest and keenest analyst. They had eventually, and only after some clever application of radar and ultrasound on site, found the discharged round, that single shot which had so instantly terminated a devious and somewhat inglorious life. It had been when the landlord of the property had mentioned its renovation, carried out some years ago, that they had begun to wonder about irregularities – hidden cavities, old metal fixtures embedded in the masonry, soft spots, wire stone ties, a myriad of possibilities – that they called for more sophisticated equipment. It transpired that the stonework had been taken down rather than demolished in order to preserve as many stones as possible for the rebuild. It wasn't, and had never been, a protected structure, but the natural beauty of the imported Kentish Ragstone lent itself to the imaginative architect whose vision could be realised without the need to replicate the old shell in its old form, stone by stone. Thus old brackets and hinge spigots were simply turned sideways or inwards so as to leave the lustrous refreshed sandstones resplendent in their subtlety. The rebuild had incorporated two areas of bare stonewall inside the finished building – always pleasing on the eye – and its exterior elevations left the Ragstones to face the full brunt of the winter storms which rushed in off the wide reaches of the North Sea. In this commission the weather-most corner of the first floor had been carefully and aesthetically protected with local Suffolk flint stones in a spirited attempt to combat the more severe gales infamous for their association with spring high tides.

The young technician had calculated the bullet's trajectory with a clever mix of mathematics and supposition. The entry point in the bathroom wall was simply invisible to the naked eye, but microscopic examination had identified the point at which it had pierced mortar immediately beneath the angle of a large sandstone block. There it collided with the heel of an old rusty hinge plate and ricocheted into a small cavity where it tumbled through a convoluted series of voids – slipshod errors of the building work and not part of the architect's design brief – to rest, finally, in a tiny space close to ground level.

It had taken some time to retrieve the focus of their attention. Digging through stone and flint in a deliberately careful archaeological fashion was not the glamourous end of the forensic spectrum. However, their success enabled them to prove beyond doubt that it had been the fatal projectile that had removed a large proportion of Lee Phillipson's cranium. They soon added another crucial factor to their conclusions, one which corroborated their earlier assessment of the ordnance taken from traces around the victim's entry-point wound. Chemical constituent analysis revealed a bullet probably manufactured in the late nineteen thirties and without doubt a Parabellum of German manufacture and typically supplied to the German military for use with Luger and Mauser pistols. This rather satisfying confirmation was further reinforced by a truly wild stroke of luck when a police sniffer dog latched onto a small metallic object in the granite chippings of the main drive, hidden under the trailing edge of a buddleia bush. It was the bullet casing! How it had ended up there they could only speculate, but if the shooter had collected his own casing post-mortem, and clearly he must have, then why would he be so careless in losing it while making his escape –

unless that particular feature of the plan was not accidental. Surely that was simply a bridge too far on the road to credibility. In any event, that would be for DCI Lehrer and his crew to pursue further.

On the same day, in London, Daniel Crighton pushed back into his sculpted office chair and regarded impassively the television to his right. The BBC news bulletin posted the latest on a bizarre domestic shooting in Suffolk, but the lack of breadth and penetration from the reporter, in fact the lack of anything new over and above the previous day's broadcast, washed over him in his apparent disinterest.

He shifted back to his computer screen, but the spell had been cast and he couldn't regain his concentration on the current state of inventories across his chain of London pharmacies. He looked at the ceiling tiles and exhaled in a long slow sigh. He sat there motionless in his own private sanctum. He really had wanted to get to know him, his natural father, and he remained bitterly disappointed that their first – and ultimately last – reunion encounter had so obviously failed. He couldn't decide whether or not he would have pushed again for another meeting…had the man, his father, not been killed in such a barbaric fashion…but such considerations were entirely pointless now. After so many years feeling so abandoned, so betrayed, to have garnered the fortitude and determination to find him and to reach out to him…well, had the apprehension been worth the result? Who could say? He really didn't know, or perhaps no longer cared, and perhaps his apathy was merely a protective response, in self-defence, to a vile closing chapter in the man's drab and distasteful life. How did he really feel? He just wasn't sure. It was over. There were no next steps, no follow-ups, no second or was it third chances. A man he had never really known was now dead. That same man had walked out on him as an infant and then, more than twenty five years later, had held him very much at arm's length during their first adult skirmish. Daniel thought he'd seen the truth, thought he understood, and it seemed just another impasse in a life-track littered with barriers and obstacles. Did it matter? Not now. It was over. He picked up the phone and called his mother, but only reached that ridiculously lavish message of hers and he dropped the unit back into its cradle.

On screen he could see at a glance that the Lewisham branch was a running low on certain prescription drugs. The inventory programme very smartly highlighted depleted stocks per product and by branch. He knew their expected turn-over figures more or less by heart, certainly closely enough to spot any aberrations or unexpected levels of consumption. His weekly on-screen perusal enabled him to replenish on demand through the coordinating software which automatically fired off orders to manufacturers once supplies had been exhausted beyond a certain threshold. Only he had the authority to intervene and override the system, but rarely did he need to interrupt the very efficient process. On the other hand he could invade the process at will – and unchecked – should he need to make manual adjustments to the stock figures. This he had found quite useful on occasions.

Typically he would watch out for those obvious drugs that may prove valuable on the street. He had been wary and vigilant ever since that mess over at Blackheath when that half-wit had been siphoning off the stock for his own black-market sales. Daniel had long since suspected that blowing the whistle on that idiot had probably saved the joker's life, if not his job.

In addition he paid close attention to the variable demand for sleeping pills and a range of tranquilisers, including *benzos* for stress and anxiety control. Opiates and painkillers of various descriptions were also common currency among those for whom dependency was a daily drag. Steroids also featured on his check list, and the extensive consumption of amphetamines demanded his attention more frequently than just weekly. As he scanned the statistics before him he shook his head in dismay at the images flicking across his mental canvas. He knew only too well that London was awash with illegal narcotics. He was confronted with the stuff in all its malicious forms in every bar and club he ever visited, but the endemic abuse of prescription drugs across whole swathes of the population was a characteristic of life in the capital that he had really struggled to adjust to ever since his earliest work as a pharmacist. He knew about the drop-outs, benefit wasters and street tramps who trudged from soup kitchen to rescue shelter and very often dossed down, even in mid-winter, under the arches of the Thames bridges or beneath a red-brick Victorian railway span. He knew too that many young office workers of similar ages to his own were forever seeking the latest high as a fundamental constituent of a good night out. Fashionable it had become to adopt Thursday nights as the new Friday – start on the booze early, snort a couple of lines mid-evening then drop a few pills as you head off to some rave or other. Then later, much later, slope off home as the commuters hit the city and sleep it all off through a Friday *sicky*. He despaired at the very thought of the state those idiots would be in not many years from now. But it didn't stop there, among the youthful socialites who earned more than they knew what to do with...oh no. Further up the food chain among the ambitious, truly driven swarm of business leaders, managers and traders, there existed a covert consumption of legal and illegal substances that Daniel Crighton found truly terrifying. Money was no object, in fact irrelevant to the overall equation. Whatever they wanted, it was comfortably affordable. He believed that many, many senior figures across the business spectrum not only pursued an active flirtation with narcotics, but in addition, levels of dependency within some of the capital's most prestigious corporates were, in his opinion, dangerous and all too prevalent.

He tripped from branch to branch and spreadsheet to spreadsheet checking trends with a practiced eye. He decided that their current status was more or less as expected, so he switched across to Firefox and opened up the London Fashion Week website. He visually sifted his way through the event diary just to be sure that he had the catwalk exhibitions correctly timed in his own Outlook agenda. Then he stepped quickly through a number of exhibitors' websites and clicked on their own links to the event itself at Earls Court. He wanted to see how competitors were aligning themselves to one of the world's most exciting fashion jamborees, and he was delighted to note the favourable comparison made with the slick functionality and lavish style projected by the website of his own associates. A year earlier he had invested a small but significant developmental sum in a vibrant new fashion house in which he'd had more than a passing interest for three years or more. As an external and fairly dormant backer he was finding his interest and attention more and more frequently distracted away from the drudgery of his core business in favour of the perceived glamour and thrill of haute couture. He continued on screen and marvelled at the flowing elegance of the ball gowns and evening dresses. The clean-cut lines of the lounge suits and casual jackets made those square-jawed boys look so cool and yet so stylish – that sloppy, dishevelled look no longer signalled *attractive* to their bold aspiring designers. He smiled subconsciously. He liked what he saw. He looked back at the news programme – cricket. He picked up the remote and killed the screen.

17 – parlour games

Lehrer and Addison slipped in just as the steward was moving to close the doors of the funeral parlour. Doleful organ music greeted them as they settled into the light-oak pews of the fairly new and rather soulless main hall of the crematorium. The chamber was brightly illuminated as the sunlight streamed in through modern stained glass high above them, and to one side the expansive clear glass of the floor-to-ceiling windows invited mourners to look out at the rich lustre of the spring-flower borders in the garden of remembrance. They shuffled along to the far end of the bench as quietly and discreetly as they could, not wishing to alert anyone to their uninvited presence.

The congregation was sparse. To the front, predictably, they could make out Lynsey Bastion and her father Ric. She appeared to lean in towards him as if relying on him for physical as well as moral support. Her quiet sniffles could still be heard right at the back of the hall despite the melodic incantation of the organ as it cast a requiem spell on the mixed gathering. To her right, but obviously sitting with the Bastions, was a young man unknown to Lehrer. When he nudged his colleague gently and motioned a question about the man's identity, Addison whispered that it was Daniel Crighton, the deceased's estranged son, and the same man who had recently attempted to connect with his real father with less than favourable results. Lehrer remembered the Bastions' differing reports of that apparently abortive trip. He looked quizzically at the three of them, the backs of their heads, as they sat there in the front row – and odd association in many ways, and yet a small group that may yet prove useful to his investigation.

Half-way down the right hand side sat a gang of middle-aged blokes – presumably some of Lee Phillipson's drinking buddies and fishing mates – who had clearly pre-determined to make the man's departing ceremony not quite such as damp a squib as might have been anticipated. They rumbled in upbeat conversation, and sporadic but muted laughter could be heard escaping their immediate enclave. Clearly they had come to see the man off in something of the style and manner to which his recent memory could adhere.

Here and there were scattered small huddles of mourners, and Lehrer noticed the pub landlord from Compton, Jimmy Judge, engaged earnestly in conversation with the small band about him, presumably members of his staff from the Midshipman. Also there were a number of office types in predictable livery, and a variety of miscellaneous visitors who sat respectfully awaiting the commencement of the brief service. Lehrer knew that all of them would have to be checked out and eliminated from his list. It wouldn't have been the first time that a murderer attended the funeral of his victim, even though he felt it something of a leap of faith on this occasion.

To the left, and sitting alone in that front pew, was an elderly gent who sat with military stiffness and looked only forwards, towards the lectern, which stood in the corner of the room and to the left of the coffin where it rested centrally on trestles. A modest wreath adorned the oak lid. Lehrer took a guess that this would be the dead man's father. His fearful reputation – according to Janice Swinton at least – appeared to be reinforced by his rigid, upright form. Several rows behind him sat an elderly woman with her middle-aged daughter, or so the detectives assumed. Even from their oblique vantage point they could see a clear likeness between the two generations. Addison proffered the notion that this must be Phillipson's mother and his sister, Pippa. Both women appeared abject in their distress and they clung to each other in mutual support.

In the few minutes it had taken the police officers to absorb the retinue before them, known attendees had been mentally ticked off and interesting parties listed for further examination. Then the subtle tones of the organ recital lifted to an elevated cadence recognisable immediately as Blake's emotive Jerusalem, and the celebrant entered from the side to take up his position at the lectern. As all present rose in sombre attention, Lehrer realised for the first time that Janice Swinton had also sneaked in at the back, on the other side of the aisle. She smiled and nodded in acknowledgement as he spied her, but he could see that she was beset by grief, her red and blotchy eyes brimming over, handkerchief held to her nose, and she looked away and was lost in her own thoughts of earlier, happier times.

The service drew on the more gregarious characteristics of Phillipson's personality. A fishing mate regaled them with hilarious yarns of soggy days on the river bank, emptied hip flasks, slippery catches and too many escapes to a local boozer in favour of warmth and a few rounds of darts. Another, one of Jimmy's regulars, recalled trips abroad immersed in that curious mix of serious art galleries and touring cricket test matches. Between the wise-cracks and funny gags several of the attentive throng wondered just how Lee Phillipson had afforded such lavish excursions, but just as many, those who really knew, lowered their heads and mumbled their own discomfort just to themselves. Janice Swinton's tears dried up as her frustration simmered inside, and Lynsey Bastion blanched at the same moment, imagining the severity of her former friend's unforgiving anger.

The state celebrant guided the service along with managerial efficiency and demonstrated a practiced ease as the various contributions to the ceremony were given up. Rousing hymns were sung , readings read and, for those of a religious persuasion, a closing prayer was offered – something about the meek inheriting the earth – as Lee Phillipson's wooden coffin glided away, nosing its way through the short drapes to the furnace beyond.

DCI Lehrer felt sure he had seen Janice Swinton breath a final sigh of relief as the elongated box had disappeared from view. He wanted to ask her how she was truly feeling, and that opportunity presented itself later in the day, but not before a polite but small gathering, the rump of the congregation, had come together over tea, cake and scones in the garden room beyond the main hall.

DS Addison steered the boss artfully towards young Daniel Crighton and the three of them engaged in a courteous bit of fact finding masquerading as sympathetic soul searching. It became clear very quickly that Addison's earlier summary of Crighton's stance had indeed been very accurate. The man seemed truly morose at his somewhat tenuous loss, and his wretched disappointment at not having had the chance to rebuild that paternal relationship, missing for all his years, had marked him most evidently. It interested and perhaps surprised the detectives that Crighton had just as many questions for them as they fired at him. It appeared that he wanted the investigation into his father's death brought to a close just as soon as possible – for closure, they were given to understand. Their discussions were interrupted when old Ric Bastion joined them with his tea cup chinking against its saucer, held in his gently shaking hand. He seemed to warm to the young man who had once, and so very recently, visited his own daughter's house only to return to London so unexpectedly, thus denying the two men of very different generations the opportunity to get to know each other. They chatted closely, the younger chap quickly developing a real affinity with his senior sparring partner, and they began to drift away from their police escort, a manoeuvre Lehrer suspected was entirely deliberate on the part of the grandfatherly figure.

No-one seemed to mind that the police officers had not only turned up to the funeral, but were mingling comfortably within the assembled clusters of sombre folk. Every person there knew of the dark purpose behind their attendance, namely to glean as much information as possible in the pursuance of their investigation. They were, after all, only there to advance their search for the man's killer, but they demonstrated deference and sympathy and were tolerated. To some it seemed an affront to the dead man's dignity, to others a brazen cheek that they should be there at all, but Lehrer sensed that they enjoyed mute acceptance from within the gathering so he chose to press on as best he could, mindful not to be indiscreet or in any way provocative. Unfortunately his quiet exchanges progressed his project not a bit, although he was able to reconfirm a number of aspects already registered, but then an altercation erupted on the fringes of the group.

Stan Phillipson, the bereaved and angry father, grumbled and growled his discontent in poorly camouflaged, terse exchanges with his former wife. Neither Lehrer nor Addison could make out the precise nature of his complaints, but as the confrontation continued the volume quickly rose and soon everyone felt compelled to listen to the grudging malice being dispensed in a very public forum by a very bitter old man. His ex-wife, Anne, who had severed the marital ties nearly three decades earlier, pleaded in vain with the twisted old misery that he should calm down and show some respect – for their own late son and eldest child, if for nobody else. But urging restraint only seemed to excite him further and he launched into a hurtful tirade of accusations about how she and their feckless daughter had colluded over many years in their attempts to subdue any sense of ambition and industry in poor Lee's difficult and often tempestuous life. Quickly he cast the net of accusation farther and dragged in Lynsey Bastion, her father Ric and a loose cannon's range of peripheral figures – chief amongst them that tight bitch Janice Swinton – all of whom had unfairly dragged his boy through the mud and slime of their own filthy gutters. His daughter Pippa shouted at him to stop, to see the reality, to take off those life-long blinkers and to see her brother for what he really had been, but in response he raged even more. Her mother stood there, tears rolling down her cheeks, mourning the loss of her son, and watching just one more time the same spiteful ignorance that had so very nearly destroyed her own life, and those of their children, rolled out before her for all to witness.

    One of Lee Phillipson's fishing club friends stepped in to try to assert some control over the fractious and embarrassing older man, but he was swiftly dismissed for his troubles. Even Daniel Crighton, the man's own grandson, tried to intervene, but he too was cut down with scathing barbs. It soon became clear that Lee Phillipson had crafted a fascinating tale of deceit and deception targeted not just at his first wife, but also at his own estranged son for the way he had avoided and undermined his poor caring father for so many years. Eye brows lifted in wonder at other potential distortions Stan Phillipson had been treated to, but little could be done to ease the man's histrionics and people began slowly to drift away in confusion and defeat. How could a man of his years and associated experience be quite so naïve? Such were the questions carried away with the leavers as they quietly sloped off. In the end however, Stan Phillipson ran out of steam and he crumpled in distress and retired to a quiet corner to lick his wounds. Jimmy Judge took the man under his wing and promised to drive him back to the railway station at Woodbridge. The old man dried his eyes, cleared his throat and suggested they should go, there and then.

    The remaining entourage relaxed as the tension of the moment ebbed away. They remembered their collective purpose and tried to import more flattering memories of the fun loving Lee Phillipson who had been stolen from them in such tragic circumstances. Inevitably such reflections rebounded back to the police officers in their midst, and Daniel Crighton again pressed them on the current status of their task. He asked a number of pertinent – borderline intrusive – questions about forensic details, of what they knew and where the gaps in their knowledge lay. Lehrer handled it all with the gravity appropriate to a murder investigation. Addison wondered at the manner and persistence of the lad's interrogation.

In a different corner Janice Swinton reconvened with Anne and Pippa Phillipson to share their sadness at a middle-aged man's premature death, a man with whom all three of them had enjoyed great days and grim. They didn't need to say it. They knew that that the grim days far outnumbered those of a more pleasant, often fun-filled disposition.

Lehrer stood back from the small thinning crowd. Exits were multiplying now and soon all would be gone to carry on through the day-to-day turmoil of normal life – lives the murdered man had, for so many of them, tarnished beyond redemption.

The detective churned his way through the few details of which they were sure. The aged bullet and casing signified a real breakthrough. His team was already pursuing every possible lead provided by the reams of data being spewed out by computer searches of firearms outlets, shooting clubs, antique dealers, first and second world war battle theatre societies, battle re-enactment clubs, memorabilia collectors and a host of associated sources which surely must be hiding that vital missing link that would take them to the next step. A needle in a haystack it undoubtedly was, but having something specific to focus on would almost certainly carry them forward. So far they'd had no immediate breakthrough from McLellan's assignation with the bar-room brawler, but his trade in collection pieces had set a few more hares running and a lot of people were running down leads as fast as humanly possible. Lehrer felt fairly confident that something would give soon enough. On the other hand he remained unsettled by some of the unattributed forensics taken from the crime scene, day one. He knew from years of experience that unidentifiable trace elements had a nasty habit of either catching you out or letting you down, and he frowned with that silent consideration just as DS Addison reconnected with him on the edge of the group.

She discreetly played back to him a few of the conversations she'd just had. Little additional information had been extracted, at least nothing of any apparent value in her normally perceptive view. Even so, Pippa Phillipson, now Pippa Jensen, had given Addison a measured account of her relationship with her brother as they had grown up together.

It started as something quite ordinary, a younger sister's in-built respect and admiration for her older brother. They had been quite close, good friends and close companions as much as siblings as they stretched beyond their teenage years and into adult independence. Soon however, things began to drift, rudderless into a varied assortment of frustrations, questionable judgements and disappointing outcomes. In all of it she had tried to play the loyal sister. When some of Lee's early, more serious relationships had suffered some kind of setback or even ruptured completely, his little sister would try to convey something of the female perspective in an attempt to encourage him to consider the other side of any twosome. It had appeared all too often to Pippa that her brother's sincerity was too easily compromised by his driving urge to enjoy himself to the full irrespective of some of the natural obligations upon which any liaison would fundamentally rely. Too often he had appeared cavalier and uncaring, worse still selfish and demanding when faced with difficult or sensitive decisions. Not many years had rolled by before she and her mother had winced at every callous twist and carefree turn in what had become a blaze of laddish behaviour typical of a college student rather than a young man pushing thirty.

For him there had been no sense of shame as each and every chaotic melodrama unravelled. Their father's ever more poisonous interference only encouraged Lee down the same self-obsessed track. Pippa and their mother would wrestle with the futility of the balanced approach, something more mature, a sense of consideration, of duty even, but Lee had slipped around those arguments with ease. He just wanted to enjoy life. He had grown into the caricature of the life and soul of the party. He loved to be in the thick of things: the last one thrown out of the pub in the wee small hours, the first one to sign up for a fishing trip or a coach trip up to Lords to see the cricket. But as his hectic social calendar expanded, the rising costs of his happy-go-lucky entertainment budget just mushroomed beyond his own financial means. While he still lived at home he got away with it by simply not paying his agreed rent to his mother and that put him seriously at odds with her and his sister. From afar the old man had continually taken his son's side of any thorny debates at home, pitching in remotely with his toxic comments and opinions designed only to enhance the familial pressure. The younger man would see his father quite regularly and after each encounter the women sensed a surly atmosphere about the house, more antagonistic, almost combative. They knew full well what Stan Phillipson had been up to. He was simply trying to make life as unbearable as possible for the woman who had ditched him all those years ago. From that perceived injustice he had never recovered, and he had spent the rest of his life apportioning blame in lieu of his own personal failings.

For Pippa, the first really significant indication of the extent of her brother's potential stupidity had been the way in which he'd courted that girl he'd met on the train and married her within just a few weeks. He'd had no game plan: no means of supporting and developing the relationship. It had been pure infatuation – but to marry the girl? Who does that kind of thing? Her father had bleated on about romance and spontaneity – all the things his wife, her mother, had apparently lacked – but Pippa had seen it as reckless, almost juvenile. Then...and you could have put money on it... he was caught playing away from home and his new wife declared herself pregnant. Exasperation turned to rank disgust when he had simply walked out and left them after the baby had been born. She'd had some rambling telephone conversation with her brother some time later during which he'd expressed his remorse and his wish to visit the child and perhaps to rekindle the family flame, but that never happened. To think that the same child, now a man, was here today at his own father's funeral having only ever met the man once, and so very recently...well, she'd said, it just seems like a tragedy of stage and screen or something you'd read about in a romantic novel.

Pippa had realised quite quickly that her brother's deliberate escape from, and persistent evasion of any parental responsibility over many years had been all about money. He had been very reluctant to face up to the need to work harder and to earn a little more in order to cover his family dues. Lee had fabricated some ridiculous yarn about his involvement with the girlfriend of a known small-time gangster in London. It wasn't that he didn't want to go back: he was afraid for his life. The criminal fraternity in the capital were supposedly renowned for the retaliations they would visit upon their enemies whenever slighted in matters of the heart or of business. At first Pippa had scoffed at such a pathetic ruse, but then she considered the candour with which Lee had confessed one of his many infidelities and she was left wondering just what sorts of people her brother had been rubbing shoulders with. Either way, when Lee had moaned about not being able to visit his son, because of the risks of returning to the big city, Pippa had made the simple and yet crushing comparison with the potential for her to visit her own child, her little boy who had died at just five with a rare blood disorder, and after two years of indescribable hell in hospital – Pippa would have given her own life to be able to see her little boy one last time and to know that he was well again. Lee had hung up the phone.

Later, much later, disgust turned to revulsion at the very transparent, cold and calculated manner in which he had set-up Janice Swinton and just systematically stripped her to the bone over an entire decade. Sister and mother had actively intervened, trying to get their boy, now a man immersed in his own sense of self-importance, to pull hard on the handbrake and to stop the destructive juggernaut that was his own ego from crashing further through the vulnerable lives of the Swinton clan. But it was all in vein. Constantly propelled forward by his blinkered father, Lee Phillipson had simply carried on just as he had for his entire life – looking out for himself without a note of compassion for any victim he left in the lurch.

And no, by no means was it unthinkable that someone might have wriggled out from under one of Lee's many catastrophes and come looking for revenge and retribution. Lee had never seen his effect on others as anything more than fate or accident. It was life to him. It was just the way of the world and he saw the strong-willed as those who made things happen while all around them, the gentle caring considerate types allowed themselves to be trampled in the rush. Pippa had long since given up trying to influence him. Moreover, she had, for some years, learned to simply ignore her elder brother on the basis that his distortions of the truth were so complete that he had eventually convinced himself that his version of history was the only accurate one. In that specific regard he had already caught up with his delusional father. In this he'd recruited his father as his staunchest ally and the two of them had railed at the world and all its imperfections that had conspired to deny them their just rewards in life.

For DS Addison such a frank and open exchange, a dissertation almost, had only reminded her that, on the one hand, they probably hadn't significantly misjudged Lee Phillipson's character and weaknesses. On the other hand however, Pippa Jensen's account only reinforced the alarming scale of the task in which they were currently engaged. A negligent, devil-may-care attitude of such proportions must surely have scarred many a passing acquaintance during the last forty years or so. How would they identify the one victim amongst so many who could, would and in fact did visit revenge upon the dead man?

Her thought processes were interrupted as Janice Swinton moved in alongside DCI Lehrer. She asked how they were, the two coppers who stood out from the crowd, but she was more interested in what they had learned. They honestly reported that they'd not picked up much, but any help she could give in identifying some of the unknown faces in the congregation would be readily appreciated. She offered to drop back to the station when they told her that hidden photographers would have captured the images of all those present just in case the perpetrator had indeed turned up to witness the closing chapter of Lee Phillipson's life. DS Addison offered to lead the way and Lehrer accepted Janice Swinton's invitation to ride in her car back to HQ in Ipswich.

18 – love's labours' liabilities

Josh Swinton lay supine in a rather full bath of steaming hot water. He lay completely still, soaking up the relaxing warmth all around him. He looked at his own naked form through the refracting prism of the water and he couldn't decide whether or not to be pleased or displeased with what he saw. He considered the potentially debilitating effects of countless hours pawing over the draughtsman's board in the lower boat shed, or even the long late hours bent double in some God-forsaken inaccessible corner of the old boat to which he had given so much of his own private time in recent years. He concluded though, that those infrequent gym sessions, together with his sexy wife's recently elevated physical demands must be having some positive effect on his rather lean and wholesome torso.

It was another baby, he knew that of course. She had talked about having another for some time and he suspected, without having put it to the test, that she had stopped taking those all-important daily tablets some months ago. He didn't mind. In fact he approved – at least in his heart if not in his head. Another little one running about the place would be nice, not just for her but for the whole family. Sadie, their daughter, would just love a little cherub to spoil – until, that is, the inevitable veil of jealousy descended to add spice to a brand new sibling rivalry. But she simply hadn't caught, his sexy little diva, even after months of deliriously exciting bedroom antics – not like the first time when she turned out pregnant with barely a look at her in those outrageous red suspenders. Where had she got those from? Who cares, he counselled himself silently. And now she really was ramping up the activity – much to his continued delight – and in addition she was beginning to calculate her monthly timings very carefully in an attempt to ravage him at just the right moment. What bliss – could a man ask for anything more? He doubted it.

He slowly slid beneath the surface of the water gently exhaling bubbles as he went. His mind drifted away from the domestics and found itself back at work – a retrograde step he was sure – but even as he tried to recover that lost ground he remembered the young detective who had been to see him. From there it was a depressingly short step to the miserable ghost of Lee Phillipson, an unavoidable focus which could only leech out of him the disdain and disgust he had cultivated for that man over many painful years. Then he smiled to himself, and the warm ingress pushed him back to the surface to draw breath before immersing himself fully once again. That cheating thieving bastard was gone once and for all. No more lies and self-purging fabrications. No more tales of others pillaged just as they themselves had been. No more chance encounters in unexpected places – the difficult moment in the supermarket aisle or that hollow void in the garage forecourt, urging the petrol pump to gush faster having spied the creep driving in to fill up at the very same pump. How many times had he wanted to rearrange that fucker's facial features? How many times, in stark truth, had his hatred for that man raged so violently in his chest that he had wanted to kill him – and not just to end his days, but to make him really suffer before the end for all he had done to them.

He raised his chin and took another breath. Submerged again in his watery world he wondered just how many others had harboured those self-same feelings for that despicable fraud. But it was done…he was gone…and they really should celebrate a happy wake for a man most wouldn't piss on even if he were on fire in the street – at least not if they knew him, really knew him, and knew of all the shocking scams and schemes he had enacted over so many years, and knew too of the great line of victims left behind littering his path in his rear-view mirror of life. And then he thought again about the young police detective. He wondered how those boys were getting on. That must be one hell of a task, sifting through the debris of that slippery bastard's affairs in a desperate attempt to find the truth amongst a lifetime of deceit and deception. My God, he reflected, that'll sort out the Suffolk Bobbies. We'll soon see if they're up to snuff.

With a gentle push of his feet against enamelled cast-iron, he raised himself just an inch or so and breathed in long and slowly through his nose. With his eyes still shut, but rising further out of the water, he swept the excess water from his face with the palms of his hands. As he laid his arms along the sides of the bath he suddenly sensed that he was no longer alone. He immediately questioned whether or not he had shut the bathroom door properly, and in mild alarm he opened his eyes and in the same moment looked round to check the old brass lock.

She stood there in the frame of the door, her petite and shapely form declaring purpose, intent, a clear proposition that he recognised immediately. No matter how many times he had seen that look in recent weeks and months it still never failed to arouse him instantly. He felt that carnal stirring in his loins and the predictable driving anticipation was already irreversible. She had always been a sensuous and exciting lover, but of late she had experimented with new and erotic diversions and he had willingly found himself extending his own repertoire in order merely to match her ever more imaginative demands.

She wore the flimsiest of silk camisoles in a delicate pearl grey with a matching thong which barely covered and therefore emphasised the closest of Brazilian shaves. Her enticing nipples pushed hard into the light fabric, and she raised a hand under the silk to knead her left breast firmly catching the nipple between fingers and drawing in a thin audible wisp of air as the sensation rippled through her body. With her free hand she pushed her thong aside exposing her gaping warmth and fingered herself with a slow deliberate rhythm, her eyes closing, her head dropping a little as she liberated any last vestiges of modesty. He sat there in the water completely transfixed by the visual imagery before him. As her breathing quickened he stood up in the bath. His proud erection rose to meet her as she stepped quickly forward. Bowing her head, she took his swollen glans in her mouth. He gasped out loud. Cupping his tightening sac with one hand she gripped his stiffness with the other and licked him softly, deftly but quickly until his penis ached for the explosion not far off. But then he looked down at this gorgeous creature, her head bobbing gently before him, and he slowly lifted her away. She looked up at him slightly perplexed, but he stepped out of the water pushing her gently away as he did so. He dipped quickly, and catching her under her arms he tossed her lightly in the air and caught her masterfully with his strong hands under her buttocks. Her legs splayed wide in anticipation and gripped him around the waist, hands locking together for a moment behind his neck. He groped quickly and carefully for her wetness. Pulling her thong roughly aside, he lowered her forcefully and thrust himself deep into her welcoming softness. She cried out gleefully, and then chastised herself in a hissing fit of whispering admonition lest she should wake up their sleeping daughter, but he ignored her. He took two quick steps to the window sill where he rested her pert bottom. She kissed him long and hard as he pushed into her and she writhed on his rigid totem. Their eyes met with a burning intensity, and as he pumped into her with accelerating vigour she pushed her arms out to each side to steady herself within the casement. The perspiration ran from the two of them, her damp blond hair sticking to her face and yet throwing forwards with every penetrating thrust, and she threw back her head and moaned at the magical pleasure of it not thinking for a second about babies or pregnancy or any of that. As the hot wet waves swept through her innermost self she gripped him inside as his pulsing ejaculation shuddered into her and he gasped a muted guttural release to match her own orgasmic exultation.

He stood there stock still not daring to break the spell. She clung to him with hot sticky hands locked behind his head and rested her grip around his hips as his hardness subsided. Her cami top was drenched with a mix of bath water and salty sweat and the translucent silk laid bare her firm breasts. He scooped her up and swished her round into a gentleman's carry – one arm behind her back, the other under her legs. He prised the door open with his foot and they peaked along the landing listening instinctively for sounds of wakefulness from their daughter's room – nothing. Quickly he tip-toed across to their own bedroom where he threw his girl in a wide arc right into the middle of their king sized bed where she bounced with a mischievous giggle. He quickly locked the door and joined her on the bed. He wanted more, and she knew perfectly well that his second coming would be her just reward only after some serious fucking. He dispensed with her clammy underwear in a second. Naked before him she looked shockingly beautiful and riotously rude. He licked her with lavishly long strokes, tracing her labia up and down and needling her clitoris with the tip of his tongue. She gasped and mewed her appreciation, her head thrown back, her fingers pushed into his hair and her nails scraping his scalp as the intensities welled and passed. Then he pulled away, flipped her over, parted her legs with one swift and delicate movement and plunged his rejuvenated penis into her gaping flesh. She cried out again, but then she pushed back against him raising her bottom and kneeling on all fours so that she could absorb him completely. He fucked into her pulling her hips back towards his own and smacking against her taut buttocks as each and every thrust elicited a gentle cry of satisfaction. Increasing his pace he leaned forward and reached around her slender waste slipping his hands up to her breasts at which point she sat back against him, still squirming on his strident member and she welcomed his firm grip as she bounced him into orgasmic overload. His pumping ejaculation greeted her own feverish clitoral cascade, and the two of them collapsed breathless to the horizontal gasping for air and marvelling at their own pounding heart rates.

They lay there for some time totally spent. They looked lovingly at one another through glazed expressions commensurate with sexual exhaustion and late night weariness. They linked fingers, exchanged gentle kisses, expecting at any moment that they might slip into deep slumber only to be rudely awakened at the start of a busy Sunday by the demanding little girl asleep just along the corridor. They drifted in satisfied torpor and soon fell asleep. Josh thought he might be dreaming as he recounted that steamy session. He dipped in and out of consciousness and as he did so he lurched from this encounter to a previous one and then to another and another. He remembered the provocative lingerie or suggestive negligees she had chosen on each occasion. His dream-like recollections delved deeper into the physical acts themselves... and he could see himself banging her up against the headboard or pushing up into her as she rode him hard up on top...and there they were, at it again, fucking up against the back of the bedroom door... jeez, was there no satisfying his girl, as the door thumped in its frame... and there it was again that banging...the now celebrated kitchen table diversion which must surely have been before Sadie was born...but the banging seemed incongruous, somehow not the sound of a creaking old oak top cleared of all its contents with the deft sweep of a passionate an eager hand...and again, that same banging. He stirred and twisted in his submerged state as he struggled to match their somatic endeavours with the resounding rhythms at the periphery of his senses. And yet again...

what is that noise? What is that banging? He sat bolt upright. Something wasn't right at all. He'd been dreaming and yet not dreaming. What was it? And then again...a heavy banging downstairs and raised voices... perhaps on the street out front. Christ, it was someone at the front door. What could be so pressing as to raise such a racket? His wife rustled in her wakefulness, but he shushed her back to sleep saying he was just going to pull the plug on the bath water and pop downstairs to switch off a few lights. He threw on his dressing gown and headed for the front door.

"Joshua Swinton?" asked the uniformed policeman.

He rubbed his tired eyes with the heels of his hands. "Yes, I'm Josh Swinton", and then he recognised the detective who had visited him earlier in the week. There were three officers in all.

"Can we come in sir?" the policeman continued.

"Sorry?"

"May we come in sir, please?"

Josh pushed his fingers through his hair and licked his lips tasting sex. He wondered just what the hell was going on. Hadn't he offered to come down to the station to talk them through some of Phillipson's less well-known excesses? Bloody hell it must be about eleven o'clock, maybe closer to midnight.

"What on earth is going on? What is this all about? Have you any idea what time it is?" he objected.

"The law doesn't always wait till breakfast time, sir", the bobby offered with a stern look on his face.

"Oh for fuck's sake...", he grunted, anger building at such a ridiculous intrusion. "Detective didn't we have an agreement? Didn't I offer to come in to see you if you needed a better briefing about you know who?"

"Er...yes. Yes, that's true", Barnes responded, "but that was before our forensic results produced a number of...er, shall we say...potentially damaging indicators which place you somewhat more centrally in our investigation, Mr. Swinton."

"Eh...come again... and perhaps in English this time?"

"It's really very simple, Josh", said Barnes tersely. And then in a depressed whisper he added, "We can arrest you right here on your doorstep or we can come inside and keep this little performance to ourselves without including the neighbours, but either way we are arresting you for the murder of Lee Phillipson."

Josh Swinton just gaped at them. He was momentarily speechless. Then, gathering himself, he exploded. "What? You cannot be this stupid. I had nothing to do with it. You know that. I even have a clean alibi. What is it? Are you that desperate to show people just what good cops you are that you have to make a quick collar? I mean... this is madness. What possible evidence can you have against me?"

"You might be surprised...very surprised...or maybe not surprised at all," and with that they pushed past him into the hallway to be greeted by a confused and tearful Mrs Swinton in a scanty robe, who genuinely looked as if she'd been having sex for hours.

Josh's mother Janice hadn't taken a man for some years. She hadn't intended it to happen, well...not really, but it had happened nevertheless. Several hours after her son's arrest – and still oblivious to that fact – she slept the early-hours sleep of the dead. That heady mix of unexpected excitement, the frisson of two older partners remembering their lines and discovering after all that sympathetic lovers can create and derive great mutual pleasure; had it been more a case of the emotional rollercoaster that had knocked her out or was it the surprising physical demands of the night which had carried her into a comatose world where dreams were her reality and reality couldn't reach her? There she canvassed an entire spectrum of random events and listless meanderings none of which held her subconscious attention for more than a few seconds. She slumbered face down in her own bed in her own home, but deprived of that comforting realisation she drifted through the nether-reaches of her mind in a state of mild confusion and floating anxiety. Here and there chaotic images came and went. Her immediate environment changed repeatedly at irregular intervals. Sounds and voices clamoured for her focus, but she spurned them all as if drawn by something more urgent, perhaps more threatening and, most unsettling of all, something unavoidable.

She twitched in her somnolence and the fingers of her left hand reached out for an unseen target and then withdrew into a balled fist. She ground her teeth and growled softly, but still she remained lost to her own mental processes. The agitated crowd roared as she rounded the corner of an ancient building and froze at the sight of a surging medieval throng. Filthy people in rags and tatters jeered and scorned a hapless soul who had been dragged before them for some form of public retribution. They threw insults at the victim of their wrath and pelted him with rotten fruit and vegetables – not to mention the odd stone – and then they turned to her beseeching her to ratify their displeasure and to support the acts of rough justice about to be dispensed. She pleaded ignorance. How could she possibly judge a man for things unseen, although his purported crimes had been tawdry and extensive? But as she tried to withdraw they seized her and forced her to pass sentence on him, this unknown wretch who cowered before them, and they demanded that she should choose fifty lashes or the hangman's noose. She cried out in despair – a muffled plea lost into her pillow – and as she resisted the mob she stole a look at the defendant. To her abject horror she saw him standing there between two heavily armed sergeants at arms – the captain of the guard close at hand but aloof and remote from the seething masses – and it was him. It was Lee Phillipson. He stood there in a shabby sack cloth, his wrists and ankles bleeding from the shackles that bound him and he met her inquisitive glance without waiver. Immediately behind him stood a tall triangular frame to which he would soon be tied should she, the presiding magistrate, deem the lash to be suitable for the purging of his lost soul. But then, what despair? To the right, and reaching out into the raucous crowd, stood an elevated wooden platform complete with trap doors below a heavily knotted rope. She screamed her objection to the severity of the proposed sentence, but she was shouted down by the angry gathering. Rough peasants and stinking whores stepped forward to recount the many sins and misdemeanours perpetrated by the accused. Disgraced wives and vengeful husbands, washer women and inn keepers, barmaids and scruffy tradesmen all threw in their vitriolic assessment of a no-good waster who deserved to swing. As the accusations swirled around her, her anguish rose ever more steadily. She couldn't decide. She wouldn't decide. She thrashed and turned among the heaving tumult, searching in desperation for an escape, and so it seemed that she would be rewarded as she floated up above the masses, leaving behind their swelling hatred. But then she heard it, the mechanical release of the trap doors. Looking back in terror she saw him drop and the great cheer from the mob overwhelmed her as his pathetic form tugged hard on the rope. She made to turn away, to continue her flight, but in the last moment of cognisance she was distracted by the scrawny lad who had pulled the great lever to send Phillipson to hell, and she cried out in recognition of her own son Josh whose scabby face sneered back at her in triumphal celebration. She reached out to save him as she drifted up and away through the angry atmosphere, and at once she thought she had succeeded when her hand met firm warm flesh, but shocked into semi-consciousness she wilted with the wakening realisation that she was in bed with her lover and the horrific spectacle had all been imaginary.

She lay there motionless in relief. She was wet with the perspiration of anxiety. She touched him again as if to reassure herself that it had indeed been just a bad dream. A thin smile creased her lips. The joy of the real world – how rarely had she thought like that in recent times? He hadn't responded. His breathing rhythms hadn't changed and he continued in peaceful satisfied sleep. She wondered how often he slept so soundly. She suspected not very often at all, but that was another train of thought and not one for this soft soporific morning after. He'd been wonderful. Controlled, commanding even, but subtle and sensitive. It had been so long. The feeling of him inside her had been truly exhilarating, but what she was most grateful for was his humility and his modesty. Somehow they hadn't felt embarrassed about being naked together, nor even about peeling each other's clothes off in the subdued lighting of her bedroom. She hadn't really reckoned on another lover at her age – and after three ex-husbands, no less – but the entire experience had seemingly just unfolded quite naturally. She hadn't tried to pass judgement on his physique or his manhood, and neither had seemed all that important. The physical encounter had lacked nothing...nothing at all she reminded herself with a private smile.

More important to her had been his own acceptance of her with all the flaws of middle age – the looseness around the tummy, the breadth of her beam, the orange-peel thighs and sagging boobs – no, none of that had apparently disappointed him or challenged his rising passions. The weight of him pressing on her, the warmth of him, his gentleness…these were the things she reflected upon. They had each discovered in the other a tender and compassionate lover, and as she lay there on her own damp sheet, the duvet discarded hours earlier, she felt flushed with drowsy joy that life could still confound her in the positive despite all her previous disappointments.

She dozed again. This time she flitted lightly in and out of happier recollections from the years gone by. Then she remembered with a wakening jolt that she had been legally barred from sharing her home with another partner by the cruel restrictions placed upon her by her dearly departed. She quickly decided that she didn't care. He was gone. Yes, his estate may clamour for contrition, but he……Lee Phillipson…would never know her secret pleasure.

She slipped off again, snoring softly into her pillow. Sometime later, she really couldn't tell how long – but she did at least recall that it was Sunday morning and she didn't have to back in Bedford until later that day for the weekly shift – she was vaguely aware of someone crunching urgently through the gravel on the front drive. It was a familiar sound, one re-played countless times over the years, but this wasn't the postman or the milkman, not on a Sunday. And anyway, whoever it was moved with some pace. Then came the alarming rap on the heavy front door knocker. That too was a familiar refrain – Yvonne from the village – but odd that she hadn't heard the car. Too sleepy perhaps, and she smiled again, before easing herself up from the bed, slipping on her dressing gown and creeping out without disturbing him.

As soon as she opened the heavy wooden door she knew that something was terribly wrong. Yvonne looked fitful and tearful. They each looked at one another and an untimely pause hung in the air just waiting to be broken.

"Oh Janice, I just had to come. I'm so sorry. I know it's early, and on a Sunday too, but it's just terrible. I just had to come…"

"Woah...hang on, Yvonne. What's so terrible, and what time is it anyway?" she responded, rubbing the sleep out of her eyes and trying to bunch some shape into her dishevelled hair.

Her good friend just gawped at her, mouth open, and then stammered something about Josh, and surely she must know about it already. And then she raised her hands to her face as the shock of her own friend's ignorance hit home.

"Yvonne, please...just gather yourself. What are you trying to say? What's happened to Josh? Just tell me straight."

"Oh God, no. You really don't know, do you?" she sighed in desperation.

"Know what?" she insisted, anxiety having hijacked her wakeful calm. "What's happened? What do I need to know, Yvonne?"

"They've arrested Josh!"

"What? Who has? Christ...what's going on? What's he supposed to have done?" And then it crashed down on her, that sickening realisation. Her son had been arrested for the murder of his own former step-father. The awful dream reasserted itself. The complexity of the task ahead clouded her senses. Then the anger began to simmer inside at the thought that her son might, just might have done something utterly unforgivable. Then her rage brimmed over as she thought of just one man – not that shifty louse who had met his maker in the protective comfort of his own bathroom only seven days earlier, and not even her own reckless lad who had, quite possibly, taken the law into his own hands, but another man entirely.

She busied herself with her distraught friend and neighbour who clung to her like a limpet. The poor woman was more distressed about having broken the news than the news itself, or so it appeared to Janice. Then, having despatched the tearful messenger with an agreed urgent need to get her skates on and get down to the police station, she closed the door, took a deep breath and headed directly for the stairs. As she turned at the half-landing, the ire spilling over within, she spied him leaning over the bannister wearing his boxers and an expression of innocent curiosity.

"You low-life scheister," she bellowed as she advanced up the last short flight. "You slimy bastard...Jesus Christ...are all men the same? Is there an honest one among you? Is there?" she screamed. "How dare you?"

He looked completely vacant. He stared blankly at her and retreated step by step into the bedroom pursued by his inquisitor who was beginning to build a real head of steam.

"You come swanning into my life via the side door, through the most haphazard of circumstances and at a most difficult time. You sweet talk me about the need to do things well, to get it right, to have integrity, and then you sweet talk me over dinner and schmooze your way into my bed and all the while your dirty little lieutenants are ferreting around through the back doors and dark alleys of your tacky little world and making an unholy fuck-up of everything they touch...," and the emotions threatened to over-power her completely with tears welling despite her futile attempts to quell them.

David Lehrer held both hands up and begged for a truce. "Wait Janice, wait...just hold on," he called, but she drove on.

"What right do you have to behave in this despicable fashion? You have undermined me and my family at precisely the time when we should have expected only help and support from you and your office. It's disgusting! To think that you would use me in this way: knowing all along that your team was skulking around in the shadows waiting to pounce when I was most vulnerable." In pausing for breath she cast her eyes to the ceiling in dismay. Then she angrily threw open her wardrobe door and began throwing out a mix of clothes into which she might hurriedly dress.

"For goodness sake Janice, just stop," he implored. "What on earth has happened?"

"Oh no...no you don't," she spat back at him. "Don't you even try to make out that you're not behind all of this. You're the boss. You can't wash your hands of this one."

"Of what?" he pleaded in visible exasperation.

She halted her busy preparations. She looked at him, and the first flickers of doubt floated across her eyes. "You don't know? You really don't know? Is this a bad joke in very poor taste?"

"What...Jehovah give me strength," he hissed through gritted teeth, "what has happened? Just tell me."

"Your people have arrested my son for murder, that's all..." and she broke down and sobbed uncontrollably.

Lehrer's head was swimming. Holy shit! From many different angles this just looked about as bad as it could possibly get. His mobile phone had been switched off all night; a calculated error. He reached for it, and opening it up the missed calls tumbled into his inbox.

19 – May 2007

Sunday 13th

What was he doing there? What does it mean? Should I be worried? Christ...I don't know what to do. The whole thing went off without a hitch – the bastard is toast now, well and truly toasted. Couldn't have happened to a more deserving son of a bitch. Got out the Bolli and drank the whole bottle. Smoked a bit of weed. Couldn't stop smiling for the rest of the day and by the time I'd been out with friends for a Friday night blast...wowza...head like a medicine ball this morning.

But what the fuck was he doing there? Feeling uneasy, must be careful.

---

20 – if the cap fits...

As Lehrer burst through the door a sea of gaunt tired faces looked briefly in his direction and then turned back to the task, their unspoken disappointment tangible. He ducked into his office to offload his raincoat and briefcase only to be confronted by his immediate team in heated discussion about their midnight arrest of Josh Swinton and the subsequent search of Barrington's Boatyard. Silence fell upon them as he pushed through the door. Blank faces greeted his arrival and some very obvious questions lined up in their minds, but remained mute for the moment. He threw his coat on the rack and edged round the desk to his chair. Addison vacated the spot to allow him to sit down and she padded over to the low cabinet to take up a new perch. He looked at them and cleared his throat, but Addison beat him to it.

"Where've you been boss? We've been calling you all night. Me and Barnsey have just got in from Barrington's Boatyard. Mac and Adi have been here with the whole shop all night. We just couldn't reach you..."

McLellan interrupted her curtly. "Back off, Amy! It's the boss. He's earned more respect than that." Amy Addison raised her eyebrows in sarcastic refrain and was about to press her case further when Lehrer himself held up his hands in submission.

"She's right Mac. It's a fair cop. I had my phone actually switched off all night – no idea why...just hadn't realised...bloody fool, and that's the truth in more ways than one..."

"Bloody hell, I hope she was worth it," Addison quipped, but MacLellan shot her the fiercest of glances and she buckled under his gaze. Lehrer reddened with the accuracy of her jibe, but he had no way of knowing just how well informed she might have been so he brushed off the admonition, offered a further apology and then pressed them for an immediate update.

It had all kicked off late yesterday afternoon when an urgent email from the forensic lab splashed into Tommy Barnes' inbox. They had made a direct and incontrovertible match between a single strand of hair found at the crime scene and the DNA profile of Josh

Swinton. Adi Hughes had counselled caution at first. It wasn't entirely implausible that such specimens could have been transported from one place to another entirely innocently – say a hair deposited at the Midshipman and accidently collected and carried to another site by a different person. In a larger, more populated area like a town or big city the chances of such transmission would be slim, but in a tiny village like Compton these things appeared more credible. They knew that the dead man and their recently arrested suspect both frequented the same pub. Hughes' arguments had dampened spirits a little, and not surprisingly. They had thought him probably right. But then not half an hour later the lab confirmed a pure match for a thumb print lifted from the bannister on Phillipson's staircase with the prints taken directly from the young Mr. Swinton. Hadn't their suspect sworn blind that he had never been into or anywhere near the dead man's home? At that moment the mood within the task force had lifted considerably, and the whole team moved seamlessly on to the next stage of their habitual process.

Barnes and a small support team had been despatched to apprehend their suspect.

When Addison, Hughes and an entire forensic unit arrived at the closed gates of Barrington's Boatyard, the manager was there waiting for them to grant them immediate access. It took them many hours working through the night, and specimen samples were rushed off to the lab at intervals throughout, but two specific discoveries led the team to believe that they really did have their man.

Hughes had led a small band down to the big boat shed and directed them over to an old boat cocooned in hay bales in the top corner of the shed. He told them to rip it apart if necessary. They were looking for an old pistol of some sort and any kind of ammunition.

Addison had sat for several hours chucking one CD after another into the video player from the firm's CCTV recordings. It should have been a simple task to review the previous weekend's activities, but the discs were changed daily, thrown into a large wooden chest (with a hasp and staple on its leading edge) and left there for three months. Once every quarter they were wiped clean and put back in the box to be used again. Naturally she chose those discs closest to the top, but such logic didn't reward her. Eventually she found a disc with the right date and time range attached to the playback and she sifted through an entire stream of different views of a variety of locations around the site. Unfortunately the cameras covering the workshop and changing rooms seemed to have been disabled for some time, but the main yards and sheds had been filmed fairly consistently. When she located some footage of someone opening up the front gate and driving off in a company van she sat the firm's manager down in front of the screen and asked him to describe what he saw. He had been unequivocal. That had been Josh Swinton unlocking and pushing back the sliding gate and then driving off in the van, Barrington's Boatyard emblazoned on its side for all to see. The recording registered a date and time from Sunday afternoon the previous weekend. It also showed the van being driven back through the open gate sometime later and the gate being carefully padlocked thereafter. Addison challenged the man's perception of just what he had been observing on the basis that the subject's face couldn't be clearly seen under the grey sweatshirt hoody.

"Aw no love," he said in quick response, "that's Josh alright: same hoody he wears most days at work – East Anglia Uni printed on the back – same dark jeans with the pocket hanging off at the back, same boots, same build, same gait...what more can I tell you?" Addison had been comfortable with the identification, but she would have been happier with a facial match, and she cast her mind back to Mad Mo Moston's similar description of the van driver he had tailed through the country lanes back to the same boatyard.

They had gathered a variety of bits and pieces from Josh Swinton's regular work spaces and from his locker in the changing room. Certainly some of the clothing they lifted provided a perfect match for everything they'd seen on camera.

When the scientific team in the boat shed confirmed the capture of a pale grey, East Anglia Uni hoody from a small locker in a bulkhead of the old shrimper they were scouring, Addison and Barnes began to relax, confident that they were getting somewhere at last. Then they hit the jackpot. They found a bullet casing on the floor of the boat shed nestled comfortably against one of the hay bales which flanked either side of the boat. Its dull metal was almost lost to human sight covered by a few loose strands of hay that lay on the floor. They found more than one bullet embedded in the end wall of the bales under the bow of the vessel. Under a powerful lens they identified similar marks on the casing to those they had seen from their single round back at the lab – the casing recovered from the murder victim's drive way. They felt sure that the composition of the bullets would be the same as that back at base, but naturally they couldn't confirm that until careful assessment and cross referencing had been carried out. Their Eureka moment occurred at about 3.00am when a small, barely hand-sized compartment, hidden behind a fixed locker in the forward cabin of the boat, relinquished a thickly wrapped but heavy item. Unravelling the sack cloth bundle, there, in the palm of one investigator's hand, lay a Luger pistol.

At this point an attentive DCI Lehrer leaned back in his chair and whistled softly in surprise. Could it get any easier than this, he speculated?

But that wasn't the whole of it, Addison had insisted.

Only half an hour ago the lab had confirmed that gunshot residue traces on the arms of the grey hoody matched those taken from the victim's entry wound and married perfectly to the ordnance recovered both with the gun and at the crime scene.

Josh Swinton leaned casually back in his chair. He seemed unruffled. The police station coffee was dreadful – he let it go cold in its plastic cup. He looked up at the dark glass habitually. He assumed he was being watched. He sneered at the unseen observer behind the pane and listened to the passing footsteps in the corridor wondering when his mother's solicitor would arrive. He knew he was to be formally interviewed, and what a complete waste of his and everyone else's time that would be, but he really couldn't see the need for legal representation. Then he remembered just how old fashioned the old boy had appeared when he'd failed miserably to extricate his mother from Phillipson's greedy clutches – if he couldn't manage that what use was he going to be here? Then he slipped further down in the uncomfortable bright orange plastic chair, splayed his legs wide under the table and folded his arms in resignation. One way or another he'd be out by lunchtime. These guys just had to be kidding, right?

His mother sat in another room, anxious, fraught, looking at the door every minute or so expecting to see her solicitor at any moment. She had been granted the privacy of a small ante-room just off the main foyer so that she could at least brief her aide before he was pitched into the lion's den. She knew nothing of the details of the case against her son, and therefore she knew that she couldn't really prepare her brief for his next most testing challenge. Her heart told her repeatedly that her son simply couldn't have done such a thing – cold blooded murder of the most clinical kind – but her head intervened in that comforting mental progression. She simply couldn't question or doubt her son's evident hatred of her former husband. She couldn't deny having heard him, many many times over, clearly state his wish that the creep were dead. She recalled with growing anxiety the number of occasions when the two of them had rubbed up against each other with increasing frequency and escalating confrontation. Many times – especially as Josh had been pushing through his teens, growing quickly, building physical shape and stature – their abrasive, fractious relationship had spilled over into ugly threatening scenes. She recoiled now from those recollections. With a sharp, tense intake of breath she remembered the day when Jimmy Judge had taken her to one side to tip her off about the angry melee of aggressive young lads who had laid in wait for Phillipson at closing time. The alarming note that sounded in her mind was that Josh had been the bovver-boy-in-chief among that aggressive contingent. She bit her lip and fretted some more. Could it really be possible? Could it be true?

The door flew open and in marched old Simpkins, her loyal legal lieutenant. In truth he had been Jeff's legal adviser when she had first met her second husband and she had stuck with him since those early days, but often she felt uneasy with that allegiance. Was he really up to this? Could he honestly claim to be sufficiently experienced in this kind of work for her to be able to entrust him with such a critical test? In for a penny, in for a pound…or, in this case, in for the greater part of the rest of her son's life! She looked at him blankly, and then simply burst into tears.

He did his consummate best to calm her. Slowly she settled and then turned herself to the job in hand. After ten minutes of heated debate she realised that she had nothing else to say, and yet still her adviser looked distinctly uncomfortable. Between them they knew little of the case against her son. In the void her apprehension subdued him. He would be going in to bat with virtually nothing on the scoreboard unless the accused himself could enlighten him in the positive. Simpkins left and Josh's pretty wife and daughter arrived at the same moment, and the two women embraced and cried together in their shared torment.

When Simpkins entered the interview room he was followed immediately by two police officers in plain clothes. On depositing his briefcase on the table top he shook hands with Josh Swinton and then deftly instructed his chaperones to get out. He demanded some private time with his client and, he insisted, whoever was sat behind that one-way glass really must ensure that the recording microphones and audio systems were to be disabled. Hughes and Addison scuttled off feeling firmly rebuked and a little less confident before they'd even started.

Ten minutes later the solicitor rapped on the door and the detectives re-entered the room. Hughes made the necessary preliminary announcements. He verbally recorded the names of those present, the time of the interview, and he cautioned the accused about what he might say and how that might be used against him in court. He openly and very clearly repeated the charges against Josh Swinton. Then they got down to business and Simpkins offered the opening gambit. Swinton still slouched in his chair with an air of vague disinterest about him.

"My client wishes to refute any and all charges against him," the solicitor stated. "He asserts his absolute lack of involvement in the recent demise of his former step-father, Lee Phillipson. He insists that he hadn't seen the man for several months before his death, that he has never visited the man's home, and that he has a solid alibi at the time of the alleged murder."

"Well...let's start with that alibi shall we Mr Swinton?" began Detective Inspector Adrian Hughes. "Run us through that if you wouldn't mind, please."

"With pleasure," the younger man quipped with only veiled sarcasm. "On Sundays I make a point of watching the big match on the telly. Last weekend it featured my team, and I certainly watched the whole game live on sat-TV. I'd been looking forward to it all week. I wasn't going to miss that one, and the boys delivered."

"Can anyone vouch for you at that time?"

"Yes, of course, but didn't I have the same conversation with that other chap, one of your colleagues, when he came down to Barrington's?"

"Ah yes, that would be DS Barnes I think, but you see here's the thing: we need to have you repeat that for our formal recording. Why don't you just go through that again for us?" Josh Swinton shook his head to indicate his reluctance, and sighed heavily in frustration, but he responded.

"My wife can attest to my presence at home on Sunday afternoon and specifically during the hours of four o'clock and six o'clock that afternoon – that's the time of the game itself, you see."

"Well...here's another thing: she denies knowing whether you were at home or not."

"Sorry? That can't be right."

"Apparently so," Hughes confirmed. "Is it not the case that she takes your daughter to Sunday afternoon swimming club at about 3.30pm every Sunday and that she doesn't normally return until about 6.30pm, after treating the little girl to some tea at the café in the leisure centre?"

Swinton blanched a little and squirmed upwards in his chair. "Well...sure...that is the case, but she saw me there just before the game as she was leaving. She must have pointed that out. And then she'd see me still at home when she got back, heard me talking about the game and all that..."

"Well sure she did, of course," Hughes interrupted, "but that would have given you something like three hours of free time to yourself. Could anyone else have been with you or seen you during that time period?"

"No! I was in my own house watching the television," Josh Swinton shrugged.

"And what do you know about the manner of the crime against Mr Phillipson?"

"Eh...sorry, that's a bit of a change of tack isn't it?"

"Yes it is," urged Hughes, "and what do you know about it?"

"Say nothing, Josh," the solicitor chimed in. "My client doesn't have to answer that question on the grounds that it might be incriminating."

"Don't worry Mr Simpkins," Josh Swinton retorted, "it's been common gossip all over the village since before the police knew anything about it themselves." He looked back to the detectives and added, "It's generally understood that Phillipson was shot dead in his bathroom at about 5.00pm: at least that's what I found out down at the Midshipman."

"Oh, really...and who told you that?"

"One of the barmaids: her parents live next door to Phillipson."

"And you know which house belonged to Phillipson, do you not?" prodded Hughes.

"Yes, it's not far from the pub actually."

"And you've visited the house before: you would know the layout and so on?"

"No. Like I said to your other bloke, I may know where it is, but I've never even stepped foot in the place. Why would I? I've had nothing to do with that waster since my mother kicked him out of our old farmhouse and tried to glue the family back together again. That bastard broke us into lots of little pieces, and no mistake."

"And you wear that animosity very vividly on your sleeve, if I may say so Mr Swinton. Such an unfettered level of aggression towards another person is indicative of someone who may just go one or two steps too far in seeking some kind of lasting revenge for any perceived violation, wouldn't you say?"

The solicitor held up his hand. "My client will not answer that question and you, DI Hughes, will retract that from the record."

Hughes nodded acknowledgement and continued. "So how long would it take for you to drive from your house back to the village on a quiet Sunday afternoon Josh?"

Simpkins growled his dissatisfaction at the line being taken.

"Okay then, let me put that another way. You do frequent the village quite often don't you Josh? You've admitted that much freely in your chat with DS Barnes. How long does the drive back to the village take?"

"You know that already. Why ask? It must be fifteen minutes max," Josh Swinton said.

"And if you went...let's say via the post office in Woodbridge, how much more drive time would that add to the journey?" Hughes pressed.

"What the hell as that got to do with anything?" objected Swinton, and the solicitor held up his hands in exasperation as if to ask just where this bizarre line of questioning was leading them.

"Would you agree that the journey, as described, would take you no more than say, twenty five minutes in normal traffic?"

"Well, yes, that would be a reasonable *guesstimate*, but what's that got to do with me sitting here talking to you?" rasped the accused, now becoming a little more agitated.

"Josh...you don't mind if I call you Josh, do you?"

"What? Just get on with it for Chrissakes."

"Josh, did you go into work last Sunday at any time?"

"Eh? Bloody hell man, where are you off to now?"

"Just answer the question. You work at Barrington's Boatyard, we can at least agree on that, but were you there at any time last Sunday?"

"No. Like I said, I was at home on Sunday. On Sunday afternoon I watched the football on the television. Is that clear this time?" Swinton's brow had begun to look a little feverish. His eyelids flickered a little erratically and he drew his long sleeve across his top lip to mop the beads of sweat there. The damp patch on his cuff looked conspicuous.

"Tell me Josh, what sorts of clothes do you wear at work?"

"Sorry?"

"You know...overalls, company uniform, jeans and t-shirt, that sort of idea?" It appeared to Hughes and Addison that the deliberately shifting, outwardly random nature of their questioning was beginning to leech its way into Swinton's subconscious.

"Er...well, usually very casual stuff, you know...," and he hesitated and cast a look at ceiling as he quickly exhaled, "jeans and soft boat shoes sometimes. Other times it would be working boots to protect the feet when doing heavier jobs. Often it would just be trainers, jeans and a sweat shirt, but look, why are you asking me these stupid questions? It's beginning to look like you're either fishing for clues or trying to deliberately confuse me into saying something rash."

"Do you often say rash things then?"

"Shit! What is this?" Swinton barked at them.

"Detectives, please: is this entirely necessary?" queried the solicitor.

DS Addison contributed for the first time. "Mr Simpkins, we're trying to establish an accurate study of Josh's movements last Sunday. Some aspects of his story as we have understood it hitherto simply don't add up. We need clarity."

"Which aspects?" Simpkins shot back.

"All in good time," Hughes retorted. "So Josh, which university did you go to?"

"Fuck's sake," Swinton spat out, and he flung himself back in the chair again with great flamboyance and sat there shaking his head in growing irritation.

"Let me suggest East Anglia. Now what colour sweat shirts are the most popular there and what kind of motif would they normally carry?"

"You jokers are just doing this deliberately to wind me up. Come on Mr Simpkins, it's time we left," and he motioned to stand and head for the door.

"Sit down Josh. Don't make a prick of yourself. You are under arrest. I shouldn't need to point out that you are not free to go, and if you go anywhere it will be to the cells."

Simpkins jumped in and reminded them that they could only hold his client for up to forty eight hours pending release, but Addison pointed out the error of his judgement. "That only applies if your client is here under questioning and has not yet been charged. The evidence against your client is robust and will be duly presented in court, but make no mistake, he is under arrest for murder and he isn't going anywhere in the short term."

Swinton swallowed hard. He looked at the flushed embarrassed face of his legal adviser and wilted.

"Let's get back to those work clothes and that university sweatshirt shall we, Josh?"

In his gut Josh Swinton sensed a quivering nerve of uncertainty. He was suddenly afraid of where the interrogation was going. He sat upright again and eyed his inquisitors.

"The one I wear at work is a pale grey colour with white *E A Uni* lettering on the back."

"With a soft grey cotton hood attached, isn't that right?" And then the accused looked genuinely alarmed. As far as he could remember he'd left it hanging in his work locker in the changing rooms there. Why was it of significance to them, he wondered? His right knee started to bounce nervously up and down at pace and he placed a hand on it to try to dampen the movement.

Amy Addison leaned forward, flipped up the screen of her laptop, touched the screen with a stiff finger, and then turned the machine around so that the accused and his solicitor could see the imagery on-screen. As she did so Adi Hughes leaned towards the recording machine and announced her actions for the record.

"Does this look familiar Josh?" she asked.

The video flashed into action and they watched, fascinated, as a young man hopped out of a Barrington's Boatyard van to open the boatyard gates. The figure looked about Josh's height and weight and was clearly wearing Josh's clothes, as described by Josh himself not minutes earlier. Josh Swinton recognised the physical location immediately and he knew instinctively that the little cameo on screen had been filmed by Barrington's CCTV camera just beside the main gate. It was certainly the main access to the Woodbridge site.

"It looks like me taking the van out. I guess you could have recorded quite a few of those at different times," he conceded.

"Ah yes Josh, but just take a look at the date and timeline at the bottom right corner of the screen".

He squinted closer to get a better look and then gasped in horror. "That's last Sunday at about four o'clock. But that just can't be right...I mean, er...that's not possible. There must be some sort of timing glitch on the security system." He turned to his solicitor and looked desperately for some assistance, but his adviser just gaped at him unsure of what to say or how to say it.

Josh stumbled on. "Have you checked the timing on the system?"

"Yes. It's accurate."

"No, no. That's impossible. I mean...I just wasn't there."

"That's not what your factory manager seems to think. He identified you too, just as you have identified yourself just now."

"Fuck you lot," the young man exploded. "This is bullshit. There has to be a very simple explanation for this. I wasn't there. I was at home."

"On your own, like you said," Hughes added with a flourish of mockery in his tone.

Josh Swinton seethed.

Then, in the same meandering style, Hughes asked, "What can you tell us about the old boat you've been working on down there at Barrington's?"

Swinton was completely thrown and he bristled with indignation as he recognised their repeated ploy. "What's there to tell? It's a renovation project. I've worked on her for quite a few years, but I don't spend as much...hang on a second, I've done all this before with your other plod down at the yard. He must have reported back."

"To repeat, it's for our mutual benefit that we hear it from you, first hand, and for the official record on disc."

"Mutual benefit, my arse! This is some kind of stitch up and I'll work it out given time and come back at you lot. You should be ashamed of yourselves. All of this for some ridiculous statistics that you hope will show the public just how clever and diligent you are. I promise you, I will get to the bottom of this."

"Are you threatening us with some form of reprisal?" Amy Addison asked.

"Don't answer that," interceded the solicitor.

"It's okay," Swinton replied, as he continued to stare at his oppressors. "This filth is trying to get me banged up for something I didn't do, and I will flush them out in time, I promise you. You could make a packet on this little jamboree," and he turned to smile at the

164

solicitor whose eyes bulged not at the thought of any rich pickings to be derived from suing the police, but at his client's audacity.

"Stick with the boat, son?" Hughes challenged, more assertive this time. "How did you come by her?"

"What's that to you?"

"Neither here nor there, if truth be told, but I am interested in its history. It seems to be a bit of a relic, but I'm sure the old vessel could look like a fine example of its kind with a lot more time, money and hard work. Of those, you might find yourself pushed for time if you're in Barlinnie for the next thirty years for murder. More interesting still is some of the very old equipment that seems to have come with the craft. Do you want to talk about some of the odds and ends on board?"

Josh Swinton froze. He looked down. He knew exactly what the detective was driving at and he found himself bereft of any quick-witted, humorous response with which to throw the copper off the trail. Only two people on the planet had ever known of the existence of that old pistol, and one of those, his old grandad Walter, had long since passed away leaving Josh secure in that secretive knowledge. His head was swimming. For the first time he began to doubt his ability to counter the tide that seemed to be rushing against him. Something was seriously wrong and very definitely out of his control. He tried to bluff it out.

"What the hell are you talking about?" he flashed back at his inquisitor, but the crackle in his voice stole the bravado in his rebuttal. The solicitor sat forward on his seat, an innocent bystander unable to come to his client's rescue.

"Come on Josh, quit messing around. Tell me about its weaponry!"

Swinton slumped before them. How could they know? Obviously it wasn't a man o' war of the line. It was just an old Suffolk shrimper: no deck cannon to consider. They could only be referring to one gun. He used to get it out every now and again when he was working late in the boat shed. Sometimes he just needed a break and he'd check that the entire place was empty before firing a few rounds into the old bales at the far end of the bay. It had been idle fun, and that was all. How could they know about it? Surely he was just becoming paranoid.

"It's a shrimper for God's sake."

"And I'm sure neither the first shrimper nor the last to carry clever little cubby-holes and hidden compartments containing all sorts of interesting goodies like old war time memorabilia."

The copper was referring to the gun, but why? What was the relevance of it? The weapon had been concealed for more than seventy years. They couldn't possibly think he'd taken it out and gone off to kill that bastard Phillipson.

Addison cleared her throat and adopted something of a presentational approach to what appeared to be a summary of their collective circumstances so far.

"Josh Swinton, we confirm that you are under arrest for the murder of Lee Phillipson on Sunday last at about 5.00pm. You are not obliged to say anything, but anything you do say will be taken down and may be used as evidence against you in court." Swinton looked as if he might break down at any moment.

"This is crazy," he yelled.

"We have detailed, conclusive evidence which, contrary to your own statements, places you very definitely in the home of the victim at some stage in the recent past. We have detailed and conclusive ballistic assessments of the murder weapon and related ordnance both at the crime scene and at the site of your old boat in Barrington's Boatyard. The forensic science applied to gun and bullets leaves little room for speculation. The pre-war Luger concealed by you in the hull of that boat and used in close proximity to that boat, is also the weapon used to despatch the victim. Gunshot residues on the victim's entry wound and on your clothing, especially the sweatshirt hidden in the same vessel, tie you directly to the murder scene and the same murder weapon."

A wave of panic overwhelmed him. He looked at them. He was quietly terrified and the perspiration trickled down inside his shirt from his chest into the waistband of his trousers.

"Wait, wait! For goodness sake, hear me out. Yes, I admit hiding the gun. It was a gift to my great grandfather from a British soldier at Dunkirk. The squaddie must have taken it from a German officer, presumably some poor sod he had killed in the last frenetic moments of that beach-head siege. He must have been so utterly grateful to my great grandad, old Walter, who, like so many brave men in the flotilla, had sailed very close to the beach at great risk to themselves just to pick up as many men from the water as he could. One of them must have rewarded the old boy for his courage by giving him a Luger, a highly prized hand gun of that era. Walter hid it in the hull of the forward cabin and I discovered it by accident. I admit it here and now. I have fired that gun into the bales around my boat, but that's all. What's more, to my knowledge that gun has never left the boat from that day to this."

"CCTV footage shows you taking a company van out from the boatyard at a corresponding time. You identified yourself in the video here in this interview room, as did a senior member of staff at the yard. Furthermore your return journey was followed by a third-party witness whose descriptions of you in the van are commensurate with the descriptions we have seen and already discussed."

"But if any of this garbage was even remotely accurate, just ask yourselves, why would I take the trouble of going to the boat yard to retrieve the weapon? Why wouldn't I have simply taken it home with me and then done the deed from home?"

"We can only speculate at this stage as to the finer details of your plan, but our forensic examinations leave us with little doubt about your applied methodology, and aspects of motivation and opportunity seem crystal clear.

"We know, and have many witnesses to this effect, that you have regularly and consistently talked of revenge against the dead man. Your dislike of him, born out of years of rancour, appears to be a powerful motivator, and even as a youth you had attempted to way-lay the man in order to beat him up or possibly even to kill him then, when you were just a callow youth. Such evidence is compelling."

Swinton just sat there, head bowed, silent. Then he looked up slowly and fixed Amy Addison with a searching stare. "In all seriousness, isn't it worth looking at the idea that someone is trying to frame me? Wouldn't it be so easy for one of so many aggrieved parties to exact some form of retribution for all the horrible things that man got away with in life, and at the same time to position me as the culprit? Is that in any way realistic or do you already think I'm peddling a conspiracy theory? I'm innocent of these charges, but I have no means of combatting them."

"Mr Swinton, we're looking at every angle, but I have to tell you that every signal sends us in your direction," Addison said firmly.

With that they terminated the interview and the accused was swiftly taken out by two uniformed officers to spend the night in custody at the police station. The following day he would be despatched to a remand prison pending court proceedings. Addison thought Swinton looked scared and miserable as he was carted off.

When Simpkins reconvened with Janice Swinton, and also with her daughter-in-law, he was devoured by them in search of immediate and hopefully positive news. Their hopes were quickly dashed. Not only did the old stalwart appear a little hollowed out by the interrogation he had witnessed, but he confided in them quickly and simply that Josh's position did indeed look dire. Some specifics of the tale really took the women by surprise. For Josh Swinton's young wife the very idea that her husband had not been watching football at his usual time the previous Sunday just didn't sit well with her. She hadn't noticed any unusual signs. In fact Josh had talked incessantly about his team's exciting performance that day and now she just couldn't bring herself to believe that he hadn't been camped in front of the big-screen TV throughout her regular absence with the little one at the swimming club.

Janice Swinton too was rocked by some of the revelations relayed by her solicitor and old friend. She gasped when he said that the police had recovered forensic identification of Josh in Lee Phillipson's home. She was equally startled to learn of the old German pistol stashed away in her grandfather's old shrimper. She had heard the story of the Luger from her grandfather Walter directly. Josh's assumption about the grateful soldier rescued from the waves off the French coast in wartime had been right in the key details, but the eventual whereabouts of the weapon were never discussed and the family had surmised that it had been lost or sold many years earlier. On learning about this vital piece of evidence she began to fear the worst. The information surrounding the ballistics and gunshot residue hit her hard. It appeared to indicate an insurmountable barrier to proving her son's innocence. She became thoughtful and broody, slightly removed from the discussions at hand. Her daughter-in- law didn't miss the point, but questioned the logic of her husband's supposed circuitous route via the boatyard to do the despicable deed. That seemed wholly incredible. She just didn't think his mind worked along those lines. However, the solicitor counselled her that trying to apply normal daily routines to a man outwardly intent on murder may be fundamentally misleading. She flashed a look of objection at him, but she failed to pursue the point further.

The two women left in a serious state of disquiet, not knowing what would happen next, or even when they might visit their loved one in the holding cell.

Two floors above them DCI Lehrer had re-run the interview with DI Hughes and DS Addison. He really wasn't sure that they had learned much more, except that the accused had offered nothing tangible by way of an alibi or even an alternative story. His colleagues professed their satisfaction that their case to the Crown Prosecution Service would be robust and water-tight: they were convinced that they had nabbed the right man. They also declared a degree of sympathy with the alleged murderer when considering the disgusting litany of malfeasance perpetrated by the late Lee Phillipson. However, murder was murder they said, and he should be put away for a very long time.

DCI Lehrer couldn't argue with much of their case against Josh Swinton. His heart ached for the agonies the boy's mother would be churning through at that moment, but to his colleagues Lehrer seemed distracted, almost pre-occupied with something on the periphery. When they urged him to sign off the next phase – preparations for the CPS file – to their astonishment he told them to hold off until he'd had time to talk to the Chief Superintendent. They took that as an unnecessary delay, but when they pushed a little harder he dismissed them from the office telling them to get all loose ends tied up over the next twenty four hours.

In his office, alone for a moment, he swivelled in his chair and looked out at the bright sky. Within his own mental summary he acknowledged that the case against Josh Swinton, someone he'd never met, looked remarkably solid. The powerful combination of motivation and opportunity, together with laser-guided forensics and ballistics, appeared to brook very little argument. Nevertheless, he remained suspicious of the use of the Barrington's van in the fatal episode. It just seemed incongruous, somehow over-complicated, a very high risk element of what must have been a carefully thought out plan. He homed in on Josh Swinton's own rather tepid claim that someone had set him up. That, of itself, seemed a huge leap. It would require not only someone who hated Phillipson enough to have killed him, but also an intimate knowledge of Josh Swinton's everyday movements and some of his innermost secrets to boot. The idea looked outrageous, and yet Lehrer just couldn't put it to bed. Finding people who had developed various forms of pathological hostility to Phillipson had proven all too easy, but to combine that with a drive to incriminate another in the act of murder, well…that must surely be a field of one or, more likely, none.

Then there was the lack of a facial ID from the video taken at the main gate of the boatyard: fortuitous or carefully contrived? If someone were mimicking Josh Swinton he certainly wouldn't want his face to be seen, but such a blatant declaration on film could easily qualify for a perpetrator who wanted to leave a visible trail in Josh Swinton's name. Just listen to yourself he argued. You're making it look like Rendell, Poirot and Holmes all rolled into one. The case looks very strong. What's the problem? Was it actually the boy himself who was holding him back, or was it the boy's mother and what she had become to him so very, very recently.

He resolved to get back to the forensics team and to take another look at the few remaining samples that still eluded identification. Was there something vital in that list? Was there a con-man killer out there who had very effectively killed two birds with one devastating stone, and if so, what could be his connection to Josh Swinton?

Out in the main office Adi Hughes was doling out wrap-up procedures in anticipation of going to trial via their CPS submission.

It had been a very long, arduous and trying couple of days, but to have nailed the case in just one week was, frankly, unbelievable.

21 – another diversion?

It was very clear to him. They still had seven unidentified traces taken from Phillipson's home. What if... just what if one of those turned out to be a crucial oversight, one which had condemned an innocent young man to a life behind bars? He sat at his desk, elbows splayed, fists supporting his jawline as he chewed remorselessly on his cheap biro.

Several days had passed and his frustrations had been steadily building. Not one of his close-knit and very trusted team had expressed even a pinch of doubt despite his own plainly contrarian views. He felt he was being railroaded by his own squad, and after some early hints and rather vocal skirmishes they appeared to have retreated and drawn up the wagons in their defensive laager. He could sense their resentment at his continued reluctance to submit the case to the Crown Prosecution Service.

Then a higher authority had intervened: the Chief Superintendent had overruled him and forced him to get on with it. He'd been working through some of the back-log attached to other cases when Adi Hughes had stuck his head around the door to inform him that the big boss had demanded an audience. So he'd trapesed upstairs wearing an anxious look, fully expecting his twelve unaccounted-for hours last Saturday night to be a very serious problem – possibly sufficiently awkward to have him removed from the case. In fact, he considered while slowly mounting the concrete steps of the rear stairwell, the prospect of any form of reprieve seemed simply too unrealistic. He'd been having sex with a critical witness in a murder investigation – the main suspect's mother as it turned out. What else could it mean? He was cooked, and it wouldn't end there either.

To his enormous relief however, the Chief Superintendent had asked him about his reluctance to proceed to the CPS on the Josh Swinton case, and when he'd begun to outline his reservations his boss had simply interrupted him and instructed him to submit the file. Apparently the Chief had gone through the details with Adi Hughes. As one of the most senior officers in the Suffolk force, the Chief had taken the view that the prosecution had an incredibly strong case and that anything less than a conviction would be a travesty of justice. He ushered Lehrer out of his office with a stiff rebuke for his evident apprehension and a clear instruction to make haste. As Lehrer padded back down the same stairway he smiled ruefully at having dodged a serious reprimand for his own ridiculous behaviour, and simultaneously he gratefully tipped his imaginary hat to Hughes's loyalty. Obviously his own out-of-office exploits had not been discussed. He wouldn't forget that.

So there he sat gnawing the end of his pen and reflecting on how he could pursue the Swinton case discreetly when there were so many other operational issues to contend with. He'd had no further contact with the boy's mother and he knew he couldn't hope to reinstate that conduit, certainly not at this juncture and probably forever more.

Just then a tap on the door announced the arrival of Hughes and McLellan. They carried with them a couple of hefty files, one clearly marked *Tattoo* and the other *Cove*.

Operation Cove referred to their long-established and painstaking infiltration of the trafficking networks associated with the busy ports of Felixstowe and Harwich. Despite great risks to themselves, Lehrer's snouts, working covertly with transport firms, hauliers, stevedore unions and the like, had penetrated a number of clandestine organisations. From the inside they had been remarkably successful at ingratiating themselves with people-traffickers, drug smugglers and weapons dealers from a range of different host countries, all of whom were plying their illicit trades through two of Britain's most active ports. Tip-offs were sadly infrequent – secrecy was always challenging – but almost always accurate and timely. Lehrer's units, working closely with the Port Authorities and Her Majesty's Customs Officers, had achieved some spectacular victories over gun runners from Eastern Europe and illegal slave traders from the Middle East and North Africa who seemed to manage a perpetual supply of young women and girls to the unscrupulous underground sex industry lurking in the shadows of every major town and city in Britain. The global narcotics moguls also appeared confident that rewards justified the risks of shipping their filth into the UK in the hidden compartments of trucks or the false floors of shipping containers. International law enforcement relied heavily on local, inside intelligence, but also on global information gathered across a vast hi-tech web of specialist electronic surveillance.

On any one day Lehrer and his allies could just as easily be talking to their counterparts in South America or Hong Kong, Pakistan or the USA in their fight against the world's most lucrative and illegal money spinners, but they might just as easily be sweeping up their own local offenders and victims who, in their growing numbers at street level, represented the demand side of the same international equation. This was where *Operation Tattoo* connected with *Cove*, at a very local level in the back streets and alleyways of a myriad of small regional towns and villages across East Anglia. And the region was by no means unusual when compared with any other corner of Britain. If there were key differences by comparison, they certainly lay in the scale and scope of their efforts at the main ports. Not every region in the country could claim to have one of the biggest container ports in the world. For the Suffolk police that equated to an elevated sense of duty as their own patch effectively represented one of the biggest gateways into Britain for a lot of evil, undesirable business interests.

The three officers took seats around Lehrer's small conference table in one corner of his office. Hughes fished a couple of notes pages out of each file and they fell into a quick review of both on-going projects.

It appeared that a group of Polish lorry drivers had been particularly persistent of late with their attempts to smuggle illegal immigrants from Europe's eastern reaches into the gang-master empires of England's rural working population. In the previous year they'd been stopped and simply turned around once their human cargoes had been removed and confined to processing centres behind barbed wire. Then some of the same men had tried again, but this time some of them appeared to have armed themselves, or been armed, in order to better impose themselves on their counterparts in the trafficking syndicates on this side of the North Sea. Some arrests had resulted, some deportations had ensued, but perhaps more important, and certainly of more interest to Lehrer, were the recently discovered identities of two leading lights of the cartels who operated on the ground in his patch. The three detectives knew that secrecy would have to be absolute – the lives of their own colleagues literally depended on their discretion. A withering pressure was building among the criminal fraternity and they suspected that their two known lynch pins were under real strain. Intelligence suggested to the police teams that an internal spat between gangs had not been managed to any kind of moderated conclusion. Tensions were still running high. Something would snap soon, it was a question of when and where, and whether or not the force could engineer an opportunity at the same time.

Another tap on the door heralded the unexpected arrival of DS Symes from the drug squad. He was one of a number of officers actively involved with *Cove* and *Tattoo*.

"Sorry to interrupt DCI, but I thought you might want a quick update from our all-nighters. They had quite a busy old night, I must say."

Lehrer pushed his chair to one side and motioned Symes to take the vacant seat.

"What have you got for us?" he asked.

"Well...how shall I put it? It's Barrington's Boatyard again!"

"What's that?"

"Wasn't it Barrington's where you picked up that lad with the old Luger last week?"

McLellan and Hughes looked sheepishly at one another, wondering if the boss might blow his cool altogether.

"Yes, yes, of course it was, but what are you referring to now?" Lehrer sneered, aware of the sensitive reaction from his two immediate colleagues.

"Well...you know how it is when something like that...you know, a specific connection...is somehow lodged in your brain, and then out of the blue, or the dark night in this case, you get an unexpected reminder of it right there before your eyes?" He paused for impact.

"Go on then," urged Mac, "you've got us all on the same hook now, so get on with it."

"It was quite remarkable really. There we were, a few of us staking out a couple of known dealing locations – acting on good info' too, I should point out – and coordinating our efforts on foot and on four wheels. We'd had a bit of luck early evening. We picked up a handful of scum bags sniffing around the usual spots just behind the marina in Ipswich. You know the sort: nose rings, dyed hair half shaved off, Doc Martens some of 'em, tattoos all over the place, even tongue studs and probably pierced knobs or nipples for all I know…"

"As you say, we know the sort," Hughes pressed in frustration.

"Yeah…right…well, we carted a few of them back for a de-coke and a kip in the cells, and we were wondering about the chances of getting any further after such an early score, but we decided to stick at it. Nothing happened for hours, and there we were, two of us getting cold in a transit under the red-brick arches, when we spotted an approaching headlight coming in from one of the back lanes. Going by his main beams, he appeared to be looking for someone or something. The motion of the vehicle was just too slow and careful. Lo and behold, as he approached us, and we were all parked up, lights out, no-one at home… obviously, he drew to a stop close by and in direct line of sight. Even in the subdued light I could see the name of the boatyard on the side of the van. No sooner had it registered, I saw two scrawny figures emerge from a side ginnel and head directly for that van. The business was done in no more than two minutes, but by that time we had closed off the same ginnel as a potential escape route. We flicked our lights on and rushed them. It was a very easy collar, I can tell you, and the van had a glove box stashed full of various highs and lows for any number of needy addicts out there on the street."

"So what happened? How far did you get? Why the Barrington's Boatyard van?"

"We dealt with the youngsters first and put the driver of the van in the cell block for a bit of thinking time. He looked shocked at first, but now he's pretty subdued."

"You mean he's still here? Lehrer enquired, surprised.

"Oh yeah, I thought you might like a crack at him, you know…seeing as you're already perfectly familiar with Barrington's Boatyard."

Lehrer smiled. He wondered if maybe, despite everyone's apparent reluctance, there was an extra lead to pursue which might lead him back to Josh Swinton. But then he posed another question.

"And the youngsters as you called them: what of them?"

"Late teens, early twenties, I'd say – drop-outs in every respect, in my view. We packed them off with a slapped wrist as soon as we'd got the basics. The girl was a tad abrasive to say the very least – quite well-spoken for someone with about six piercings in each eyebrow and jet-black lipstick, tight jeans and tits on show through her skimpy top. She claimed to live in her own flat and that her grandfather paid the rent, although I doubt he pays for her habit too. Cocaine is an expensive fix these days. She denied it of course, but her nostrils were blown and when we body searched her she'd stuffed a couple of sachets up her *you know what* in an attempt to avoid detection."

"I thought coke was more a rich girl's sport," Mac threw in.

"Me too," Symes replied, "but she must be putting herself about to earn that sort of dough. She had needle marks in her forearms too, so God only knows what cocktail of poisons she normally enjoys. When all's said and done though, she's a victim, not the cause, so we ticked her off, gave her a formal caution and chucked her out. As for the lad, well...bit of an odd fish really."

"How d'you mean?"

"Sullen, uncommunicative, resentful... and I mean of life itself not just of us for making the catch. He was more a needles and smokes man, or so it seemed. He lives in a small cottage out in the sticks. Like her, he too doesn't work. Again there was mention of some sort of financial support, but he refused to talk about his parents or anyone in the family line. I think he's a proper loaner...on his own almost all the time. We've asked him to check in with us each week for the next month, but he'll not keep that promise, I guarantee it."

"And the van driver is their regular Mr Fixit, yes?"

"In one, Chief, in one."

"All right then, can we go and see him?"

"It's your shop Chief."

"I think you know that's not true. It's the big Chief's shop, just to be pedantic." Lehrer looked at Hughes and McLellan. "Which of you is feeling most open-minded at the minute?"

Paul Bromsgrove sat hunched over the edge of his low-level bunk in the grey and lifeless holding cell. He hadn't slept at all. A uniformed officer led him out of his confinement, along a windowless corridor to an interview room where two plain clothes detectives sat at the far side of a simple table. One of them pushed a plastic cup of murky brown machine-coffee towards him by way of welcome. He sat down tentatively, eyed the coffee with a grimace, and then looked blankly towards his interrogators. Lehrer couldn't decide whether the man was just timid and frightened or wholly implacable. He stared at them through his round glasses and seemed perpetually on the brink of saying something but nothing came forth. Hughes pitched in with a robust starter just to see what reaction he could get.

"You've got just about every fucking type of toxic filth available in that van of yours. What the fuck do you think you're playing at?"

Bromsgrove appeared to flinch slightly, but said nothing and concentrated his lifeless stare on Hughes alone.

"Oh I get it...hard-nosed bastard are we? Okay then, if you want to play it rough we can accommodate a low-life pusher like you to whatever level you choose. Let's get the cards on the table shall we...," but Lehrer motioned him to stop.

"Mr Bromsgrove you are entitled to legal representation. We have not officially started this interview...that's to say we are not yet recording this conversation, but we are about to, so if you wish to exercise your right to legal assistance please speak-up now."

He switched his focus to Lehrer and held it there, mute for a few moments more. Then he said, "Oh no, no old chap, quite unnecessary. One should know when one is in a bind of one's own making, and when in such a bind one simply has to take one's medicine in large measure and with minimum fuss, wouldn't you say?"

Both coppers just looked at each other. Hughes barely managed to supress a smirk and Lehrer couldn't fathom either a total fruitcake or a well-educated middle-class fraud. He gathered himself.

"Mr Bromsgrove you are in an invidious position, one which will almost certainly result in you facing a prison sentence for the possession and trafficking of serious, high-end narcotics. I really do urge you to think about this very carefully and to seek some form of support here."

"Repeating oneself can appear rude Detective Chief Inspector, and at the very least is somewhat tedious. However, I have been pulling this little, er... what would you chaps call it...er, scam, yes that's it, this little scam for several years and to be frank I'm astonished at having avoided detection for so long. It has been quite an adventure, and if I may say so, quite a lucrative one to boot. So no, thank you, Detective Chief Inspector, I will not avail myself of your proposed legal advisory services knowing, as I do, that such unexpected and unjustified privileges can only be accorded at great expense to the public purse, and I have every last sympathy with the British tax payer for the many injustices he must bear." Hughes slowly shook his head and turned to look again at Lehrer, with raised eyebrows telegraphing his own bewilderment.

"Very well, sir, you have made your choice clear to us and in very eloquent terms, for which we thank you." Leaning forward and activating the recording system, he stated the introductory preliminaries concisely and pressed on.

"Tell us about your activities, please, Mr Bromsgrove. I am, of course, referring to that, er...little scam... to which you referred just a moment ago."

"Well, I say...there really isn't all that much to tell. I am something of a failed professional, at least as far as professional ambitions might go, and for some time, many years in fact, I have been seriously in need of extra income to support a rather mundane lifestyle."

"But drug running? Supplying feckless kids and wino drop outs with the hard stuff is one hell of a side-line," Hughes argued.

"Granted...it came about quite by chance through a fellow I know in London. One or two other links to the chain were forged in a similarly fortuitous and perfectly accidental fashion and there I was delivering small packets of hash and weed to pathetic layabouts in dark corners around town on Wednesday nights. Before I knew it I was beginning to accrue some rather impressive sums. The environment and the customers were usually equally unpleasant, but there seemed little risk and I always calculated my ability to withdraw at short notice if things turned nasty."

"Always Wednesday nights?"

"Indeed."

"How so?"

"By dint of circumstances."

"Explain, please."

"It's remarkably simple when one takes a step back." He paused and exhaled with a forlorn extended sigh. "My life was not always quite so dismal, gentlemen, but I work in a rather shabby office performing very basic accountancy functions and running errands for those who are too idle to do the same. Once upon a time I was a glittering Cambridge graduate with a role in the city beckoning, but getting a young girl in the family way scuppered any illusions, or should that be delusions of grandeur I may have harboured at the time. I never got fully and properly qualified...chartered status and all that comes with it, and I was therefore condemned to run a second or third tier life as a book keeper for a variety of tepid, unambitious organisations. The girl I had stood by in her hour of maternal need did, it must be acknowledged, stand by me for many subsequent years despite the rather limited horizons open to us. We had two children actually, but in the final analysis they opted to move with her when she eventually abandoned my rather boring existence for an alternative which appeared so much more exciting. In the process I lost everything: not just my family, but my business, my home and all my savings too."

"You mean you allowed her to keep the house for the sake of the kids?"

"Goodness gracious, no! At the risk of contradicting myself gentlemen, allow me to state that the convulsions our family experienced at that time were a little more complex than that, but I'm really not convinced that the period in question is of any relevance to our discussions beyond clarifying that my financial circumstances were dire and, well, needs must, must they not? That was my motivation. Making extra money quickly and easily came to me as a much appreciated and very timely adjunct to my banal daily routine."

"And the Barrington's van: I don't suppose you work there?"

"Oh, but I do, you see. Running the books there is a function I could perform in my sleep. So mundane is the rigmarole that I jumped at the chance of a regular day out of the office in the van to collect basic supplies and to deliver small items, special post and so on every Thursday. They offered me the van to be taken home on Wednesday evenings in preparation for the Thursday sortie. Parking up for a refresher on the way home threw me into an entirely new subterranean world of vice and sleaze. Once my London friend had whispered in my ear, and I'd developed the courage to give the distribution business a try, it all just accelerated from very humble beginnings to a pecuniary intake I simply could not afford to staunch. It hasn't been so life-changing to take me out of Barrington's as yet, but I am getting close to being able to buy a very nice home and to be able to escape the brutality of squalid rental accommodation."

"You do realise Mr Bromsgrove that those funds will be sequestered by the courts at some stage in this process."

"Only if they can be located, Detective Chief Inspector." More raised eyebrows.

"I think we'll be able to work it out. Cambridge graduates we may not be, but our techy chaps are fairly adept at tracking down money, believe me."

"Or I might make it easier for you if we can do a little trade or two," Bromsgrove suggested.

"What, something like a reduced sentence in exchange for the cash?"

"Oh, you disappoint me Detective Chief Inspector. I had you as a man of great perception. What say you to this: a reduced sentence for the name of my supplier, and I keep the cash?"

"You really would shop your contact just like that? You truly are a contradiction Mr Bromsgrove. There you were not ten minutes ago fretting desperately for the British tax payer and all the many burdens he must endure, and now you're perfectly happy to chop off the hand that feeds you without a care – what price loyalty, eh?"

"Ah yes, but you see, the hand that feeds me is conjoined to a disgusting bone-idle wretch who has never done a steady day's work in his life, let alone contribute to Her Majesty's tax revenues. He's just like all of those pathetic louts who immerse themselves in their jumbled, garbled hallucinogenic world of needles, spliffs and pills. He's just like them, but he's managed to shin his way up that rank slimy pole to a level where he can exploit more of them to his ultimate benefit. They have never pressed their shoulders to the wheel. They don't pay taxes – on the contrary, the tax payer pays for their rancid one-room bedsits, and their doss houses, and he pays for their welfare, their needle exchanges, their soup kitchens…," and he halted as he realised that they were gaping, speechless at his tirade. But then he carried on. "People like him and people like the dregs you arrested me with last night…those people are sub-human. They always take and never give. They will soak up everything given to them if it's free and when they have to pay they will prostitute themselves in the most heinous ways possible to ensure that they can achieve their next mindless high."

"Doing deals with drug pushers is like walking on quicksand," Lehrer countered. "You can't ever tell when you'll start to sink into oblivion, and the pusher is the last man to stretch out his hand in an effort to haul you out of the mire."

"Trust me gentlemen, there is a code of ethics among right-minded criminals," Bromsgrove asserted. "The principal contention, that of the cynic you might say, is that most but not all people are charlatans who, given the chance, would wilfully harm one for some perceived gain or advantage. There are exceptions to that rule, of course, and I consider myself such an exception."

"Really? Who's to say that your friend of dubious nature in London is your only supplier?" Hughes threw across at him. "We could be forgiven for thinking that in this neck of the woods you might also be furnished with illicit materials by some of the syndicates operating in and around the ports. What about a few more names in exchange for securing your ill-gotten gains?"

Bromsgrove looked momentarily perplexed. Lehrer knew instinctively that the very idea had never crossed the man's mind.

"Gentlemen," he stammered, "I am simply bereft of comment. I know nothing of what you speak. I have only ever worked my own discreet and rather modest channel. There is nothing else to divulge in that regard."

"All right then," Lehrer interjected, "let's back up a little here. How long have you been doing this, and how come your employers never intervened?"

"Oh, now let me see," Bromsgrove responded, stroking his bearded chin as he cast his mind back in time. His dark button-like eyes glimmered in the subdued lighting of the featureless room. "I would estimate about five years. I have been with Barrington's for longer, but the coincidence of outlet and opportunity only presented itself at about that time. The van was a real boon you understand. No-one ever questioned a local firm's van being parked up of an evening, either in Ipswich or Woodbridge or a variety of places around here. It just seemed to fit beautifully into the background. I was always very careful not to leave any traces in the van lest a colleague discover something inappropriate when using the vehicle. There were one or two false alarms I must confess, heart fluttering moments, as in the case of last week's raid on the boatyard commensurate with young Josh Swinton's current predicament, but I was always fortunate not to have been too careless too often." Hughes again turned to the senior man with a more than inquisitive expression across his face.

"So you know Josh Swinton. How well do you know him?"

"Quite well I should say, but we are birds of a different feather who don't often fly together. He's an industrious young chap, I'll give him that, and I have great admiration for his skills as applied to that old boat of his in the ferro shed there, but we are at least a generation apart and he has more exciting company to keep in my humble opinion."

"How often do you see him about the yard?"

"Oh...infrequently I would say, but that's because I'm in the main administration office most of the time and he's out on site or often in the naval architect's drawing office as I understand it. I don't have much cause to go there."

"But you knew of the boat renovation in the main shed?"

"But of course, it's something genuinely close to our hearts. We want him to succeed. He deserves to."

"And what else can you tell me about that boat?"

"Simply that it was once a brave little craft that sailed the Channel to Dunkirk under the guiding helmsman's hand of Josh's great-grandfather no less. A finer tale we shall never hear, gentlemen, and how fitting that the great-grandson should bear the onerous responsibility of such a significant refurbishment. Oh, yes...er, there is one other snippet I can reveal, but of course you must know of this already. The boat itself was where the Luger was found. Who could have predicted such a twist?"

At that the policemen squirmed uncomfortably and Hughes coughed artificially in an attempt to conceal his jolted reaction.

"How long have you known about the presence of that gun, Mr Bromsgrove?" Lehrer demanded.

"Since your eagled-eyed young forensic chap emerged with it from within the shallow bowels of the vessel. We all heard that little yarn in an instant. The office network had that juicy morsel before your team had even vacated the boat shed."

The officers looked less than convinced, but their gut reaction told them that his account was entirely feasible. Bromsgrove cleared his throat and continued.

"Gentlemen, please, I sense some misgivings, but I can only remind you of my entirely transparent and very candid approach to this interview. Young Mr Swinton and I may indeed share some common ground, but a clandestine pact to conceal a second world-war pistol does not bear serious consideration."

"And what would bear serious consideration in connection with young Mr Swinton?"

"Do you know, Detective Chief Inspector, I may not possess the most sensitive radar in matters such as these, but last week I would have sworn that Josh was actually delighted with the recent victim's demise, and that is a view which I wholeheartedly endorse."

Hughes, who had been pushing back on his chair as he listened to this most bizarre of confessions, almost toppled backwards in shock and instead pitched forward knocking the plastic cups and their remnants right across the table. He apologised quickly, but neither he nor Lehrer could mask their astonishment. Lehrer's mind raced back to that worrying list of unidentified forensic traces, and Hughes knew exactly where his boss's thoughts were heading.

"Tell us about that victim, Mr Bromsgrove. What do you know?"

"Far too much than is good for me, if I'm any judge, but I am confident that any suspicion of my involvement there will soon be quashed. To answer your question, I need to take you back to the happier, brighter times in my life when I had growing children and a loving if somewhat unglamorous wife at home. All of that was destroyed by a certain Lee Phillipson."

"This is a wind up," spluttered Hughes.

"Carry on," urged Lehrer, looking earnestly at his interviewee.

"Phillipson was a cheap accountant, a book keeper just like my good self," Bromsgrove added. "We worked together at a small business on a trading estate which is now the BT complex at Martlesham. He persuaded me that going into our own joint venture would propel us into a more rewarding and thoroughly independent corporate arena. He was such a good salesman. I seem to recall that he had in fact sold life insurance door-to-door earlier in his life and that should have been sufficient warning to me. But those bright lights twinkled in my imagination. I could see the bubbles rising in the champagne. I could sense the warmth of the Italian sun on my back as I sat with Beverley, my wife, by our own pool at our villa in Tuscany. I promise you gentlemen, that man really could have taken coals to Newcastle except for several fundamental flaws in his make-up. The man was a liar and a fraud. More importantly, he was allergic to hard work. He convinced me to finance the project and then I very quickly discovered that he was not prepared to knuckle down with the determination any new business needs in order to survive, let alone succeed. It folded, naturally, that was pre-determined. I simply couldn't get through enough contractual work and, at the same time, seek to win new contracts sufficient to keep us afloat. I had been a one-man-band from the outset and our debts swallowed my entire contribution. Like a fool I had re-mortgaged the house in order to make that ambitious step and shortly thereafter I lost the house too."

"What about the family? Where did you go?"

"Ah, and there's the rub, gentlemen. I didn't have to worry about the family. It was then I discovered that he'd been bedding my wife for months. When it came to that unavoidable binary decision, him or me, his was the more exciting lifestyle. But of course she hadn't seen through the fairy tales and fabrications as I had. I begged and implored my dear lady to see the reality, but he'd already imbued her with his version of my weaknesses and ultimate failure, and she left with the kids to share his tiny dwelling in Church Ivy. It lasted a few months. He'd had his way with her and by then she bored him. He was already moving on to who knows where, and I understood later that he sold that house anyway because he simply couldn't sustain the mortgage. My lady never returned. Who could blame her? There was nothing to return to. She scrimped her way through life for a while. But she soon found someone who could support her in a manner she preferred and I gradually saw less and less of my dear offspring as they grew. It would not stretch the realms of fantasy too far if I were to say to you, here and now, that I rejoiced when I saw the news bulletin about Phillipson's death. Frankly, I have no way of discerning Josh Swinton's understanding of my own reaction to that same news. I could see real pleasure in his recognition of the man's passing, but could he see the same joy in me? I just could not vouch for that, and it hardly seems relevant."

"And you have no knowledge of where Phillipson went next after ditching your wife and kids?"

"No, none."

"If I said that he turned up shortly afterwards within the Swinton household would that surprise you?"

Bromsgrove gave a sharp gasp and then fell back in his chair as the shock took hold. He looked at once complicit with their understanding and then, quickly thereafter, he appeared very angry.

"Mr Bromsgrove, I am going to return you to a cell here pending the taking of some DNA swabs and the like. I can't yet tell you what will happen next, but I will endeavour to keep you informed. You will be charged with possession and trafficking of illegal substances in the public domain. I reaffirm my belief that you should seek some form of legal counsel and this officer," pointing to the closed door, "can help you arrange that."

With that Lehrer stood and called the uniformed officer back into the room. As he did so he shot Hughes a penetrating glance as if to suggest that the Swinton case was not done and dusted yet. Hughes saw that bristling look and knew that they were in for a lot more hard work in very short order.

22 – what's in a name?

Janice Swinton returned to work in Bedford, as was her obligation, but she left behind her normally focused attention to detail, submerged as she was in the quagmire of her son's arrest and subsequent remand. Her boy, her only son, in her mind still the same little boy who had so playfully engaged in his childhood escapades on the high seas in boats of every kind, had been despatched to Manton prison following a short but disheartening bail hearing at Ipswich Crown Court. Neither she nor her distraught daughter-in-law could fathom that judgement. Even if Josh had indeed committed the terrible act for which he had been charged, surely common sense alone would have persuaded any magistrate that this had been an act of calculated retribution, a crime of so many passions but one directed at one individual and therefore, surely, the accused would not be classified as someone dangerous to the community at large. And yet, despite all cogent consideration, Josh had been remanded into custody pending trial.

Janice had come very close to calling David Lehrer directly, but she simply couldn't bring herself to make that contact at the risk of further complicating the investigative process. She had gone over that night with him time and time again, and she had resisted the temptation to blame him in some way for the way in which the dominoes had tumbled in the ensuing hours of that subsequent, hellish Sunday morning. That look of genuine shock plastered across his features when she had confronted him in her bedroom had belied any suspicion of complicity on his part. She somehow just knew that what had passed between them that night had be wonderful, caring and sharing, but also fundamentally sincere. She had sensed the potential for ˜stability in a rewarding relationship, and that was something she had given up on many years ago. She also guessed that he had, so far at least, not been held to account in any way for his absence during those critical few hours, and she had determined not to further compromise his position by appealing directly to him for help. That decision had not been reached easily. She had remembered his earlier insistence that her son should and would be properly investigated, and for a lot of justifiably good reasons too.

Now she just hoped that this was just a mistake of incalculable proportions, but her wayward emotions carried her backwards and forwards through her son's only explanation – that someone else was deliberately trying to stitch him up. That appeared to be so far-fetched as to be impossible, a view shared by Kerry, his pretty young wife, in deep and distressing discussions with her mother-in-law.

Park Green had been electrified with the disturbing news that the adult son of their highly respected leader had been arrested for murder. Many of Janice's fiercest supporters, Mrs Meakins and the Wing Commander among them, had scoffed at such a ruse. They pretended that all would become clearer soon enough, but later they conceded that the fact that the lad had been remanded really did not look very promising.

As for Janice's staff, well, she quickly discovered who were her closest allies and, just as quickly, where her misplaced loyalties had been accorded. She was not herself. She was often short and irritable and seemed to spend a lot of time apologising for her irascible mood. She struggled to maintain her concentration and spent long periods alone in her office picking her way absent-mindedly through a blurred, ill-defined list of administrative tasks, none of which could surmount the all-consuming trepidation with which she wrestled hour after hour.

She was aware however, that for her team and for the Wingco's fellow inmates the world had not stopped turning. Their needs were just as pressing, their own duties just as challenging, and she would emerge from her lair periodically to walk the floor and to try to put a brave face on her situation for those who cared to notice. On occasions she would indeed be distracted by the on-going demands of the nursing home, and sometimes she would be relieved to collapse into a chair in one of her staff rooms to share a cup of tea with a small band of nurses or cleaners, happy just to be able to mix with those she knew and felt comfortable with. At other times however, she would react too sensitively to a minor problem before her, and then find herself scurrying back to her office bolt-hole to lick her wounds and to avoid the critical looks from her own people and the quizzical expressions of her residents. Everyone knew and understood the peculiar and quite unprecedented causes behind her volatile behaviour, and for the most part she was tolerated by a largely supportive ensemble that did its best to keep her going.

When the Meakins troop reappeared one bright sunny morning with their solicitor in tow, the home team recognised immediately that this was just another attempt amongst many to have the old girl sign away her fortune long before she was ready to do so. Janice Swinton was tipped off that there was something of a ruckus going on in the corner of the day lounge and she marched aggressively down the corridor and breezed into the lounge looking more like Queen Boudica than the serious professional manager of a respected institution. She blasted the motley crew of avaricious leeches, and even when the legal chap objected to her intrusion she cut him dead with a swingeing assessment of the value of his kind to society in general. She not only instructed them to leave forthwith, but she accompanied them to the main entrance and closed the doors very pointedly behind them once she had ushered them over the threshold. Then she hurried back to her own retreat, sat down heavily in her leather desk-chair and burst into tears once again.

Her thoughts wandered off to her son in some imagined cell of cramped dimensions where he shared that limited space with a couple of regular offenders of questionable ethics and disagreeable personal hygiene. Then she thought of her latest love once again, or should that have been lover. She had rarely felt so safe, so secure, so wanted in recent years, and oh…how she could do with those same comforts right now. Her sense of insecurity persisted, and it appeared to her that the more she thought about David Lehrer the more exaggerated her feelings of isolation became. Had he walked through the door at that moment she convinced herself, all of those doubts would quickly dissipate, and she wondered about the power of the man who could influence her in such a way from afar.

As the days rolled by into weeks, and as Janice Swinton's anxiety grew more conspicuous, the home developed a tense and often fractious atmosphere. Frictions between staff appeared less camouflaged from fellow team members as well as residents, and hitherto minor altercations or interruptions to a typical day seemed to take on an inflated profile and a damaging significance. Janice fought hard to pour soothing oil on these turbulent currents, but the eddying tides of disaffection sucked the balance of compromise from some of her less well-adjusted charges and she found that relationships began to fray where previously there had been reasonable harmony.

The Wing Commander discovered, much to his disappointment, that the earliest of their newly arranged chess matches seemed to charge his fellow players with a more combative approach. He felt certain that the elevated tension of the place was indeed feeding through to some of his friends and he became exasperated by one or two confrontational moments thrown up in the heat of table-top battle. He was also delivered of a withering blast from the normally delightful widow, Genevieve Allthorpe, when she chose to offer her candid views of his visiting grandson. True enough, he had inwardly conceded, the lad had looked a mess. He had shaved one side of his head to the skull and dyed the other half a whimsical pale turquoise blue colour which matched the garish swirling tattoo creeping up his neck from under his collar. The older man had never really taken any notice of this particular feature among many in his grandson's itinerant display of what the lad liked to call body art. Now however, with the bristling depravity of the half-bared crown, not only did the pictorial horror beneath his left ear and jawline appear so unavoidable, but onlookers were actively drawn to it like a homing beacon. The lad's other artistic adaptations, or deformities as the older generation considered them, now became so much more overt and therefore intrusive. The eyebrow studs represented the only gleaming characteristic of an otherwise pale and sallow visage. The nose rings had perpetrated two swollen red sores to one side of his nose and for those who chose to engage the young man in conversation, the saliva-soaked tongue stud captivated and disgusted them within the shortest garbled sentence he could muster. The Wingco reminded himself that in this day and age he was by no means the only elderly inmate of Park Green whose younger relatives dabbled in the mystical cult of smokes, snorts, pills and needles. He was confounded by youth in this regard and wondered, on many occasions, why the younger generations seemed so unhappy that they needed to invest in such dangerous pastimes only to make themselves feel better. What was wrong with them? Perhaps they should have flown an air raid or two over Essen to equip them with a heavy dose of reality before delving into such murky pools for their casual kicks. None the less, anointing the Wingco's only living flesh and blood with the dismissive label of disgusting human trash was perhaps not Mrs Allthorpe's best ever contribution to neighbourly relations. The old chap magnanimously gave her the benefit of the doubt however, and consigned the episode to one of many fuelled by the divisive intrusion of their leader's unfortunate domestic circumstances which had clearly permeated the place like a dangerous virus from which there appeared to be no immediate respite. They were not alone in their state of mild and unsettling turmoil.

David Lehrer too found the loneliness of his position extremely testing. The diversion introduced by the erudite and well-educated drug dealer, Paul Bromsgrove, had proven to be a rewarding distraction, but only to exploit Lehrer's singular view that the case against Josh Swinton did not look entirely sound. Forensics had failed to link Bromsgrove with any aspect of the Phillipson case, a result which hardly surprised Lehrer, but which disappointed him nevertheless. The impact on Lehrer's team had been initially disconcerting: they had reluctantly accepted that left-field surprises like this one could only reinforce the notion that other possible options remained out there, untested. With so many uncorroborated traces from the crime scene there may just be another unforeseeable twist in the tale that might throw serious doubt on the anticipated Swinton conviction. However, as time ebbed away his normally trusty band settled for the easiest option and showed an eagerness to pursue their many other cases in preference to tackling the very difficult nature of the unknown.

Lehrer thought about Janice a lot. He had no way of knowing, at least not with any real certainty, that she had accepted the innocence of his plea. Yes, he was in charge of a murder investigation, and yes he had made it clear that even her son was a potential suspect, but he had taken what appeared to be sincere affection to the next stage as naturally as it had occurred and without any intention to distract her while his diligent officers had continued in the pursuit of their goals.

He thought he had seen enough in her eyes, as she threw clothes on to the bed and made haste to get dressed in order to get down town to see her son. He felt sure, fairly sure anyway, that the arrested fury with which she'd initially erupted had, in the end, been stemmed before she'd driven off. He really hoped so. He wanted this to be right, if a relationship remained a realistic possibility, and of that potential outcome he didn't dare think. He remembered feeling completely relaxed with her. He remembered her firm figure and her warm heart. He remembered drifting into that slow and satisfying rhythm, a mutually fulfilling bond, and a thin smile pursed his lips for which he quickly castigated himself in the face of her undoubted suffering in the days which followed.

And he thought about her son – bail denied and carted off to a remand prison. How would he be feeling now? Would his story now change under the pressure of incarceration, or would he continue to claim his innocence despite so many condemning factors stacked up against him? He may not have been convinced about the younger man's guilt, but like so many onlookers, the desperate assertion that someone else had done the deed in his name seemed to challenge any notion of realism. He wondered what the conditions were like for young Swinton: crowded for sure, and mixing with all sorts of characters from the wrong side of the street. Such a place could break a person's will very quickly, and that could have disastrous effects on the eventual outcome of his predicament. People say and do some terrible and often ridiculous things when they lose hope. Lehrer recalled Barnes's description of the lad at interview...calm, relaxed most of the time, forthright and occasionally very aggressive. He wondered how that might look now in the interview room after a few challenging weeks bereft of life's normal reference coordinates.

On the other hand, and biting his knuckle at the shock of the recollection, he remembered his own very old grandmother's harrowing tales from the camps and, despite the awful misery of it all, how she insisted that true adversity can sometimes bring out the very best of character and nature in a determined individual. He marvelled again at that, and allowed himself the descent into a mine of outrageous stories which he'd heard as a boy, when his Jewish heritage was being asserted by those around him who fretted about his obvious reluctance to maintain the code. Old Esther had spared him little of the gruesome reality of her time in Buchenwald. Her own daughter, David's mother, had shrieked her objections at the debilitating history of such a forgettable period of man's malevolence to man, but he, even as a child, had encouraged the old woman privately. He had wanted to know what barbarity really looked like and she had not disappointed him. Ironically, it had been the cold, heartless truth which had led him away from the very religion that the older generations around him had urged him to follow. He had simply not been able to qualify the need for faith, when some of the physical aspects of that code had placed his kind in so much danger in the first place. And he knew, growing up in London as a Jewish boy, that those same damned prejudices that had wiped out nearly all of his extended family in Germany and Poland before and during the war, lived on in rude health in and around one of the world's increasingly cosmopolitan cities. How his mother had been smuggled out as a child in the late thirties remained a mystery to him, but he knew from his grandmother's reflections that she and her husband had taken immense risks to achieve that despatch, risks which eventually came back knocking on their door – the same door that bore the devil's brand of that other David's aspirational star.

He bit his lip in long-practiced dismay as he realised that those flashbacks to his own childhood usually left him morose and needy. He stiffened in his chair and straightened the knot in his tie before buzzing through to Hughes in the open office.

"Adi, I just wanted to check that our man Bromsgrove is getting some legal support. Do you know if that came through? That man's in deeper shit than he realises and he could be spending a longer time at Her Majesty's pleasure than he gambled on."

"Yes Chief, he's all assigned. It looks grim, I'll grant you, but there is still something of a plea bargain in the offing so we might be able to direct our mates in the Met to run along and catch his supplier in due course."

"Okay, good. Have we traced his wife and kids yet?"

"Roger that, too. They took a bit of finding…somewhere up north off the top of my head, but she appears to have remarried quite well and it seems to have smoothed off any rough edges she may have picked up through her earlier experiences."

"You mean that she's comfy now, and as well off as she was ever likely to be with our ever-so-pukka drug dealer, so she really doesn't give a toss anymore, is that it?"

"Yup, that's the gist."

"And her kids?"

"Not so clear-cut. Just scanning the notes now as we speak...Manchester by the way...and it appears that the boy did pretty well for himself and is now out in Singapore, but the girl seems to have dropped out and is still taking subsidies from the parents, or should that be from her step-father...clean alibi for the Singapore connection...er, the daughter, well, whereabouts at the time of Phillipson's death unaccounted for...the only potential alibi is her geographical location, but note that she does spend time down here with her former teenage hippy friends, so there is more work going on there to try to pin her down with some accuracy."

"Good work Adi. I just can't imagine why those two would look on Phillipson with any of that soft warm glow of heartfelt affection, if you know what I mean? Just keep me informed, please."

"Aye aye, skip!"

Back at Park Green Janice Swinton had just concluded one of her important management meetings, and had navigated the session without any major mishaps. She was cossetted in her own private office, having collected a stiff cup of instant coffee upon her return, when there was a crisp and immediately recognisable triple-tap on the door. She knew it to be Wing Commander Lionel even as she emerged from searching her lowest drawer for the biscuit tin.

"Wing Commander, how good to see you. Please do come in. Here take this one," she gestured to an armchair within the office and beyond the imposing barricade of her desk. Her elderly visitor recognised at once the conferring of special privileges. He smiled warmly and edged around the two harder, less-forgiving chairs nearer the door and deposited himself in the splendour of the deeper chair, lining up his canes to one side and leaning them against the arm.

"To what do I owe this distinct pleasure, Lionel?"

"A mission of mercy, Janice, if you don't mind me saying so?"

"Oh really, are my circumstances so patently obvious that my closest friends feel the need to comfort me in my hour of need?"

"Well...in short ma'am, yes, that's what we're here for, in part at any rate. We've all had some ups and downs of late, but this terrible business over your son's recent arrest has upset more apple carts in this normally tranquil place than we could ever put right."

"Oh Lord, is it really that bad?"

"In all honesty, no, and yet in combination with some of our own unsettling disruptions I would have to describe the combined effects as something less than perfect," he smiled again with warmth and sincerity.

"Lionel, do you know, you are a wonderfully generous and perceptive man, and I can readily appreciate the many allegiances you enjoy out there amongst our richly diverse community. Where would we be without you? Where would I be without your support?"

"Janice, as always you are too kind, and yet we are of the impression, I refer to the not insignificant collection of those who care, that support is precisely what you need. Naturally we mustn't overwhelm you in any way which might undermine your leadership status, but if there is a way we can lift you out of the interminable anxiety which must be gnawing away at you day and night, then let us uncover what that remedy might be, shall we?"

"If only it were that simple, Lionel. You see, it's bad enough that I have made some very poor decisions in my life which have had a material impact on me, my family and our overall financial well-being, but it's another level of stupidity altogether when I recognise that my son's dreadful position can be directly traced all the way back to those same blinkered views I carried around with me for far too long. How on earth can I recover twenty or thirty years of naivety, I ask you?"

"You can't, and it's no good pretending otherwise. I really can't comment on the granular detail of your past life and any hazardous relationships you had to negotiate when you were obviously younger and less experienced than you are now, but there must surely be a positive way forward that can help build something from here."

"You know Lionel, in all honesty I think I'm close to throwing in the towel." The Wing Commander leaned forward, a tinge of frustration, or even anger flickering across his grey eyes. "Oh, do please forgive me," she continued, " I wasn't suggesting anything as drastic as that which overtook your poor daughter, heaven forbid, but I've been battered down and got myself up again and back into the fight so many times I just don't know if I can do it again. If the court case goes against my boy I think shall simply implode." She fished out a tissue form her handbag and blew her nose gently.

"Do please calm yourself my dear," he urged. "Surely the legal system will prevail. I am by no means close enough to the detail of the case to be able to make an assessment of my own, but I trust your judgement implicitly."

"But why would you? Look at the mess I've made of things for so, so long."

"Ah, but in this instant, my dear, it's about honesty and sincerity. When you say to me, with evident conviction, that it is simply inconceivable that your boy could have and would have done this terrible thing, well...simply put, I believe you. It's now for the jury to see that same sincerity. Why would they not?"

"Because the jury doesn't know me or my son as you know me. They cannot possibly gain that reassurance over the relatively short course of a trial."

"I do concede your point, Janice," he said dejectedly, "but does the evidence not present any significant doubts or questions?"

"Only one of any note, and that's the very public nature in which the accused, my son, was seen to make use of a company van with which to transport himself to the crime scene – why would he do that? It makes no sense that he would deliberately publicise his movements, even to the extent of appearing on the firm's security cameras..."

"Devices he would have known about and easily have been able to avoid had he wanted to," the Wing Commander concluded.

"Precisely, Lionel, and yet in the absence of any other tangible explanation, my son has been committed to trial."

"Well my dear, it all looks very flimsy indeed. I can't help but anticipate an acquittal from what you have just told me."

"Do you really think so?"

"I do…," and then he faltered, "but I should also counsel you that my own nerves are a little tetchy these days, and I'm beginning to question some of my own judgements too."

"And that's a feeling I know only too well, I must say."

"Yes…hardly encouraging at my age. One automatically assumes that one is losing another faculty…going gaa-gaa for want of a better description."

"And I suppose unnecessary confrontations with fellow residents do not exactly help to ease those niggling doubts, eh Lionel?"

"Ah, and I'm supposed to be the perceptive one. Do I detect an understanding of my recent spat with good old Mrs Allthorpe?"

"I'm afraid you do, Lionel. It sounded a little ugly and rather unfair. How do you feel about it now?"

"More forgiving I should say. As I mentioned earlier, there is a wearisome tension about the place and we are not ourselves. In defence of Genny Allthorpe, when my wretched grandson rolled up the other day he did look a sight, and not a pleasant one either. He was wearing those hideous, washed-out jeans with the rips and tears blatantly obvious for all to see."

"That's fashion for you," Janice Swinton added.

"But clearly not haute coutour by any standards," and she giggled mischievously at his old-fashioned values. "It was the boots and the dangling chains," he continued, "and we shouldn't overlook the black nail varnish and that ridiculous hair-cut of his. If I thought for one second that if he's spending my meagre but regular stipend on that sort of frivolous nonsense I think I'd stop the tap forthwith."

"But of course he is, Lionel. I suppose he's still unemployed, still drawing benefits?" she asked, more serious again.

"Oh, most certainly, and that galls me beyond belief. Was it really all worth fighting for? I often think not, and Genny Allthorpe clearly agrees even though she was way beyond the line with her forceful character assassination."

"So what did she say?"

"Janice, I believe it was more about what he said, or at least tried to say out there in the open lounge. By God he could hardly speak. He was a high as a kite and initially very emotional. He burbled on about all manner of meaningless drivel. Half the time I simply couldn't understand him...I mean... I just couldn't make out the words. But he seemed very agitated – just couldn't sit still for a single moment – and I realised that his miserable performance was being taken in by a host of irritated onlookers, of which Mrs Allthorpe was just one."

"And what was he trying to say, oh...and what's the lad's name again, do remind me Lionel please?"

"Seth!" the Wing Commander announced with a visible cringe and a gentle shake of the head.

"Seth?" she queried, nonplussed.

"Indeed, Seth after his father I believe, but there was an ineffectual drifter if ever there was one. He ran out on our girl within the lad's first year. The boy never really had a father figure about the place and I often wonder if that's what scuppered his chances from the outset."

"And he never came back, the father?"

"Correct, he disappeared from the face of the planet as far as our Maisie was concerned." The old man looked tired and rueful all of a sudden as he reflected on those darker days. "Back to the lounge entertainment however," he started up again, "the boy was almost delirious, so much so that I really did wonder how on earth he'd made it over here on the bus. At one stage he talked about revenge, and I imagined that he was asking me to do something or perhaps that he should be doing something for me. Then, a little later when my attention had drifted into damage limitation mode with our audience, he mumbled and cackled about avenging my daughter. I simply couldn't fathom it out. I took it as a challenge, as if in some way he blamed me for his mother's suicide and expected me to do something unimaginable to put things right. Really Janice, I could not decipher his code, but I was mollified that he seemed to relax a little during his time here – the effect of his latest fix wearing off I assumed – and I was simply relieved to see him take his leave.

"But if you think you have your own errors of judgement to contend with Janice, I promise you that Maisie's many mistakes would give yours a very good run for their money."

"Don't tell me, the wrong sort of men – you have mentioned her weakness to me before, Lionel."

"Yes I do recall, but the hurtful memories don't go away, do they? She had so many different chaps in her life at that time. The boy must have wondered what his poor mother was up to. Unfortunately her search for security, and of course for some love and affection beyond that from her parents, only made her appear vulnerable and weak. In truth that's exactly what she was. So many new boyfriends, and with each one new hope for a fresh start and a better life, but it simply wasn't meant to be."

"Were there no encouraging glimmers?" she prodded, gently.

"Oh there was one chap who hung around for a few years. What was his name? Do you know Janice, I keep having these senior moments when I just can't pull a name out the hat and apply to the right face," he huffed in exasperation. "I don't think I ever knew his surname, but his Christian name is right here on the tip of my tongue…but damn and blast, can I get it…it'll come, I'm sure. In any event he seemed good for her. Maisie worshipped the man, and Seth idolised him. They would spend weekends down at the beach or on the river bank building huge sand castles inside which they could stand as the tide came in. Seth got so excited as the gentle waves slopped over the parapet and they had to run for drier ground. I have some fond memories of the lad enjoying those carefree days. They'd play cricket on the sands too, take picnics, you can imagine the sort of thing. But in the passage of time her man became a little disinterested at first and then steadily more detached. His work was a bit patchy, and that brought with it some obvious benefits, but also some real pressures. I think he moved jobs a few times in a short period. At once he had loads of free time to give to Maisie and especially to Seth, but just as quickly he'd be working late or rarely at home. Maisie put on a lot of weight then – comfort-eating my dear old girl said at the time – but to us it looked as if her man had little interest in the larger, softer, more cuddly version of my poor daughter."

"Don't tell me," she interjected with a dead-pan expression, "another one who just went out one day and didn't come back."

"Your powers of perception again, my dear...yes, he just took off and that was that." He looked melancholy at the finality of his own statement, but Janice knew that his mind had already pitched forward in time to the tragedy that befell them all only a few years later. "Little Seth was simply swept away by the emptiness of it all. At such a tender age he had no means to comprehend such a colossal shift in his domestic landscape. And Maisie...well, as you know..." and a tear gathered in the corner of one eye, "she took all those tablets and sloshed them down with half a bottle of vodka and I blame him for her demise as much as if he'd administered the poison himself."

She too dabbed a tear away with her tissue and they sat there drained of so much emotion. Had she not experienced men of that calibre herself she may have considered the tale all too fanciful, but real-life had long since breached any idyllic outlook she may have harboured.

"Forgive me my dear, please," he implored her softly. "My purpose was to offer a shoulder to cry on or, more constructively, to lean on in your hour of need, and yet here we are weeping over our broken hearts instead of finding the positives to latch on to."

"Don't worry Lionel, no, really...just talking about these things always helps, as I think you said to me some weeks ago when we sat in the leather chairs in the corridor."

"How right you are."

"So, you're right. What can we do next? As for your grandson, Seth, it would appear logical to try to link him through to our social services and to begin the process of tackling his addictions. He's had a very, very tough upbringing it would appear, and while we can't express surprise at some of the outcomes now evident, we should be able to take concerted action to begin the process of winning him back from the brink of self-destruction."

The Wing Commander shuddered at the prospect of a double suicide, a frightful result he had simply not considered before that very moment. With a sudden sense of urgency he acknowledged the threat she had envisioned and swore a commitment to himself, and to the lad, to get some important wheels in motion.

A knock at the door interrupted their newly ambitious flow. It was Janice's secretary with a pile of opened mail for her to digest. She also mentioned to Janice that she'd had a call earlier from a Detective Sergeant Amy Addison of the Suffolk Constabulary, and could she call her back when free. She slipped a post-it note onto the desk with a hastily scribbled but clearly visible phone number. A little flutter raced through her heart at the mere mentioned of the prosecuting force that actively pursued her son's conviction. She couldn't decide whether or not the innocent mention of the police had also tugged an emotional string back to David Lehrer, but she chose to suppress the idea immediately.

As her colleague left and closed the door behind her, Janice Swinton suddenly realised that she had been sipping away at her coffee all the while and rudely overlooking the refreshment needs of her guest. Her offer was politely declined however, the Wing Commander now pushing himself up on his canes and beginning to make his own exit. He thought he had kept her too long already, and he now knew she had more pressing things to attend to in the immediate sense. However, he also appeared keen to get to grips with the new challenge and as he ambled towards the door he wanted to keep their early momentum going.

"Janice, you must have all the necessary official connections at your disposal to enable us to coordinate the appropriate services in the right way."

"Ordinarily that would be true, Lionel, but only for this region. You mentioned that Seth travels over to see you by bus or coach, isn't that the case?"

"Yes."

"From where... how far afield is he, or is he actually quite local to us here in Bedford?"

"No, no. He's actually from your neck of the woods. He lives in a tatty little cottage down Ermiston way, near Rendlesham Forest...you know, not far from Shottisham"

Janice Swinton looked at once intrigued. "I had no idea Wing Commander. How long has he been out there?"

"All his life! That little cottage was once my daughter's. I bought it for her. She never had to make mortgage payments or anything like that. In fact, on reflection," he offered as he edged closer to the door, "I suspect it was one of the worst things I ever did for her."

"You mean it made her too comfortable?"

"Well, yes, but more significantly it attracted the wrong sort of hangers-on. You can imagine I'm sure...the lazier types who saw a free billet as something just too good to be true. Rightly or wrongly that's how I played it, and that's where the lad grew up and has always lived. So once again you see, my dear girl, you are not the only one who has made difficult and potentially catastrophic decisions born purely out of good will and the wish to offer a helping hand out there in the modern jungle of life."

She shook her head empathising with his torment, but added, "In which case I need to reach across to the Suffolk service people and hopefully to get some cogs engaged in the right sequence. I'll need to offer you and me together as endorsing contacts here, and of course I'll need contact details for him you understand?"

"Yes, yes, of course," he responded in gratitude. "I'll get those to you this afternoon," he insisted with an affirmative nod.

And then as he opened the door and turned to leave she threw out one last, parting enquiry. "And did that dreadful chap's name come back to you in the end?"

"Yes...er, I had it just as your post was delivered...er, yes, it was Lee. The fellow's name was Lee, Lee something or other, and I hope never to clap eyes on him ever again."

As he strutted out into the corridor he failed to see the look of alarm etched into her features, as she reached for the phone.

23 – June 2007

Saturday 2nd

Where the fuck is Michael? Haven't heard from him in weeks. He doesn't return my calls or respond to text messages. Hadn't really thought about it before now, but I have no other means of contact beyond that damned mobile phone. I can't even find him listed anywhere in London. Anxious doesn't cover it. I miss him. I need more supplies too, my needles are running low. I'm out of ecstasy and benzoes. Even the smokes are down. I still have viagra – doh, as if he needs that!

Shit, where the hell is he? What's more, what was he doing back there? And my head is banging like a huge fucking drum. My hands are shaking. I can't think straight for more than a minute at a time. I'm sweating like a pig and my heart's racing like the clappers.

Did I go to see the old dog yesterday? Fuck, I can't remember. Christ I'm a mess. Something's gotta give soon.

24 – pennies from heaven?

7th June, 2007

Stevens & Stevens
Solicitors at Law
12, Hams Court
Orwell Fields
Ipswich
IP2 7XZ
Tel : 01473 999888
Fax : 01473 999887
Email : info@stevens.stevens.com

FAO Mr Seth Chinner, Rose Cottage, Ermiston, Rendlesham, Suffolk, IP27 2FQ

Ref : Last Will & Testament of the late Mr Lee Phillipson, formerly of Briar Garth, Compton-by-Westonfield, Woodbridge, Suffolk, IP21 5TJ

Dear Mr. Chinner,

As Executors acting for and on behalf of the estate of Mr Lee Phillipson, recently deceased, it is our duty to advise you that you have been named as a beneficiary of the above mentioned Will. The Crown Coroner has issued an Interim Certificate of death, pending a Grant of Probate, however, as our client's death is currently the subject of a police investigation it is possible, and indeed expected, that the distribution of his estate will be delayed until after that investigation has been completed.
Nevertheless, in the execution of our duties as Executors we are arranging a series of private readings of the Will so as to ensure that all beneficiaries are suitably informed about the deceased's estate and how it is to be managed and divided. It is important that you, as a beneficiary, understand the implications of any anticipated inheritance and any formal responsibilities adhering to it.
We would like to invite you to meet with our officers at the above address in Ipswich at 10.30am Thursday next, 14th June 2007, so that we may outline your position for you and advise you of how to proceed once the estate is released from the constraints of the said investigation.
We respectfully request that you telephone us to confirm your attendance at the specified time and date, and we look forward to meeting you then.

Yours faithfully,

For and on behalf of Stevens & Stevens

Stevens & Stevens, Solicitors at law. Regulated by The Law Society of England & Wales

25 – moral equations

He'd done his level best to smarten himself up, but he still felt distinctly conspicuous as he walked through the centre of Ipswich heading for the business hub and Orwell Fields. It was hardly a part of town he knew or even recognised. Not normally for him the well-worn sandstone slabs of the old town or the neat brick paving of the pedestrian retail zone. The old docks and the redbrick remnants of yesteryear were his preferred territories, and not normally in daylight hours either. He'd chosen to shave his head completely, rather than sporting the wild turquoise locks to just one side. Then he'd dyed the remaining stubble to a close approximation of his own natural brown, and rummaged through some old togs to find his once trendy flat cap. He removed his piercings, but retained the stud in his tongue. That had just been too awkward and he'd lost patience with it. The dark nail varnish came off quite easily and he found an old pair of casual shoes as a substitute for his shin-high Doc Martens, but his jeans proved a little more problematic. In the end he'd dragged a pair of old army green cargo pants from a box on the top of a wardrobe and he'd actually pressed them. He hadn't been able to remember the last time he used the iron. Finally a casual bomber jacket completed the set and he'd looked at himself in the glass with barely a flicker of recognition. Before he left he snorted a single line of cocaine straight off the kitchen bench and left the cottage with a noisy crash of the closing front door.

When he'd first read the letter he'd quickly decided that it was just some sort of game: some sort of sick joke perpetrated by one of his fellow users. But then he'd racked his dope-befuddled brain in a desperate attempt to remember who could have linked him to a dead man. A quick check online soon established the validity of the legal firm and its address in town, and then he'd nipped along the road to the centre of the village to place the enquiring call from the old phone box that still stood sentry there. To his complete surprise they had been expecting the call just as they'd said in the letter, so he confirmed the appointed meeting time and scurried back home to see how he might change his image in time for the trip into Ipswich the following week.

Turning a corner into a spacious square, with floral gardens at its heart confined by wrought iron railings and impressive Edwardian symmetry in all directions, he spotted the name plate high on the opposite wall. Hams Court: he just had to locate number twelve. As he walked purposefully along the nearside pavement he counted the numbers on the heavy wooden office doors, every one beautifully painted and adorned with shining brass handles and gleaming nameplates adjacent. His sense of apprehension rose steadily. This was unfamiliar territory indeed, but he held his nerve. If that bastard from the past, long gone but still as guilty as sin in his own mind, had unexpectedly decided to rebalance the scales of morality then who was he, Seth Chinner, to turn down a few grand. It would never make amends. It would never change his view. More importantly, it would never assuage the death of his mother, driven to suicide when that vile, selfish monster had so cruelly abandoned her. But if there was some money to come his way now, so be it. That would take the edge of some of the harsher realities of his own miserable existence, at least for a while.

He crossed the street to cut off the corner of the square. He reckoned that number twelve would be across the diagonal in the opposite corner. Cutting through the gardens he approached the exit gate on the far side of the square. He was just satisfying himself that the bright red door was indeed the target of his current quest, when that same door opened and an older couple descended the steps not thirty metres from him on the other side of the road. The middle-aged woman looked irate and voluble. She turned to the elderly man at her side and as she helped him down the stone steps she berated him constantly with her free arm waving in agitated fashion as if to press home a series of important points in her argument. When they reached the level pavement, the man took the woman by both hands and seemed to remonstrate with her in a calming, controlling manner. She listened intently at first, but then she wrested herself free of his grip and gesticulated again. Seth, observing from behind a wide dwarf willow, could hear the rise and fall of intonation and cadence as their obviously heated discussion played out, but he simply couldn't make out what they were saying. Instinct prevented him from getting closer. She looked familiar, in a vapid sense of someone seen before but not located in memory. But then he spotted the facial similarities and he knew he was watching father and daughter not in conflict necessarily, but in confusion, seeking answers perhaps, and then he knew who they were.

He let them pass by, their tensions slowly subsiding as they walked off down one side of the square. Then he mounted the same steps and pushed into the entrance hall of Stevens & Stevens, solicitors at law. The hallway ran off into the gloom of heavily panelled walls and dark, well-worn carpets with a heavy old staircase reaching up to the next floor and out of sight. He felt his apprehension pressing in on him again. He anticipated an elderly greying legal chap lecturing him about the complexities of legal documents while looking down his nose and beyond his pinching spectacles to the uncomfortable youth before him. He quickly discovered the reception area, and a pleasant young girl welcomed him and took him immediately into the bowels of the building where she left him in a similarly traditional oak-clad meeting room. There she asked him to wait for Miss Watts and she closed the door gently as she left. The introduction of a Miss Watts suggested a slightly different prospect, but still he suspected a degree of condescension and professional snobbery, and he fought hard to quell the rising belief that he just shouldn't have come.

How relieved he was then, and frankly quite overawed in a very different capacity, when a stunning young woman appeared in the frame of the door and stepped forward to warmly shake his hand. She was a ravishing beauty of that tantalising professional kind: fabulously but discreetly turned out in a very efficient and yet thoroughly glamorous trouser-suit, with fetching heels, silk blouse and a modicum of bare cleavage on show. Her auburn hair hung long and free, and she'd twisted the tresses into a loose, unkempt turn thrown down her left side. On her right he could see a sparkling diamond stud punctuating a soft delicate lobe, and her soulful brown eyes were captured exquisitely by the super-modern, large red frames of her spectacles. Her hand was warm and comforting, and he might easily have lost his bearings once those beguiling dark pools locked onto his, but she guided him to a seat on one side of a low coffee table and urged him to make himself comfortable. As he lowered himself and shuffled into the back of the chair she turned away, stretching up to the side of the window frame in order to ease open the louvered blind for a little more external light. He found himself treated to a most exciting glimpse of her shapely bottom and thighs as she stretched for the draw cord and lifted her rearward leg for balance, pointing a splendid four inch heel in his direction momentarily. Then, just as quickly, she turned to face him, smiled the purest white grin he had ever encountered, and settled down at the other side of the table. In the enhanced natural illumination of the room he marvelled at her subtle blusher, the matching red lip gloss and pristine red nails all brought together by those bold glasses and he just sighed in admiration at the image before him.

How it must be, sharing a life with someone like this, he wondered silently. Undoubtedly some lucky guy, or maybe even some lucky girl, would already be swept up and immersed in the great richness of life itself with a radiant beauty such as this to share every experience. He was instantly envious, but simultaneously glad for them, whoever they were. However captivating she most certainly was, he knew she was simply not for him. His taste in partners trawled different channels, and he smiled gently at that recognition within.

She returned his smile with her own perfect glinting symmetry, and then she opened her file on the table and picked up a sheaf of papers.

"Mr Chinner... may I call you Seth?"

"Er, yes, yes of course," he stammered.

"All right then. Seth, you are here today to learn about your anticipated inheritance from the estate of our recently deceased client Mr Lee Phillipson. Do you understand?"

"Yes...yes, I do."

"As Executors of the late Mr Phillipson's estate we would like to point out that there are certain legal requirements which must be satisfied in circumstances such as these. In the letter of invitation we sent out to you last week we made reference to a police investigation surrounding our client's untimely death." Seth Chinner stiffened in his chair and hoped that his anxiety wasn't too transparent. She carried on. "The primary intrusion of such an investigation is simply to impart some form of delay to our administration, but although the overall timing of the process is difficult to forecast we can, even so, advise our anticipated beneficiaries of the likely outcome of the division of the relevant Will."

Seth nodded meekly.

"Any last Will and Testament is ultimately a public document and one which can be freely viewed through the right channels. Here at Stevens and Stevens we prefer to manage our clients' affairs in, shall we say, something of a more hands-on fashion. That's why you and all of the other beneficiaries will be taken carefully through Mr Phillipson's instructions to ensure that you understand the full implications of your subsequent position. Do you understand?" she asked again.

"Yes, I think so. Are you saying that you will take me through the entire Will and all of its...er, division...is that the right word?"

"Yes, and all of its provisions, might be a better way of putting it," she suggested.

"Not just my own provisions then, whatever they may be?"

"That's correct – the entire picture – although I should tell you that in this case the Will is remarkably simple and there are few beneficiaries, as you are about to find out."

Seth sniffed and shrugged his shoulders. He smiled at her again. He knew it – that waster would have barely two shekels to rub together. That's why the Will was so simple. Coming here was about to prove a complete waste of time.

"Tell me Seth, please, what was your relationship to our late client?" He froze. He looked right past her as if studying the picture on the wall.

"Er, he was my mother's partner many years ago, when I was a child," he responded as casually as he could manage.

"Your step-father perhaps?"

"Of sorts, but they never married."

"I see," she mused, looking down at her notes.

"And you enjoyed a very close relationship with him apparently?" Seth was completely thrown by her overtly positive report.

"Well...er, I guess so...yes, in those days, yes, but I really can't remember too much about it. Like I said, I was just a kid back then."

"Rest assured, Seth, Mr Phillipson left ample justification in his legal letters attached to his Will that he specifically wanted you to benefit, in the event of his death, because of the...and I'm reading his own notes here...many happy hours I spent with the lad down on the beach and on the river bank. Those days were a blessed release from the pressures of real-life and I will always be grateful to him for that."

Seth just looked at her impassively. Maybe so, he thought, but it didn't stop you from ditching us and it didn't save my mother, you bastard.

She looked quizzically at him. He said, "Shall we get on with it then?"

"Yes, absolutely, let's take a look." She sat back in her chair and studied her notes again. "First of all, allow me to simplify the details by saying that there are only two specific elements to consider. Mr Phillipson left no property and no other capital assets save for one investment fund left in trust with ourselves, Stevens and Stevens, as the trustees. He left no life assurance, no pension funds, and indeed he wasn't drawing any pension income. He was only fifty three years of age after all. He had no works of art or anything of that kind. So, the simplest provision is born by the investment fund which was initiated five years ago in the year two thousand and two. At or around that time he received a cash lump sum payment of around seventy five thousand pounds from a source or sources unknown. He invested it in the stock market via a mixed portfolio of investment funds. You may like to know, if you don't already," she added with a tinge of embarrassment, "that the markets have had a very good run during the last five years and Mr Phillipson seems to have chosen his funds extremely well. The overall portfolio is now worth about one hundred and ten thousand pounds."

Seth nodded his head appreciatively.

"This capital is to be divided equally between four people only."

He made a quick mental calculation – just less than thirty grand!

"It is worth noting that stock prices do rise and fall on a regular, daily basis, and the value of those assets will change day-to-day until a sale price is eventually fixed. At that point, those inheriting the divided assets will be your good self, Mr Phillipson senior – that's the deceased's elderly father, Miss Lynsey Bastion – his bereaved partner, and his only son, Mr Daniel Crighton."

Seth Chinner tried to remember any mention of a son way back in the distant past, but he couldn't make that connection, and he reminded himself that he had been just a boy at the time. No matter, he concluded, thirty grand is thirty grand. He grinned at his gorgeous legal adviser.

"As for the other specific item under consideration, it has no material impact on you, Seth. Like I said, the Will is soon to be a matter of public record, so you may choose to take away with you an understanding of that additional point if you wish?"

"Yes, why not? It'll save me looking it up online later I suppose."

"Very well then. Mr Phillipson's death is recognised as a chargeable event in law, that is to say a chargeable event with specific reference to a legal agreement which he established with his former wife, Mrs Janice Swinton, whereby a charge was placed upon her family home at the regrettable breakdown of their marriage and subsequent divorce. The effect of this charge is to enforce the sale of the said property in order to release eighteen percent of the proceeds of that sale into his estate for the benefit, ultimately, of his only son, Mr Daniel Crighton."

"Wow!" was all he could say. "I don't know much about this sort of thing, but that sounds pretty awful for her and her family, I'd say."

"Perhaps so, Seth, but I really can't comment further on those particular details.

Otherwise, Seth, and unless you have any questions, I think we're done here," she concluded with an air of finality.

He shook her hand as she ushered him through reception and back towards the stone steps and the square beyond. She looked just perfect. She could have been a model, he thought, in fact a model for just about anything a woman would choose to wear, and then he wondered how well legal professionals are paid as compared with successful models. Who cares, he thought. I've got nearly thirty thousand pounds coming my way – hey hey!

He drifted off through the gardens, but then spotted a cosy looking coffee shop half-way down the opposite reach. As he was soon to be rich, he told himself that it was about time he stopped avoiding expensive coffee shops. He headed for it and took a seat in the window. He ordered a large creamy cappuccino and began thumbing through the daily paper which lay folded in the middle of the table. He hoped a double-shot's worth of caffeine would help boost his waning livener from earlier in the day.

"Good morning, Suffolk Constabulary, how can I help?"

"Hello, could you put me through to Detective Sergeant Amy Addison, please?"

"Certainly Madame, may I say who's calling?"

"Yes, of course, my name is Janice Swinton. I'm returning her earlier call."

"Very well, please hold."

The silence, save for the odd bit of static on the line, seemed to stretch out before her. She guessed that they were flat out with all sorts of things on the go, but she hoped to catch the detective before the call of duty pulled her back out onto the street.

"I'm sorry Ms Swinton. I just can't reach her, and it's beginning to look like she's back on the road. Can I page her and get her to call you? She already has you're number, is that right?"

"Oh…no…er, I mean, yes, she does have my number, but no, I'd rather not wait for the pager. Is there anyone else there I can talk to?"

"Let me see, please hold."

Janice Swinton's frustration increased with every second as she waited for the connection.

"I'm afraid I can only ask you to go through to the desk sergeant to leave a message, or perhaps you'd like to speak to the head of the team, that's Detective Chief Inspector Lehrer. Shall I connect you?"

She couldn't speak. She couldn't speak to him, surely not him, not now, but it was so important. Then the receptionist unwittingly offered an escape.

"Is it to do with something specific, perhaps a particular case, or some feedback or information, something of that sort?"

"Yes, yes it is, that's it exactly," she sighed in relief.

"Well perhaps you have the name of your case officer to hand and I could connect you there?"

"Er, no, I mean...I'm sure there is a case officer, but I just don't know the name, you see."
"All right, let's try for DCI Lehrer then."
"Oh..."
"No? Not that route?"
"Er, well...oh, okay then, yes, try him...and thank you."
"Please hold, trying his direct line now."
Her heart rate quickened to match her anxiety. She heard a few clicks on the line and then the double two-tone ring at the other end sounded loudly in her ear. She held her breath, looked up at the wall calendar, and then back at her desk...and then she slammed the receiver back into its cradle and leaned forward to rest her forehead flat on the surface in front of her.

Seth Chinner had enjoyed the cappuccino so much that he'd opted for another, and he slid slowly down in his chair as he relaxed into the comforting appreciation that he would soon be in receipt of the largest sum of money he'd ever seen. He moved on from the daily rags to a couple of old magazines, one of which exhibited flamboyant glossy pictures of refurbished homes, kitchens and bathrooms the like of which he had never seen before. He immediately thought of what he might do – with a bit of capital, naturally – to his own dilapidated hovel. For a few brief seconds his imagination began to run riot through his filthy, neglected, crumbling old cottage until he spied some of the price tags subtly applied in feint, small print in the bottom corner of each photograph. He straightened up in his chair in order to shed more light onto the pages of the magazine, but as he did so he noticed a smartly dressed figure descending the steps in the distant corner of the square – those same steps beneath that same bright red door with which he had become so recently acquainted. It was fully eighty to ninety metres away, but he dropped the magazine onto the table and peered across the park at that figure.

The subject of Seth's strained scrutiny walked across the street and made as if to enter the park, but then veered right and proceeded along the pavement hidden from view by the wrought iron railings. He reached the corner, now almost out of sight for Seth who pressed his face to the window to achieve the oblique angle necessary to maintain surveillance, and then he turned towards the coffee shop and ambled casually towards it. Crossing the street again to the same side as the café he moved beyond Seth Chinner's transfixed gaze, but the observer knew that his target was approaching. Just a minute later Seth leaned back in his chair to avoid detection as he stared in astonishment at a young man he knew only too well. As if alerted by some natural reflex the man turned quickly to look into the window of the café. Seth froze at the moment of detection, or so he assumed, but realised in the same instant that his lover, Michael, had simply not recognised him.

So many questions tumbled through Seth's panic-stricken consciousness. It took him some time to remember that his own appearance had been deliberately changed to an extent which could easily supress normal recognition. Beyond that consideration however, he was confused, distressed and furious all at the same time. He hadn't been able to reach him for several weeks and yet he'd turned up at the wretch's funeral and here he was again, striding out from the solicitor's office without a care in the world when the world expected him to be at work in London. Seth looked out of the window and followed the moving figure as it edged slowly out of sight. His clenched jaw and balled fists declared his anger. The tears in his eyes betrayed his fractured emotions. It hit him like a wrecking ball – maybe Michael wasn't Michael at all!

He wiped his eyes with his coffee serviette, threw some coins down onto the table and rushed out of the door onto the street. He could still see him down at the far end of the square and he took off in pursuit.

"What the fuck is going on," he yelled, as he clamped a hand on Michael's shoulder and turned him round with a forceful yank.

Michael looked at once afraid and guarded, the fight or flight impulse kicking in immediately. He cowered momentarily from his assailant, accosted as he had been from behind, and his lack of immediate recognition compounded his disquiet. But then a quirky, confused smile flashed across his face as he realised who it was.

"Seth, love, what is this? What's going on?"

"Oh, no you don't, you snake, no you don't…," Seth screamed. "What's going on is for me to question and you to bloody well answer, and smartish too, if you know what's good for you."

"Woah…hold on a minute Seth," Michael hissed under his breath. "Just keep your voice down," he insisted while surreptitiously looking left and right. "We're on the street here, the open street, in public for God's sake. What the hell got into you?"

"Fuck you! You've led me on and stitched me up. You haven't answered my messages or returned any of my calls. You turn up at that fucker's funeral completely out of the blue, and now you're here, large as life, strutting your stuff in this poxy little country corner when you're supposed to be in London. What got into *me*…? You've got some nerve."

"No, no love," Michael soothed, as he stepped closer and placed an affectionate palm on the side of the Seth's face. He looked reassuringly into his partner's eyes and slowly shook his head in quiet dismay. "You've got it all wrong honey, all wrong."

"Yeah, right, of course I have," Seth seethed, less volatile now but raging still inside. "We had a plan, and at no point did we ever discuss you disappearing off the map. Shit, I haven't been able to reach you, I'm short of supplies, and you know how much I rely on you in every way."

"Yes Seth, but you went off piste too, didn't you? That wasn't part of the plan either, was it?"

"Eh? What the hell are you talking about," he barked, anger rising again.

"Your little detour via the sodding boatyard – what the fuck was that all about? You must have been off your head when you dreamed that one up. I told you not to mess around with that stuff. I give you your programmes, remember?"

"Yeah, but I've been home alone, chewing my finger nails to the quick, running out of poppers and running out of needles," Seth complained.

"So chase the dragon, you don't have to get smacked-up every time you want to relax."

"Shit man, it's not the same, and I've been having these God-awful headaches…"

"Hey stop – you haven't been on those china whites too, have you?"

"Well, yeah...I mean...sometimes."

"Jesus Christ...I told you to be careful with those things. What about the special K? Just tell me, please, that you haven't been mixing all this junk."

"Yeah, I guess...well, just a bit...but fuck it, Michael, you just haven't been here to keep me straight."

"I know, I know...look, Seth, I'm sorry, but I'm trying to cover our tracks here and needs must...you know what I'm saying? Anyway," he smiled conspiratorially, "I'm not sure I want to keep you straight," and he leaned forward and lightly brushed his lips to Seth's cheek.

"Okay, okay," Seth sighed with a coy grin. "But just tell me what the hell is going on. I am right out of it. I don't know what's happening. You have to tell me what's up."

"Look, love, don't fret. Nothing's up. If I'm honest, I just can't believe you fingered that lad, his step-son, for the whole job. Like I said, that wasn't in the agreed plan and it has thrown up some tricky little challenges, but I think I'm just about there. I think we're back in line, but hey, this is hardly the place to go through all of this," and again he looked casually about to indicate the risks at large. "Let's get back to my car and head out to your place. I was going to surprise you later. I can stay over tonight. We can go through it all together and once you're up to speed – excuse the pun, gorgeous – then we can enjoy ourselves. How does that sound?"

Seth exhaled his relief, long and slow. He smiled at his lover, touched a gentle fist to his chest and said simply, "Wonderful. It sounds absolutely wonderful. Let's go."

26 – a stitch in time...

The following morning was greeted bright and early at police HQ in Ipswich. Operation Cove had cracked another tier of the clandestine gangs working in and around Felixstowe container port, and the primary incident room was noisy with the urgency of successful coppers getting close to some significant collars. Lehrer's main office was also buzzing with frenetic activity. Important data was trickling down screens at every desk, and the heated exchanges across the office competed, one with another, for audible air time as officers scrambled to convert reaction into workable process.

DS Symes, from the drug squad, was sitting on the edge of Barnes's desk debriefing Barnes, McLellan and Lehrer together about the pace of events the previous evening out there on the big ships. It was time to mobilise an entire series of house arrests all over East Anglia and deep into the neighbouring metropolis. Symes was proposing a particular game plan for which he would need additional help and resource.

Adi Hughes was sitting quietly at his desk as the maelstrom swirled around him. He was studying a written report from one of Symes' colleagues which declared a posting time on their system of 4.55am that same morning. Hughes rubbed his tired eyes with his fists. He'd been at it all night and he wondered why the guy just hadn't reported in directly. He reminded himself that there were protocols to follow, and if he'd been out on the street during the night he would have missed the bloke anyway, so the protocols clearly worked.

Sensitive as he was to Lehrer's incertitude about the impending Josh Swinton trial, Hughes knew he had to support his boss on that done deal, as some of his colleagues openly referred to it, and be seen to be supporting him in the public environment of the team office. As he scanned the document before him, he began to think that there was something very pertinent about it, something they might want to investigate further and with some urgency.

At that precise moment he heard Amy Addison shouting above the din in an attempt to attract Lehrer's attention on the other side of the office. Hughes was sure he heard the name Janice Swinton, but the central tenet of the message was lost in the surrounding bedlam. He saw Lehrer disengage from his huddle and walk round to Amy Addison's desk where they both fell into earnest conversation. He didn't know why, instinct perhaps, but Hughes just felt compelled to join them, and as he did so he distinctly heard Addison say, "It's a bit of an odd name, Seth, don't you think?" Then she looked questioningly at Hughes as he stood there mute with a piece of paper in his hand, and Lehrer turned to follow her gaze.

"Did you say Seth?" Hughes demanded.

"That's right," Addison responded. "What of it"?

"Well," he said, and then paused to look at the sheet, "there can't be many of those about, can there?"

"So?"

"Odd, don't you think, that you and I each have a reference to that same name at the same time, just out of nowhere. You must be discussing Symes' drug bust that night in the old van. You know, the night they nicked that bloke in the Barrington's Boatyard van."

"Er, Paul Bromsgrove?" said Lehrer enquiringly.

"That's the one," answered Hughes with a nod.

"Actually, no," said Addison flatly.

"No. No what? Hughes persisted.

"No, we're not talking about Bromsgrove at all."

"But...," and he held out the A4 sheet in one hand and waved at it with his free hand. "I've got Seth somebody or other mentioned here, and you just mentioned the same name as I trotted over here. As you were just saying to the boss here, it's a bit of an unusual name, isn't it?"

"Blimey," sighed Amy Addison in exasperation. "I was saying to the boss that I just took a call from a very agitated Janice Swinton. In fact she was sufficiently nervous to qualify for working here in this commotion – she'd fit in quite well, I'm sure – but the gist of it was that we should be looking for some guy named Seth."

"Did she explain why?"

"Oh sure, about four or five times over, and it transpires that there is some rather tenuous connection between the nursing home she manages in Bedford and this previously unknown, unidentified man we should be working double-quick to find."

"Why? What's he supposed to have for us?"

"Damned if I know just yet, but she is adamant that locating this bloke will unlock the case against her son – that's all!"

"Wow, that's some spiel. How does she make that out?"

Lehrer interrupted the two-way tennis and addressed Hughes directly. "She had some alarming information from one of her elderly residents the other day. Apparently it centres upon the man's grandson who is, shall we say, a bit wayward. He does a lot of drugs, hasn't worked for a while, and lives alone in some tiny cottage somewhere."

"So? How does that fit?"

"Apparently he was bragging to the old boy about deeds of revenge, but in a fairly random, drug-infused diatribe in the open lounge of the home. The exchange was witnessed by a number of the dear old wrinklies who objected to the lad's condition and behaviour, and a bit of a fracas erupted."

"But I'm not following this chief. Revenge? For what? Why is this relevant?"

"Because it appears that there was a tragic suicide in the family chain – the old man's daughter to be precise – and it's possible that her son, the grandson in question, has been harbouring some ill-will towards one of her mother's earlier live-in partners."

"A step-father you mean?"

"Figuratively yes, but the old man's daughter never married, so that status was never reinforced in law."

"Okay, but I'm still not getting the link here. What has this to do with an old folks bust up over tea and biccies?"

"Because in explaining the incident to the home's manager, Janice Swinton, the old chap made it clear that the lad's real father had run out on them not long after the boy had been born. In addition however, the old boy also revealed, quite inadvertently and innocently, that he believed his grandson's stand-in step-father for a few years to have been a guy called Lee."

"Go on," Hughes joked. "You're not serious?"

"Janice Swinton certainly wasn't joking, trust me Hughesy," Amy Addison confirmed with a tilt of the head.

"Hey listen...there may not be many Seth's around, but there sure as hell are enough Lees to sink a container ship. Did she have a surname?"

"Sadly not," replied Lehrer, "and we shouldn't overlook the fact that Seth is a biblical moniker so there may be many more of those than we might anticipate."

"The question really is," tested Amy Addison, "do we take her seriously, or do we assume that it's just a desperate attempt by a stricken mother to get her son out of a jam? Or do we get out there to the home in Bedford and interview the old boy?"

"D'you know, I think I can save you that trip," said Hughes with a cheeky grin.

His two colleagues looked at him with eyebrows raised in expectation of something jaw-dropping. He didn't disappoint.

"They found that girl...you know, the one with the Manchester connection. It seems that she does indeed spend quite a bit of time in our manor – it's where all her teenage friends are, and a lot of them are immersed in our local drug scene."

"How on earth did they track her down?"

"Quite quickly as it turned out, and...guess what...it was the same girl they picked up at the Barrington's van, that same night, the one they sent packing with a slapped wrist."

"Really?"

"Oh yeah, and what's more, when they re-interviewed her she had only one tiny little scrap of info' to relay, but it really did hit the jackpot." He paused as if to gather himself.

"Go on then, man, spit it out," Lehrer urged.

"She'd been a kid at the time, so her memory of details is sparse, but when her mother dragged her and her brother out of the family home – this is before heading north, by the way – they ended up shacked up with a step-father figure called Lee Phillipson." He paused this time for effect.

They both stared at him. He carried on.

"He ditched them after a few months by the sounds of it, but she always remembered his casual mention of a previous relationship he'd had with a girl who had a little boy called Seth. It was such a weird name, to quote her in the interview notes, but she was convinced it was Seth. She never met the lad, you understand. These were just two more ports of call in Phillipson's voyage of destruction."

"You realise what this means?" prompted Lehrer.

"Yes," quipped Addison, "that we need to find this Seth bloke now."

"Not just that," said Lehrer. "It also means that Paul Bromsgrove was nicked selling dope to his own grown-up daughter. And how could he possibly have known if he'd had no contact with her since her childhood?"

"But she must have known that her pusher was her real father, surely?"

"Possibly, but she either didn't recognise him, as he may have looked very different back then too, or she just chose not to reveal herself, to remain anonymous."

"Well let's hope that *Seth the Unknown* doesn't make the same choice when we catch up with him," said Addison. "Come on, let's find him. Janice Swinton has identified the grandfather's surname as Williams, but we can't rely on that. His daughter, the boy's mother, obviously carried the same name and she never married, but her own boy may have taken on his real father's surname and we don't have that. It's highly unlikely to be Phillipson, obviously, but we shouldn't rule it out. Janice Swinton has also pointed us loosely in the direction of a remote cottage somewhere close to Rendlesham Forest. That's our best lead I think."

"But shouldn't we pursue the Bromsgrove girl? She may have had enough motivation to despatch Phillipson, don't you think?" Hughes insisted.

"Put her second in the queue," Lehrer advised. "She may be sending us off down a cul-de-sac deliberately, but the combination of the two references to this Seth character is too strong to ignore right now." He clenched his fists and stuck both thumbs in the air. "That's good work Adders, you too Adi. We have to nail this one quickly. Let's get cracking."

27– fixed once and for all

When they bashed in the front door its entire frame crashed into the pokey lounge of the cottage. The place looked not just lived-in, but chaotic in its neglect. The two filthy old armchairs appeared to offer the only refuge from the scattered detritus of months and months of an everyday existence that had simply given up on order and hygiene. Empty beer cans, discarded gin bottles and fast-food packaging jostled for space among old newspapers and magazines, items of abandoned clothing and left over scraps of food on mouldy plates and dishes. Here and there were tin cans with lids yawning open, the contents having been consumed they had been designated as ash trays and the heavy pungency of weed and dope hung suspended in the confined space.

The galley kitchen, off to one side, showed scant improvement. The sink hadn't benefitted from running water for some time. The draining board area was stacked in grimy crockery with crusty cutlery piled in the sink itself. On the tiny window sill lay a stack of thin plastic syringes, and a disgusting wad of spent, blood-stained tissues had been collecting in the corner where the ledge met the wall. DS Addison looked away in dismay, but everywhere she looked she saw a similar vision of despair.

She was glad that they'd had the presence of mind, born out of good professional practice, to don their blue plastic over-shoes, but just as she was about to shout to Hughes to get his plastic mitts on, she heard him call out.

"Oh, no," and then louder, "hey, Adders...you better get in here."

She left the galley, pushed on through the lounge to the small bedroom behind, and then she saw him, as Hughes stepped aside to let her enter.

The room itself didn't look nearly so frantic as the others, but the young man lay prostrate on his back, entirely naked, arms splayed to either side, and his mouth wide open as if screaming his own silent agonies. Beside him on the double-bed lay a multi-coloured assortment of small pills together with another needle and syringe. The crooks of his arms were hideously disfigured with countless wounds and punctures, and a small Velcro blood pressure band lay abandoned on the floor by the bedside.

The detectives had witnessed similar scenes many times. Based on those experiences they assumed an overdose of tragic proportions, and they set about initiating the forensic examination process without delay. They also called Lehrer to update him on their discovery, and then they took their time to inspect the rest of the property without compromising the integrity of the scene overall.

The bathroom appeared squalid, and it stank. The over-bath shower curtain exhibited patchy mould around its lower extremities. The acrid stench it emitted almost had Addison retching, but the unattractive stains around the toilet bowl and on the cracked linoleum in front of the pedestal left her little room for manoeuvre. The bath had a heavy tide mark around the sides and a few adherent pubic hairs. A small pile of crumpled socks and soiled underwear lay thrown in one corner, and a plastic bottle of Rexon body wash had been deposited on top. When she eased open the wall-mounted cabinet she was surprised to see a very orderly array of clear glass bottles running along the top shelf. They looked almost clinically clean, as compared with the rest of premises. Many of them were empty, but some contained collections of small, brightly coloured tablets. On the lower shelf was a hospital style syringe dispenser which was virtually empty, and alongside it lay a pale grey clay pipe, some teaspoons, several plastic straws deliberately cut in half and a box of long matches normally used for fire-lighting. Addison closed the cupboard gingerly and then carefully tiptoed her way back to the lounge.

Hughes saw her retreating and he asked her about the state of the bathroom. Her description of the bathroom cabinet took him quite by surprise. They shared a quick once-over of the fire place, peppered with fag butts and various discards, and then they inched their way back to the front door where uniformed personnel had by then taped off the main entrance and the garden gate where it abutted the narrow country road outside. The ticker-tape message was clear: POLICE – DO NOT ENTER.

"What do you think, mate?" she asked Hughes.

"Who knows, Adders? It looks like he just OD'd, but we won't know anything until the pathology and forensic reports are done. We haven't got time to hang about just to get some hints, early doors so to speak, but with a place in a bloody awful state like that you might wonder just what sorts of interesting ideas the appliance of science may uncover."

"Well, the boffins will be here soon enough, and then I suppose the big fella will want us over to the container port."

"More than likely," he agreed.

"But we should get back to the Bromsgrove girl too. She still stands as a suspect. Potential motivation is obvious, and our lack of any detailed understanding of her movements and whereabouts supports the theory that she could have had ample opportunity."

"I don't disagree, Adders, but the gun, the boatyard van on CCTV and the hooded driver shown in that footage, well...she's just too slight of build to match what we have on screen."

"Yeah, you're right there, but this here," and she nodded towards the cottage behind him, "it's all just too vague for me. What do you think?"

Hughes hunched his shoulders and opened his hands as if to imply that he really couldn't tell and he didn't want to make a judgement. "Like I said, let's see what the scientists can prove. We shouldn't forget that we can ID this guy through his grandfather at the retirement home in Bedford. If he confirms that this is his grandson then much of his story to...oh, what's her name...er, Swinton, Janice Swinton...will look a lot more plausible. In that case the idea of perceived revenge coupled with the lad's earlier connections to Phillipson will be begging for a scientific match of some description to close the case down completely."

"I have to say, Adi, that I just wasn't sure of the vengeance motive until I understood the circumstances and the timing of his mother's suicide. I can see now why he would blame Phillipson if that slime-ball had just ditched them like he ditched so many. Christ that man was unreal. How could he live like that?"

"Amy, we don't really need to ask questions like that. We see too much of this stuff to be in any doubt that there is a great swathe of human scum out there, even among outwardly decent-looking well-educated people, who just don't think twice about turning somebody over if it's to their own benefit. Maybe these people think that life is so tough, that they're so vulnerable, that they just feel forced into these things to avoid slipping into the abyss of poverty and misery. I just don't know, I mean...what else could it be unless it's just vicious human nature? In pre-history we'd just go around clubbing folks to death if we couldn't get our own way. This kind of thing is the modern human equivalent maybe."

"With one crucial difference, Adi."

"And what's that?"

"Bone idle cavemen died of starvation. Lee Phillipson wasn't about to leave himself short, but that didn't mean he was ever going to work hard for it."

28 – a flimsy pretext

Three weeks later DCI David Lehrer sat in the Chief Superintendent's relatively palatial office suite, on the rather scenic executive floor of police HQ, overlooking the grey reaches of the river Orwell.

The Chief Superintendent was in optimistic mood, but he knew, from bitter recent experience, that enthusiasm so often masqueraded as naivety and carelessness was never lenient. A modest, unassuming professional, he knew only too well that it had been his mistake to push the Swinton case to an early conclusion – too early as it had turned out. He wanted his DCI to know that the pressure was off, at least to the extent that he, the Chief, was very definitely and very publicly carrying that particular can. At the same time however, he wanted Lehrer to understand that there could be no room for a third-time-lucky stab in the dark. They had to be absolutely certain that when they presented to the CPS the second time around, their case would indeed be bomb proof.

"I know you were wary last time, David, and I just railroaded you and your team. I'm sorry. The particulars of the case did seem conclusive, and yet there were random loose ends that appeared inconsequential to me and Adi Hughes, but not to you."

"It's sometimes the way, Chief. In fact we still face something of the same dilemma this time."

"But I thought we were all done," consternation defying control.

"Oh, we are, don't worry, but it's a question of conspiracy to murder or the combination of conspiracy and murder itself."

"Damn it David, what the hell's that supposed to mean?"

"Look on it as a wealth of opportunity, Guv," he smiled.

"Okay, look...we've got as long as this takes, all morning if necessary, so let's start at the start and hopefully the end will be obvious when we get there."

"Right you are then, Guv. At the risk of rubbing your nose in it, let's go back to the details that landed Josh Swinton in a small cell with a sweaty bunch of petty crooks for a few weeks."

"Has he been released yet?"

"Er...yesterday I believe."

"Good – that's something at least."

"Yes, and the girls in his life must be so relieved. I wonder if we'll ever be able to show our faces there again."

"Arguably more your concern than mine, DCI Lehrer," the Chief delivered with a stern tone and a glint in his eye.

Lehrer felt himself actually blush, so he carried on, head down and serious. "We knew that many of our clues led us directly to Josh Swinton from quite early on. The entire case is still counted in just a couple of months, after all. But the outwardly deliberate use of his works van, Barrington's Boatyard plastered all over it, did seem a little careless. Our killer had done his homework. He knew when his victim was vulnerable, and in his drive to implicate Josh Swinton in the act, he knew that his double victims had a penchant for the live football on television on Sunday afternoons. So he had to demonstrate that Josh had the opportunity and no real alibi at the critical time. He already knew that Josh had the motivation."

"How did he know Josh's attitude, and how had he discovered their Sunday afternoon preferences?"

"He had known Josh remotely for many years, the best part of twenty years, from childhood right through their teens and beyond, and he loathed him. To put it more accurately, he was jealous of Josh."

"But why?"

"Because in his mind Josh had usurped the best father figure Seth Chinner had ever had, and Seth couldn't forgive him for it. As for Josh's belligerent attitude to Phillipson, well, that was and still remains public currency. He made no bones about his pathological hatred of that man."

"Hardly surprising really, when you consider how Phillipson just systematically dismantled the Swintons' holdings for his own financial gain. It must have been devastating at the personal level."

"Dead right, Chief, and that goes a long way to explain Josh's antipathy. We heard it from the horse's mouth when we first interviewed him. He was brazen. It seemed to me justifiable, but almost too public, if you know what I mean. Seth Chinner heard him spouting forth many times and over many years in the local pubs and clubs. He was in no doubt that he would never have to sell Josh's motive for murder – Josh had already done a pretty good job of it himself."

"What, you mean he stalked the guy over long periods?"

"Oh yes... as he did with Phillipson himself and with Phillipson's partners and his ever-changing entourage."

"So, deliberate use of the boatyard van was the mechanism used to tag Josh Swinton. I get that bit, but the gun? How could he possibly have known about that old Luger?"

"Same process of observation, Chief, but he got lucky about a year ago, a little more perhaps. He had broken into the boatyard several times in an attempt to better understand Josh's surroundings, to find something he could use or manipulate, and he stumbled across his intended fall-guy enjoying a bit of late night shooting practice. He heard the shots from just outside the main boat shed and crept inside to find his man blasting away into some old hay bales that surrounded an old boat under repair. He hid until the lad had gone home and he knew that weapon had been left somewhere on that boat. He just had to find it, use it, put it back and then draw the long arm of the law back to the boatyard. The rest of that chapter you already know."

"But how do you know all of this?"

"You are sitting down, sir, that's good," and he paused to make sure he had his boss's attention. "He kept a diary!"

"Sense of humour, David – I like that kind of thing."

"No, Chief, it's not a wind up. He actually kept a diary, a hard-backed book. We recovered it from his cottage. We have reasonable certainty that the hand writing therein is actually his, as attested by Chinner's grandfather, Wing Commander Williams, who also identified the body in the cottage as that of his grandson. Furthermore, our forensics chaps identified only one DNA profile on that diary, that of Chinner himself, and it seems highly unlikely therefore that anyone else could have created and planted that book."

"And it sounds amazingly thorough, from what you've delivered so far."

"It's almost a blueprint for murder, Chief, and it explains how and why we were drawn deliberately to the boatyard and to Josh Swinton."

"I'm assuming it explains a lot more besides as well," prompted the Chief Superintendent.

"Quite right: in particular it introduces a character known as Michael, whose name is liberally dosed throughout the diary's pages. Seth Chinner was gay. Michael was his gay lover. The two of them seemed to enjoy a riotous life of narcotic addictions – at least that's how it was presented in the writings of a love-sick young man. In reality it seems very clear that Michael was manipulating and actively managing Seth through a mix of emotional and chemical controls. In short, Michael exerted such influence over Seth Chinner that he effectively managed the assassination of Lee Phillipson from afar – all the way from London!"

"Now you're stretching credibility, David. Why would this character, Michael, be so disposed? And if he's up in London, where did he meet Seth?"

"Ah, well...that takes us back to that earlier submission to the CPS I'm afraid, Chief. I don't mean to hark on about it, but you know I was particularly unhappy with the range of unidentified DNA traces still on file with forensics."

"Yes, yes, go on."

"Our smart chaps in the forensic lab chucked a load of samples, taken from Seth's cottage out at Rendlesham Forest, into their whizzy computer and out popped a perfect match for someone we had already banked, labelled and eliminated. That was a young man called Daniel Crighton – ring any bells?"

"Isn't he the estranged son...I mean, er...Phillipson's abandoned son from way back?"

"Dead right again, Chief.

"Woah, let's just take it slowly here shall we? You're saying that Phillipson's long-abandoned son had been pursuing a gay affair, presumably for some time, with another young man who, in turn, had been left behind by Phillipson's relentless selfishness some years after he'd walked out on his own family. Is that it?"

"Yes. Phillipson ditched his wife and baby boy because the enormity of his new responsibilities was just too much for him. He probably ran away from the financial commitment as much as anything. For him it equated to a lifetime of toil, and he just wasn't the diligent type. Then, some years later, in a pattern he repeated over and over, he ran out on his then partner, a certain Maisie Williams, and in doing so ditched her son too. That boy was Seth Chinner – he had been given his real father's surname from birth, although that bloke was also a runner, and the kid had a tough time of it throughout. Seth never got over it, and things went from bad to much worse when Maisie committed suicide heart-broken by Phillipson's betrayal. Seth blamed him for his mother's demise."

"No shortage of motivation then," quipped the Chief. "But how on earth did Crighton get to Chinner? I can see why he would – to get someone else to do the job for him, and someone he thought he could rely on in terms of their shared ambition – but how did he locate him, or even know of his existence?"

"Best guess is that his mother fed him the name quite innocently. In the absence of a father figure, Kate Phillipson, later Kate Crighton, worked hard to support her son. As the boy grew it seems that she and her mother, Daniel Crighton's grandmother, talked quite freely about where the runaway might be. You see, they were hounding him through the Child Support Agency for a few years for some paternity payments which he steadfastly avoided. Kate knew at that time that Phillipson was living with Maisie Williams and her little boy called Seth. Daniel remembered that name from his own childhood and when the time was right he set out to find him. According to the diary Seth's initial encounter with Michael had been entirely fortuitous and apparently the best day of Seth's gullible young life. But Michael wasn't Michael at all – he was Daniel on a mission."

"So why the hell did Crighton make the pretence of wanting to re-establish links to his natural father? Didn't he come out here to the countryside for a first reunion meeting with Phillipson not long before Phillipson got popped?"

"He did, sir, yes, and it's our contention that he was simply trying to throw anyone and everyone off the scent. Upon hearing of his father's premature death he was reported as being deeply distressed. It all blended into a very effective smoke screen. Meanwhile his other self had been plotting his old man's murder through the instrument of his boyfriend, who he knew to be wildly determined to achieve that same mutually desirable outcome."

"Christ it hardly bears thinking about. You wouldn't find this level of complexity even in an Agatha Christie yarn, and yet here it is, large as life. Did Seth ever suspect the charade?"

"Not as far as we can tell – although a confrontation along those lines would explain why Daniel Crighton may have panicked towards the end of all this. There is certainly no reveal in the diary, except a mention of someone known to Seth who turned up at Phillipson's funeral. He didn't stipulate a name, he just wrote, 'why was he there?' or something along those lines. I was there that day and I'm convinced he must have been referring to Michael, or Daniel as we now know him."

"So alarm bells were ringing at that stage?"

"Yes, but then it all went quiet. Seth says in the book that he can't reach him: he's not returning his calls and so on. Then it turns really ugly."

"Go on, tell me, I'm a grown up."

"Seth had gone beyond the plan. His attempt to incriminate Josh Swinton was his own doing and his alone. Daniel expected Seth to take the rap. He was expendable. That was almost certainly Daniel's desired outcome and Seth's anticipated bleating about an accomplice named Michael would have led nowhere: no surname, no photos, no whereabouts, limited risk of leaving behind DNA in a carefully cleaned cottage, SIM card discarded…all very difficult bordering on impossible for us. But Seth had added a whole new level of risk to the scheme by fitting-up Josh Swinton. It's ironic really to think that Seth had so cleverly accounted for so many pointers to Josh: depositing a few hairs in Phillipson's place, lifting that fabulous thumb print from the boatshed and getting it onto the bannister on Phillipson's stair case, even borrowing Josh's clothes to ensure not just a look alike on camera, but to get the GSR traces on the sleeve…I mean, the attention to detail was phenomenal. And of course the gun – Josh never knew that another human being was aware of the existence of that gun.

"However, something went terribly wrong for Daniel, and his strategy probably changed on the very day that Seth died. It's clear from the diary that Daniel had started to withdraw from the Michael role. Seth just couldn't reach him for some time, and he was clearly becoming anxious about his dwindling supply of uppers and downers and all manner of noxious fixes. Daniel had probably decided that despite the unwarranted involvement of Josh Swinton, there appeared to be no personal connection back to Seth, so he could just drop him like a stone and let him sort out his own withdrawal symptoms. But something changed. Something happened and it reinforced Daniel's belief that Seth was too much of a liability.

"We have a supportive contribution from a young solicitor in Ipswich who witnessed both Chinner and Crighton together in the town late morning on the day of Chinner's death."

"Really? How so?"

"She is the late Mr Phillipson's executor…"

"You're not serious," the Chief interrupted.

"I know, I know…what are the chances of such a coincidence? But on that same day she had arranged for the potential beneficiaries of Phillipson's Will to visit her office to brief them on their realistic expectations. She had met both Chinner and Crighton separately earlier that morning, but had no reason to believe they were in any way linked other than through their independent connection to the dead man in years gone by. Then, during her early lunch break, she spotted the two of them in heated debate on the street in the town centre not far from her office. She reported that they looked at first agitated and angry with one another, but that their exchange appeared to end in a more amicable fashion bordering on amorous."

"What, she called in just to tell us that?"

"Only when she heard the media reports of Chinner's death, some days later. The whole thing had looked so incongruous, contrived even, that she just felt compelled to contact us. What we do know is that Seth Chinner was dead just a few hours later.

"Chinner's cause of death is registered as respiratory failure and combined heart failure. Our pharmacological report informs us that the young man had not just overdosed, in a manner of speaking, but that he had existed for many months on a powerful cocktail of some of the most dangerous substances known to chemistry. What's more, in recent times he seems to have followed a prescribed regimen of drug portfolios, for want of a better description. These were particular mixtures designed to influence or control his behaviour. Those in tablet form were put together on a colour coded basis – a different colour spectrum for each desired effect. Add to that recreational heroin, cocaine, dope, weed and so much more and this lad was just never himself. The real trick was that his understanding of the codes had been deliberately twisted."

"You mean he thought he was taking a hotch-potch of poisons to calm himself down when in reality they were upping his heart-rate, blood pressure, adrenalin...and scaring the hell out of him no doubt. Chuck in some hallucinogens, then some opiates to reduce the headaches, well, he must have been a proper mess."

"That's right Chief, and yet the one drug among many that actually killed him was Pentobarbitone, which is the lethal element in euthanasia drugs and those similar concoctions used by some states in the US for death row executions."

"What...are you suggesting suicide, David?"

"Absolutely not! My guys may have missed it, but the SOCO team didn't. The syringe recovered by the body had not been discharged. It was still full...a heroin shot in fact...and that suggests to me that Seth Chinner was about to enjoy his next fix, but he passed out before he could administer it."

"But I doubt we could prove that," said a cynical Chief Superintendent.

"You're probably right about that, but it's worth noting that Pentobarbitone is not normally administered by injection. It can be, according to our scientific friends, and a production drug called Nembutal is perhaps the best example of that form. Typically, and especially in humans, the dose is taken in solution. It's just added to water or juice and swallowed. It requires a high concentration to be effective, but that only equates to ten grams of the stuff diluted in a glass of just about anything."

"So, Seth Chinner could have been fed that lethal dose in a fatal glass of his favourite tipple. He would never have known."

"Exactly! It doesn't take long to sedate the patient or victim in this case, and many of the other drugs he was using with some persistence actually combine with this one to exaggerate its effects."

"My God, the lad wouldn't have known what hit him."

"For his sake, let's hope so," Lehrer added with a sigh.

"Time of death – does all this tally?" the Chief asked.

"Within a given frame, yes," Lehrer reassured him.

"So we have the two young men together in town around early lunchtime – what else?"

"In addition we have a FedEx van driver reporting difficulties in squeezing past Crighton's parked Audi on a narrow lane in Rendlesham Forest outside Chinner's cottage mid-afternoon. We have a tyre tread match on the Audi too. And we also have CCTV recordings of Crighton's return to London that same evening. We have a time of death estimation of somewhere between four and five that afternoon. It all fits pretty neatly, Chief."

"So it looks almost certain that Daniel Crighton killed Seth Chinner hoping to bury his alter-ego, Michael, at the same time. But a hurried clean-up of the bedroom in the cottage didn't prevent us from identifying his DNA."

"That's right, Chief. It is true that Seth Chinner had anal sex between two and three hours before his death. It's also true that DNA swabs taken from his body identify sweat, skin and hair from Daniel Crighton – no semen, and we put that down to condoms, simple as that – but all that gives us is presence not practice. I think he just lulled the guy into an entirely false sense of security, behaved in cameo in every normal respect, and then dosed the guy up and left when he'd lost consciousness. Proving that may be as near as damn it impossible."

"Hence your opening gambit about conspiracy to murder plus murder, or just conspiracy. From what you've said, David, it looks like the only known murderer we have is also dead. Seth effectively confesses in his own diary. I suspect the best we can do with Crighton is to get him on conspiracy, wouldn't you agree?"

"Unfortunately I do, sir, but he's been very cunning in his misappropriation of drugs for his specific purpose."

"Uh-oh, that's not sounding very encouraging."

"Well, the Met's forensic accounting chaps have been in there for some time, to his London pharmacies that is, on the grounds of following up a series of thefts from their Blackheath outlet earlier in the year. We already have a clearly identifiable audit trail of regular, but infrequent discrepancies between drug inventories versus orders and dispensations. It's subtle, and spread across the entire chain of dispensing chemists in the group, but it is visible. However, drugs without identification, that is without wrappers or packaging, batch numbers or barcodes, are almost impossible to track. Crighton has covered his tracks further by making sure, whenever possible, that Seth Chinner's many addictions were satisfied and exaggerated by use of tablets, powders and tobaccos rather than liquids. He knows that all of those tiny little labels on bottles and ampules are hellish difficult to get off when compared to pouring a handful of pills into a paper bag. All of the stuff we found in Seth's cottage was untraceable – just a lot of bright colours in small glass jars."

"Sod it David, are you really suggesting he might get away with this? I mean… Christ Almighty…at this rate we're going to end up getting him struck off and fired, but free to go!"

"Oh, I think the diary will sort that out," Lehrer said with a gentle smile.

"And Crighton remains unaware of its existence?"

"Yes."

"And he remains unaware that the Met team has succeeded in identifying holes in his questionable inventories?"

"Again, Chief, yes. That's why we haven't pulled him in yet."

"Good. Perhaps you're right about the diary." He looked steadily across to his subordinate and added, "Oh all right then…perhaps you're right *again*, and more power to your elbow for that."

"Thank you, sir, but we got lucky on this one, and we shouldn't forget that."

"In what way?"

"The very fine thread that connected us to Seth Chinner was fortuitous indeed. If the old Wing Commander over in Bedford hadn't remembered Lee Phillipson's Christian name, and we hadn't been able to find the Bromsgrove girl again, we may never have known to look for Seth Chinner at all."

"You're right, of course, but I always like to think that due diligence will get there in the end, and in this case, even without those guiding lights, I hope we would have made it eventually."

"I don't suppose we'll ever know, Chief."

"I guess not, David, but a celebration is in order and I'll be out on the floor with some bubbly at about noon. Tell the troops. Thereafter I think I owe you a well-deserved lunch so I've booked us in at the Orwell Brasserie for one o'clock."

Lehrer hesitated, looked a little crestfallen, and then admitted, "Sorry Chief, but I'm already spoken for at lunchtime."

"Bloody hell man, whoever it is had better be more important than me."

"Well Chief, in any event she's better looking."

"Mmm, not difficult, let's face it, and it's a long drive from Bedford for lunch!"

29 – double-barrelled discharge

Daniel Crighton reclined lazily in his office chair. On the TV screen above him Bloomberg reported the latest Wall Street share prices from the early session of the New York Stock Exchange. It bored him. He picked up the remote and switched channels several times before reluctantly muting the intrusion and returning to his desktop.

The last couple of weeks had been testing and he'd arranged the perfect escape – to meet up with his fashion house associates for an expensive dinner and a good glass or two of something rather special. He wouldn't be hanging around much beyond five.

As he checked his inbox, and with little there of any pressing urgency, his mind began to drift back through the events of recent weeks, and he considered how fortunate he appeared to have been.

Those so-called IT specialists from the Met had spent long enough scratching and scraping their way through his inventories, but they'd looked out of their depth from the outset and he'd relaxed quite early on. Of course he knew that he'd designed much of the system himself. If he didn't know how to camouflage those little missing extras then who would? And how were those guys ever going to see beyond just a few minor, irregular accounting errors?

Seth, on the other hand, had come perilously close to blowing the whole scheme wide open. Poor Seth…poor, lovely Seth…a nice boy, but so naïve and ultimately so fucking stupid! If only he hadn't high-jacked the plan like that. There was no need to stitch up the Swinton lad. That was just infantile jealousy of the most dangerous kind. It so very nearly tied the noose around both their necks, but hey, it's over, it's sorted out – emergency measures applied in a situation of last resort, and no risks overlooked. Shit…close or what? The poor sod will go down as an overdosed loser for sure, and with that mix of filth running through his veins for so long the chances of his corpse spilling some juicy little morsel will be zero. Why Seth, why? All you had to do was kill that bastard and then get out. You would never have seen me ever again, but at least you'd still be breathing.

Then he thought about the Swintons again. They'd had it rough. His own natural father had cleaned them out good and proper. How had he managed that? How did he get away with it? Well…arguably he hadn't, not in the long run, but those poor sods must be protected from the final calamity of having to sell their family home. Daniel reminded himself that he must do something about that absurd Will.

His wandering thoughts were suddenly interrupted by a sharp tap on his door.

"Come," he called.

His branch assistant poked her head around the door with a sheepish look on her face.

"Hi, Julia, what's up?" he asked in a deliberately cheery tone.

"Couple of things actually, Daniel."

"Really? Okay, you'd better let me have both barrels then."

"Well...first off, we have a serious breach over at Blackheath."

"Oh no, not again! You know, I thought we'd cured that problem when we fired that joker a few months back."

"So did I, but we're short of some Pentobarbitone apparently."

"What!" Crighton looked worried and suddenly pensive. "How do you know? What's been said?"

Well...our new manager over there is doing a pretty good job – running a tight ship or trying to you could say..."

"And she's been on the phone?"

"No...actually I spotted her inventory report in the official register. Take a look. It's just popped up on screen. She's going through the right channels, I'll give her that."

"Jesus...er, you couldn't just delete that could you Julia, and I'll give her a call directly?"

"Ah, but you might not be able to right now, Daniel"

"Sorry...what do you mean?"

"Well, that's the second thing – there are two detectives downstairs who want to see you, and they say it's urgent."

30 – another runner?

Some days later David Lehrer returned from an important meeting with the Felixstowe Port Authority. He plonked himself down at his desk and clicked open his email inbox.

To : david.lehrer@suffolkcons.gov.uk
From : charles.carlingford@suffolkcons.gov.uk
Time : **14.06**
Date : **6th July 2007**
Subject : **CPS wavering !**

Hi David,

When you get back in from Felixstowe, do come up to my office as a matter of urgency.
The CPS has registered some reservations about the prosecuting evidence as stated within our MG3 documentation on the Crighton case. In particular they are less than convinced about the 'Decisions to Prosecute' section (sub-paras 3.2 & 3.3) of the guidelines.
The 'Evidential' stage of the 'Full Code Test' (sections 4.4 & 4.5) is under scrutiny. Note that the 'Public Interest' section is not in question.
The above points automatically throw doubt onto the 'Threshold Tests' on the basis that evidential requirements may fall short, and would do if we have nothing else still to come, eg more forensic accounting feedback from London.
Trying to read between the lines and then cut to the chase, I think they suspect that Crighton will stand up in court and accept all of his links to Chinner at the personal level, even under the camouflage of the 'Michael' moniker, but thereafter he will simply claim that Chinner's diary is a complete fabrication. He will assert that Chinner was a drug-infused head-case who imagined his diarised ramblings in their entirety – that they have no basis in fact.
From where I'm sitting that may prove very difficult to counter. I'm looking for reassurance. I've cleared my appointments until we've worked this out.

Thanks, Charlie

Charles Carlingford
Chief Superintendent
Suffolk Constabulary
Email : *charles.carlingford@suffolkcons.gov.uk*
Tel office : +44 (0)1473 666262
Mobile : +44 (0)7955 626111
Website : *www.suffolkcons.gov.uk*

Privacy and Confidentiality
The information contained in this email and any attached files are intended for the recipient(s) only. It may contain legal, privileged and/or confidential information and if you are not an intended recipient, you should not copy distribute or take any action in reliance on it or disclose its contents. If you have received this email in error, please notify the sender immediately and then delete it.

Lehrer pushed back in his chair. Was this going to be another runner of sorts, yet another four faults and a refusal before the CPS? The man's involvement at the very heart of a fetid conspiracy was undeniable. And it had been a conspiracy to end the days not just of a desperate and very unsavoury character, but those of his own natural father.

The detective felt the victory slipping steadily from his grasp and he racked his brain for something extra with which he might counter the anticipated and perfectly outrageous rebuttals of the accused. He knew that the case against not only Crighton, but even that against Chinner, relied heavily on contributions from that diary. He reassured himself that a long list of on-the-ground evidence supported Seth Chinner's written assertions in absolute terms. Had Chinner survived his own conspiracy with his lover then he'd certainly be facing a murder charge. Surely the same diary would be enough to demonstrate Crighton's involvement in the same conspiracy. But that wasn't the same as conspiracy to murder plus murder in its own right.

Dejectedly he stared out of the window. He just couldn't see how to nail the guy on the final count of murder. Then he began to worry about the lack of identifiable linkage between the drugs that were missing from the pharmacies in London and those found in Chinner's cottage. Could they even make the charge of conspiracy stick?

Frustrated, he turned back to his desk and flicked idly through his encrypted inbox knowing that he could stall the Chief a while longer. Then he spotted it. The short case number attracted his attention and he recognised the reference code of the forensic accounting team in London. He double-clicked.

To :   david.lehrer@suffolkcons.gov.uk
From :   forensics.lab@suffolkcons.gov.uk
Time :   **12.53**
Date :   **6th July 2007**
Subject : **Evidential corroboration, case DL/AJJ0405/DC**
Attachments : Interim report & summary, case DL/AJ0405/DC

DCI Lehrer,

Further to my recent interim report and summary (attached again for your reference) of our examination of the Rendlesham cottage of Mr Seth Chinner, I write to inform you that the team has secured another evidential match which, I'm sure, you will find extremely encouraging.

As you know, our forensic accounting team working in London has identified an outwardly random but persistent level of inventory leakage from the pharmacy chain under investigation. Hitherto, we had been unable to cross-reference any of the missing products with those unidentified materials recovered from the cottage.

However, two clear glass ampules, unmarked and unlabelled, were also found on the premises: one in a dense collection of old used tissue on the kitchen window sill or ledge, the other in the back of the kitchen cupboard below the sink. Each appears to have had any adhesive label removed in hot water.

The lack of identifiable markings was initially disappointing, but our optical and spectrometer analyses have revealed that the ink used in the labels has etched through the paper into a remnant smear or layer of glue on the glass below, such that much of the original identifying information given with each ampule remains sufficiently legible for our purposes.

On this basis I can tell you that we can corroborate each of the two ampules as having been sourced from the inventory stocks of one specific outlet in the London pharmacy chain.

My final report & summary will be with you by COB tomorrow.

Thanks, Roger Webster

Roger Webster, APT, FCSFS
Head of Department
Forensic Science Laboratory
Suffolk Constabulary
Email : forensics.lab@suffolkcons.gov.uk
Tel office : +44 (0)1473 626888
Website : www.suffolkcons.gov.uk

Privacy and Confidentiality
The information contained in this email and any attached files are intended for the recipient(s) only. It may contain legal, privileged and/or confidential information and if you are not an intended recipient, you should not copy distribute or take any action in reliance on it or disclose its contents. If you have received this email in error, please notify the sender immediately and then delete it.

Lehrer had to read those last few lines again. He grinned like a little boy when he read, 'we can corroborate', one more time.

"Got him, Chief, got him," he said to himself. Then he clicked 'print', stepped over to the printer, grabbed the hard copy as the paper spewed forth and headed for the back stairs up to the Chief Superintendent's office.